What the press says about Harlequin Romances...

"...clean, wholesome fiction...always with an upbeat, happy ending."
—*San Francisco Chronicle*

"...a work of art."
— *The Globe & Mail*, Toronto

"Nothing quite like it has happened since *Gone With the Wind...,*"
—*Los Angeles Times*

"...among the top ten..."
—*International Herald-Tribune*, Paris

"Women have come to trust these clean, easy-to-read love stories about contemporary people, set in exciting foreign places."
—*Best Sellers*, New York

Every Wise Man

by

JACQUELINE GILBERT

Harlequin Books

TORONTO • LONDON • NEW YORK • AMSTERDAM • SYDNEY

Original hardcover edition published in 1977
by Mills & Boon Limited

ISBN 0-373-02102-X

Harlequin edition published September 1977

Printed in U.S.A.

For
Simon, Rebekah, Sarah and Naomi

O mistress mine, where are you roaming?
O stay and hear; your true love's coming,
That can sing both high and low;
Trip no further, pretty sweeting;
Journeys end in lovers' meeting,
Every wise man's son doth know.

SHAKESPEARE: *Twelfth Night*

CHAPTER ONE

'O, when mine eyes did see Olivia first.'

THE girl walking down Rotheringham High Street was unaware that passers-by turned, glancing back. Indeed, she
would have been surprised, for Olivia Darcy had no preten-
sions as to her looks. She knew that her face could never be
called beautiful, but in rare moments of self-appraisal Olivia
allowed herself some satisfaction over her eyes, which were
green, flecked with tawny gold, and the thick brown lashes
that framed them. Her hair, nut-brown and long, was also
thick, which pleased her, and straight, which didn't, but her
nose she thought definitely snub and, worse, freckled, and her
mouth she considered too full and generous.

It was this generosity of the mouth, this warm oblivious
smile, that made the heads turn. That and the swinging, bouncing step of a young woman so obviously enjoying the morning
sunshine—a young woman seemingly without a care in the
world. Yet in Olivia's twenty-five years there had been perhaps more than her fair share of cares, more than her fair
share of knocks, to bruise and sometimes scar. But hers was
an ebullient nature laced with a strong streak of optimism, and
although this optimism had a while back taken a near-mortal
blow it was beginning to struggle through once more, the
process being helped by a good portion of common sense and
then topped with an abundance of humour.

Olivia was on her way this Monday morning to Messrs
Turnbull and Shawcross, an established and respected employment agency. As always when one job had finished and the
search for another was about to begin, the streak of optimism
was bubbling away, putting a healthy glow to her cheeks and
a light spring to her step.

Pushing open the heavy double doors of the agency, she
hoped that it would be Mrs Shawcross and not Miss Turnbull
on duty today. Mrs Shawcross was plump, cheerful and easy-
going and sometimes Olivia would regale her with the more

7

comic happenings that came her way, perhaps slightly embroidering them for effect, knowing they were appreciated. Miss Turnbull, on the other hand, reminded Olivia vividly of the various headmistresses who had come into contact with 'the Darcy girl' in her early years. Like Miss Turnbull, they also found that the responsibility lay rather too heavily for comfort and tended to heave a sigh of relief when she passed out of their lives. It was, therefore, with a slight lessening of spirits that Olivia saw the thin, angular shape of Miss Turnbull behind the reception counter.

'Good morning, Miss Turnbull,' began Olivia, determined not to be intimidated, her smile bright and cheerful.

'Mm . . . good morning, Miss Darcy.' The greeting was acceptable in content, but the tone and delivery quite definitely conveyed 'so you're back again'.

'Isn't it a beautiful day? Have you anything that would suit me, please?'

Miss Turnbull, who had begun to work her way slowly through the tray of index cards before her, paused and eyed Olivia over the rim of her glasses.

'Or rather . . . that you would suit, Miss Darcy?'

'Well, yes, but isn't that the same thing?' answered Olivia bravely.

'Not quite,' was the dry reply.

Olivia decided that silence was the best policy and waited expectantly while the slim, immaculately kept hands flicked competently through the cards. Now and again one would be lifted out, considered with pursed lips before being replaced with a decisive snap. After this process had been repeated four or five times Miss Turnbull announced:

'It would be a help, of course, if you could do shorthand. Perhaps then . . .' and her voice, all resignation, died away. Olivia was back again with the innumerable headmistresses. In such a tone had they all said: 'It would be a help if your father allowed you to remain with us for a reasonable period. Perhaps then . . .' Feeling compelled to justify herself, as she had justified her father in the past, Olivia said firmly:

'Mr Longman was quite satisfied with my work, no shorthand was needed, only typing. The job came to an end when the manuscript did.' She paused and grinned. 'And what a manuscript! You ought to read . . . well, perhaps not. It doesn't have to be typing, you know. I'll tackle anything,' she added quickly.

One by one the cards were passed over and then Miss Turnbull's hand hovered, a card was brought out, perused, half returned and then thoughtfully studied.

'Take a seat, Miss Darcy,' and Miss Turnbull retreated into the inner office. Olivia knew from experience that she had gone to discuss the case with Mrs Shawcross who, being more venturesome than her partner, would perhaps give it the go-ahead. Olivia strained to hear. She could see Miss Turnbull's shape silhouetted through the glass partition and saw her reach for the telephone, obviously about to confirm that the situation still needed filling. She's not a bad old stick, considered Olivia, sitting down to wait for the verdict. Miss Turnbull had found her a succession of jobs during the past year and it was not for the want of trying on her part that none of them had become permanent. No wonder her face drops a mile when I reappear like the proverbial bad penny, thought Olivia, grinning to herself. She leant back and closed her eyes. What I could really do with, she thought dreamily, is a good steady job with a dishy employer who falls madly in love with me and carries me off to the Bahamas for a honeymoon. She allowed her imagination to take flight, but gave up after a while when she couldn't put a face to the 'dish' in question. The older I get, she rather wistfully admitted, the choosier I seem to become.

'Cressida House, Millbrook Road.' Miss Turnbull's voice made her jump and quickly opening her eyes she crossed hastily to the counter. 'It's off the main London Road, at the Castle end,' Miss Turnbull continued. 'Do you know it, Miss Darcy?' and from her tone Olivia deduced that Miss Turnbull doubted she would.

'No, but I'll soon find the place. What exactly . . .?'

Miss Turnbull frowned. 'A typist is required. You are not what they specified, but Mrs Shawcross seems to think that there is no harm in you going to try for it. As is usual your fee will be returned if you do not get the position, or we will endeavour to find another for you.' She was busy writing the address on to one of the Agency cards while speaking. 'I do have an alternative if you are unlucky. Not typing. The County

Hall requires an assistant in the canteen, but ...' The unfinished sentence spoke volumes.

'Look, Miss Turnbull, honestly, I did not lose the Peterson job because I couldn't cope,' protested Olivia. 'It wasn't my fault that Mr Peterson had roving hands! And it wasn't my fault that they roved just when I was serving Mrs Peterson!' In her mind's eye she once again saw Mrs Peterson's horrified face as she contemplated the hot, delicious Spaghetti Bolognese which should have been on the plate before her and was, in fact, lying resplendent in her ample lap. Olivia couldn't help but grin as she remembered the pleasure this accident afforded her, and even Miss Turnbull allowed her lips to twitch before saying repressively:

'A most unfortunate incident. Now, here is the address to go to, and the name is Raynor.'

'Thank you, Miss Turnbull. I'll ring you if I get it.'

'If you would, please. Good day, Miss Darcy.'

It wasn't until Olivia was outside that she wondered why Miss Turnbull didn't think she was suitable, what it was that the Raynor person specified in his request for an employee. She hesitated and then pushed the card into her pocket, reasoning that she was a competent typist and apart from reliable work what more could anyone want?

Jumping off the bus at Rotheringham Castle, Olivia looked anxiously at the ominous black clouds that had obliterated the earlier sunshine and felt a drop of rain on her face. Following the bus conductor's directions she walked briskly along the main road looking for the turn she wanted, the pavement becoming more and more splattered with large wet blobs. Millbrook Road was wide, flanked with grass verges and trees. All the houses were large, set back in well ordered gardens, and the general appearance was one of unobtrusive wealth. Which, thought Olivia as she raced up the drive of Cressida House, was the reason for Miss Turnbull's doubts! By the time she breathlessly reached the shelter of the porch the rain was a torrential downpour and she conceded an overwhelming victory to the elements. She began to mop her face and hair with a completely inadequate handkerchief, but gave up when she realised she was fighting a losing battle.

'What a mess I must look—and what a way to arrive for an interview!' she wailed, contemplating the puddle forming

10

round her sodden shoes and feeling the trickle of water running down her neck. She placed a finger resolutely on the bell and awaited results, which were not long in coming but were hardly promising. The beautiful carved oak door opened to reveal a smartly dressed woman in her middle fifties, with grey hair and brown appraising eyes, who said firmly, but quite kindly:

'The surgery is round the side of the house, but I'm afraid Doctor Raynor is out on his rounds. If you come back at four o'clock he'll be able to see you then,' and the door shut decisively in her face.

It's nice to know where the surgery is, just in case pneumonia sets in, thought Olivia in amusement, although the fact that 'Raynor' turns out to be a doctor might prove traumatic, my spelling being what it is, and medical terms being what they are. Flicking a persistent rivulet of rain from her nose, she lifted her hand to the bell-push and left it there until the door was opened once more.

'I don't want the surgery,' she began before the woman could speak, 'I've come about the job. I understand Miss Turnbull telephoned you.'

'My dear girl, I *am* sorry. Do come in. I'm afraid we're so used to people coming to the wrong door I thought you must have missed the surgery directions through dashing in out of the rain. You are rather wet, aren't you? Come through here where there's a fire and I'll go and fetch someone to deal with you. Your name is ...?'

'Darcy, Olivia Darcy.'

'Ah, yes, I remember the name now. Still, we can't be too careful, checking up, ... mean. We've been plagued out with all sorts of unsuitable applicants, you'd never believe it. Most trying. That's why we've put it in the Agency's hands. I don't know how word got about that we need a typist, but some of them couldn't write, let alone type—not that typing was what they were interested in anyway. But there, I suppose you can't blame them. It's just that it's made things so difficult and tempers are beginning to fray. Right, Miss Darcy, dry yourself off in front of the fire while I'm away.'

Olivia doubted that this was possible; her hair, suit and tights were clinging miserably to her. She knelt thankfully on the hearthrug before the cheerful fire and tried to make

11

sense of the woman's conversation. If 'they' were not interested in typing, what were 'they' interested in? she wondered. Deciding that it was beyond her, she took off her jacket and hung it across the back of a chair. Her cream silk blouse had dark, damp patches at the cuffs and neck, which she couldn't do much about, and catching a glance of herself reflected in the mirror above the fireplace she groaned at the apparition staring back at her. Quickly kicking off her sodden shoes, she flung her hair forward and spread it out before the heat, at the same time lifting first one foot and then the other towards the flames in an attempt to dry as much of herself as possible in one go.

So intent was she on achieving maximum results that it wasn't until a pair of dark leather shoes appeared in her line of vision that Olivia realised she was not alone. The fact that this was, in all probability, her prospective employer and that she was hopping about on one foot, hair all over the place and steam rising from all surfaces, didn't foretell a propitious beginning. Restoring her body to its more natural posture and brushing the hair from her face, she looked up at the man standing before her. The first hurried impression was of crisp dark hair, a pale face and cool, calculating smoke-grey eyes.

'Er—I'm so sorry, Doctor Raynor, but I'm afraid, as you can see, I was caught in the downpour.' She bent and hurriedly thrust on her shoes, wincing slightly at their dampness. When she again stood up she found him studying her, eyes narrowed, forehead creased, a peculiarly arrested look on his face. Although Olivia could hardly blame him for looking startled, knowing she looked a fright, she thought he might at least have had the courtesy of pretending that nothing was amiss. 'How do you do? I'm Olivia Darcy from the Agency.' She smiled and almost held out her hand, but something told her the gesture would be wasted and indeed, all she got was a nod. Doctor Raynor was obviously in no mood to be polite, and by the look on his face her attempt to rescue the situation with friendly amusement should be abandoned instanter.

'Have you the Agency card, please?' he asked shortly.

She turned and picked up her coat, feeling in the pocket. The card was damp and holding it gingerly between thumb and finger she silently passed it to him, and while he studied it, she studied him. Definitely a shortage of bedside manner,

12

she decided, although perhaps he doesn't need it, he looks the strong, dedicated type; his patients probably put up with his rudeness and settle for results. He looked up and caught her stare and she hastily averted her eyes, but not before gaining the impression that grey eyes could be very cold and hard.

'How long have you been with the Agency?'

'Er—nearly a year. I've never worked for a doctor before, but no doubt you'll provide a medical dictionary. I hope so!' She smiled but saw no answering smile, not even a glimmer of appreciation at what was a justifiable drawback to the job. My God, she thought grimly, no sense of humour—this is going to be fun!

'There's been a mistake,' he said at last. 'I'm not Doctor Raynor.'

'Oh ... then who ...?'

'I'm his brother, Matthew Raynor.' He searched her face as if waiting for some reaction.

'I'm sorry. I thought ... perhaps, if it's convenient, I could wait until Doctor Raynor returns?' Olivia felt her colour rise and began to feel annoyed. Whatever is the matter with the man? she thought crossly. I know I look a mess, but surely he needn't keep looking at me quite like that?

'Did Miss ...' his eyes glanced down to the card, '... Turnbull tell you anything about the nature of the job?'

'No. Only that you needed a typist,' Olivia answered shortly.

'Not the full name of who your employer was to be?'

'No ... only the surname.'

A car drew up outside the window and the banging of the doors seemed to make him come to a decision.

'I'm afraid you've had a wasted journey. I'll order a taxi to take you back in to town—at my expense, of course.' He nodded briefly and walked to the door. Olivia kept her voice as cool and as even as his own.

'The situation has been filled, Mr Raynor?'

He hesitated. 'No.'

'Then I would prefer to have Doctor Raynor tell me himself that I'm unsuitable—after he has seen my qualifications.'

He returned, only the flicking of the Agency card between his fingers betraying his impatience. 'That would be more wasted time, as it's not Doctor Raynor who requires the typist.'

'Oh.' Olivia expelled a deep breath. She would have pre-
ferred the unseen doctor to his unfavourable brother, but
beggars can't be choosers, and having gone this far ... 'Mr
Raynor, I quite realise the impression you're receiving, but
really, I'm not responsible for a cloudburst. I assure you I can
type, and if you would care to confirm with Miss Turn ...'

'And neither do I.' A dark brow lifted irritably. 'My father
requires someone to type his notes ...'

'Then ...'

'... and you are not suitable.'

'Why not?' asked Olivia bluntly, hackles beginning to rise.
He appeared taken aback by the question, as if he wasn't used
to having his words challenged.

'I asked for a mature woman,' was the reply when it finally
came.

'Well, I'm sorry I'm not middle-aged, but I'm no young
thing either,' she retorted, knowing he wouldn't change his
mind but determined to go down fighting. She deliberately
lightened her voice. 'I could, of course, put my hair up in a
bun ... that would help.' She thought she saw the glint of
momentary amusement in his eyes, but it was fleeting and
could just as well have been annoyance. His voice was as
impersonal as ever.

'My father is a very discerning man, Miss Darcy.'

'What *does* he do?' she asked with studied innocence. '*Eat*
young girls?'

'Yes,' came the dry retort. 'I'll ring for the taxi.' This time
he left the room, closing the door quietly but firmly behind
him.

Olivia found she was consumed with varying emotions,
anger and frustration being uppermost. What an enchanting
man! She wandered round the room, taking in her surroundings properly for the first time. It was a room obviously well
used and lived in and even to Olivia's untrained eye contain-
ing items that would warm a collector's heart. But it was not
a show place and had an atmosphere of ease and careless
dignity. Velvet curtains hung in the wide bay and their rich
gold, together with the moss green of the carpet, was picked
out again in the floral covers of the largest three-piece suite
Olivia had ever seen. It would be pleasant, she considered,
working in a house like this. Shivering slightly, she made her

way back to the fire, going over again the disastrous interview with Matthew Raynor. 'Mature woman' indeed! He had just taken an instinctive dislike to her, which, she told herself grimly, was reciprocated.

'Here we are, sorry I've been so long, but the telephone had to be answered.' The woman who had first greeted her came hurrying in, carrying two large towels and a steaming cup of coffee. 'Then Mr Raynor had to be sorted out and what with one thing and another ... I'm Harriet Grey, by the way, general factotum. Here, dry yourself off with these as best you can. Ah, I can hear Mr Raynor coming. Excuse me, he doesn't know you've arrived.'

Before Olivia could utter a word she was off, and feeling completely unconcerned whether she heard or saw another Raynor again in her life Olivia wrapped one of the towels, turban style, round her head and began to dry her legs with the other. She could hear Harriet Grey's slightly raised voice outside and a man's voice answering her, and then the owner of the voice came into the room and Olivia straightened. And stared.

'Of course,' she breathed softly, surprise and delight rushing through her. 'Raynor! Charles Raynor!'

'That settles it, Harry. She's definitely the one, no matter what Matthew says. We'll have a fait accompli before he sees her. The other two didn't even recognise me,' and ignoring Harriet's muttered, 'That's not what was wrong with them,' the man in the wheelchair manoeuvred his way towards her and took the outstretched hand.

'Don't you want to know if I can type?' Olivia asked with a smile, completely captivated.

'Good heavens, no! I don't suppose they'd have sent you if you couldn't. That's all for now, Harry. I'll shout if I want you.'

'What about Matthew?' began Harriet doubtfully.

'Leave him—it's me that's got to work with the girl.'

Olivia looked on helplessly. She knew she ought to say that Matthew had already interviewed her and found her wanting, but remembering the cold grey eyes and peremptory dismissal and now knowing who her employer was, she clamped her mouth shut and crossed her fingers.

'Sit down, Miss ... Darcy, isn't it? Drink your coffee while it's hot. You did get rather wet, didn't you?' and he smiled, his voice all amusement. Realising that she still had the towel round her head, Olivia pulled it away and said ruefully:

'I know I must look a mess. Certainly not a good impression to give you, I'm afraid.'

'Nonsense,' Charles Raynor said emphatically, looking appreciatively at her. 'You stand up to a soaking far better than most, my dear.' He moved the wheelchair opposite her and continued matter-of-factly: 'Well now, as you know who I am, presumably you know also that I've been in a car accident and am confined to this damned wheelchair for a few weeks. If I'm good and do as I'm told I shall come out of it almost like new.' He smiled confidently. 'Luckily I am what we in the theatre business call "resting". Had the accident happened as little as three weeks earlier things would have been more difficult.'

'You mean because of *Intervening Years*?' asked Olivia, clasping her hands round her knees and leaning forward with eager interest.

'Better and better,' exclaimed Charles Raynor, his voice deepening with approval. 'You saw the play?'

Olivia nodded, 'Twice,' adding impulsively, 'I know under the circumstances you'd expect me to say this, but I loved every minute of it.'

He considered her gravely: 'No, I don't think I would expect it. After a while we actors grow built-in antennae to sift out insincerity. Why did you love every minute of it?'

'It was believable,' replied Olivia promptly. 'These days most plays seem to go from one extreme to another; either they're so obscure as to be meaningless or so meaningless that they're unsatisfying. This seemed to hit a compromise beautifully—it didn't try to be clever and told a story with a beginning, a middle and an end. The characters were real and although the play didn't end happily in the true sense of the word, it left you with hope. If you take away hope you're left with nothing.'

Charles Raynor half closed his eyes and nodded his head thoughtfully. 'A good summing up. Yes, it was a well constructed play and satisfying to be in.' He turned as the door opened and Harriet asked hurriedly:

'Are you definitely having Miss Darcy, Charles? I've got

16

two girls outside trying to convince me they're typists and they've drama students written all over them. May I say the position is filled?'

Charles lifted an inquiring brow at Olivia, who said simply: 'Yes, please,' and Harriet left the room.

'I'm afraid the decision to compile a one-man show has brought us innumerable complications.' He smiled. 'You don't want a part in my next play, do you, Miss Darcy?' he asked with exaggerated anxiety.

'Why . . . no.'

'Good. Are you drying out?'

'Yes, thank you, Mr Raynor.'

'There's certainly more colour in your cheeks. When will you be able to move in? The sooner the better from my point of view.'

'Move in?' echoed Olivia in surprise.

'Oh, dear. Didn't they explain I wanted you to live in? Well, I do. I can't bear comings and goings and your work will be spasmodic—when I'm in the mood we'll work hard, when I'm not we'll have a holiday. I hope to be down at the Royal quite frequently, revitalising myself. I may need you to chauffeur me. You can drive?'

Olivia nodded, bemused at the rate things were progressing. Charles Raynor swung the chair round and went to the door, calling: 'Harriet!' before turning back and asking persuasively: 'You will be able to stay, won't you, Miss . . . oh, the devil take it, I can't keep calling you Miss Darcy. What's your Christian name, child?'

'Olivia, and yes, please, I should like to stay,' ventured Olivia, suddenly shy.

'Olivia!' Delight showed on his face as the famous Raynor voice lingered caressingly over the name. ' "Make me a willow cabin at your gate, And call upon my soul within the house; Write loyal cantons of contemned love and sing them loud even in the dead of night; Halloo your name to the reverberate hills, And make the babbling gossip of the air Cry out "Olivia!" ' '

There was silence as they smiled at each other in mutual satisfaction for some seconds. Olivia could hardly believe that she should be sitting at the feet of Charles Raynor, curled up on his hearthrug, listening to him quoting *Twelfth Night* on

17

an ordinary Monday morning. But hadn't she been sitting at his feet, metaphorically speaking, for the past ten years?

'I've always fancied playing Viola rather than Olivia,' she blurted out, and he smiled.

'Ah, the breeches—you could wear them too.' He raised his brow and asked teasingly: 'Have you met your Sebastian yet?'

Olivia dimpled. 'No. Do you think it possible in these days?'

Charles Raynor was about to reply when the telephone rang and with an 'Excuse me, please,' he moved over to the table and answered it. Olivia gazed round the room at the various pictures hanging on the walls, but found herself drawn back to the man who was a living legend in the world of acting and who for so long had held her esteem and admiration. There was no mistaking that resonant voice or the face she had so often seen from the other side of the footlights. On stage Charles Raynor had a riveting personality and tremendous presence. Off stage his charm was just as irresistible, the more so because he seemed unaware of the fact.

Taking advantage of his being half turned away from her, Olivia studied him with unashamed interest, acknowledging that his physical appearance had much to offer for his attraction. Hair, once fair, now silver-grey, lay in thick waves over a well-shaped head. The laughter lines on his face were deeply etched and his eyes, the deepest of blues, were compelling and expressive. His nose was Roman and the line of his jaw was strong and square. But it was the voice that was so fascinating, and Olivia remembered Charles Raynor's Macbeth and Lear and wished she could have seen his Hamlet. She wondered if she would ever dare ask him how he prepared for the character he was taking, for he had the ability to almost seem to change physically with each new part. With a start she realised that Charles Raynor had replaced the telephone and was returning to her, but before they could resume their conversation the door opened.

'Harry's busy, Father, can I ...?'

'Ah, Matthew, I didn't realise you were in. Carlyon wants you to ring him.'

Matthew Raynor nodded and eyed Olivia with a frown.

Charles Raynor turned with a smile to Olivia, who had hastily scrambled to her feet, and said smoothly: 'This is

18

Miss Darcy who is coming to work for me. Her name is Olivia.'

Matthew Raynor held his father's look for a long moment and gave a ghost of a sigh. Flicking her a glance, he said heavily: 'Indeed?'

'Perhaps you could arrange for a taxi to collect her things, Matt?' Charles Raynor held out his hand and Olivia willingly gave him her own. 'Goodbye, my dear. I'll see you this evening. I'll leave you in Matthew's capable hands, he'll look after you,' and giving her the suspicion of a flutter of the eyelid and a smile to charm the birds off the trees, he wheeled himself expertly through the doorway.

Matthew Raynor looked thoughtfully after him and then back to Olivia, who, to her disgust, felt the colour rise in her cheeks, and chin in the air she said quickly:

'You'll not believe this, but I didn't get the chance to say that you ... well, that we ... the minute your father saw me ...' Her voice trailed.

'Oh, I can believe that quite easily, Miss Darcy,' Matthew Raynor conceded dryly, 'knowing my father. You recognised him, of course, and the rest was easy.' He lifted his head and listened. 'That sounds like the taxi I ordered. When you get back with your things Harriet will show you to your room.'

'Thank you,' said Olivia stiffly.

'Are you quite sure you want to move in? You need not, if you don't wish.'

'Mr Raynor especially asked me to.'

'My father is used to getting his own way, Miss Darcy, but that is no reason why he shouldn't be thwarted on occasions.' He looked inquiringly at her.

'I shall be happy to do as Mr Raynor asks.'

He eyed her narrowly for a moment and then gave an imperceptible nod, and Olivia felt resentment returning. If Mr Matthew Raynor could see her present bedsitter he would perhaps understand her ready acquiescence!

'I don't suppose my father discussed terms?' She shook her head. 'No, he wouldn't, of course. Well, don't worry, you'll be well paid, but you'll have to earn every penny of it. You'll find yourself doing far more than just typing. Like poor Harriet you'll not call your soul your own, but possibly, like her, you won't wish to. Sure you won't change your mind? No, I can see you won't.'

Olivia picked up her jacket and slipped it on. 'Mr Raynor, do you always take such an instant dislike to strangers?'

'Only when my instinct tells me that they spell trouble.'

'And your instinct is working at the moment?'

He smiled thinly. 'Working overtime, Miss Darcy.'

'Aren't you rather hasty with your snap judgments?'

'I think not. I have vast experience of ambitious actresses gazing adoringly at my father, either with a view to marriage stakes or the furtherance of their career.'

'I see,' said Olivia, fury almost rendering her speechless.

'I'm glad you do, Miss Darcy.' He led the way into the hall and she was unprepared when he stopped and asked abruptly: 'Are you connected in any way with the theatre?'

Startled, she said blankly: 'The ... theatre?'

'Yes.'

'You mean ... Rotheringham Theatre Royal?'

'Any theatre, Miss Darcy.' The words were spaced out deliberately.

'No,' she answered shortly.

He nodded and stood aside for her to pass. Olivia climbed into the taxi and gave directions, careful not to look back. He hadn't believed her, of that she was sure.

'I've put you in the green room,' said Harriet as Olivia followed her up the stairs. 'It's not all that large, but it faces south and has a good view.'

'What an enormous house this is,' exclaimed Olivia. 'It looks large from the outside, but even so ...'

'There's been extensions to accommodate the new surgery and a larger garage and rooms were added above. We need them, I can assure you. I never know how many guests Charles will arrive with, especially since he launched into television. Things have quietened down since his accident, necessarily so. We've had a change round so that he can be on the ground floor. Luckily there's a bathroom on the surgery side which he can use. Here we are.' Harriet opened the bedroom door and looked round critically. 'We have a daily who comes in to help in the kitchen and a cleaner who comes mornings, so although the house is large I do have help.' She walked over to a small desk situated beneath the window. 'Do you think you could work in here? I've been puzzling where to put you and . . .'

'This will be fine,' Olivia assured her quickly. 'You ought to see some of the rooms I've lived and worked in—you wouldn't be worried then!'

Harriet patted her shoulder, preparing to leave. 'I told Matt you looked a sensible girl. Unpack and come downstairs when you've finished, lunch will be ready by then.'

It didn't take Olivia very long to sort out her things. Years of moving from one place to another had imposed a discipline and she had very few unnecessary possessions. She placed the photograph of her father and mother, taken not long after they were married, on the chest of drawers and an assortment of books on the bedside table, together with her travelling clock. She had just stowed away the last of her clothing and was closing the lid of her trunk when she heard a brief tap on the door. Opening it, she found Matthew Raynor holding a typewriter on which was perched, rather precariously, a box of paper and carbons.

'Oh, thank you, let me take that,' and she rescued the box. He crossed the room and placed the typewriter on to the desk.

'Will you be all right working in here?'

'Yes, indeed. I have a perfect view from the window.' She crossed to it and leant on the sill. 'I didn't realise that the Castle grounds came right down to the garden boundary. Almost like being in the middle of the country.'

He looked out of the window and nodded. 'It is beautiful, isn't it? One tends to take it all for granted, but after a spell away it's appreciated as strongly as ever. It's hardly believable that fifteen minutes' driving and you're in the middle of a thriving city—we get the best of both worlds. Do you like the country, Miss Darcy?'

'Oh, as for liking it, yes, but I've never lived there, really in the country, I mean. I'm a town girl, not from choice but by circumstance. I think I could be quite happy living in the country, though—if that was where my home was.'

'Wouldn't you miss the bright spots?'

She laughed. 'It depends. You'd have to qualify what you mean by "bright spots", I'd certainly miss the . . .' she stopped short, 'cultural aspects of city life, but unless one were living deep in the wilds there's nearly always a town of some size a reasonable distance away.' She turned and bent to snap the lock on the trunk. 'Is there somewhere I can store this, please? My suitcase fits on the top of the wardrobe easily, but ...' She looked up and found him staring at the trunk with raised brows. 'I couldn't afford to stay on in my digs,' she said defensively, 'at least, it seemed silly to keep the room, so I had to bring everything with me. If it's not convenient I'll store the trunk at the station.'

'No, Miss Darcy, that won't be necessary. I'll take it down to the garage, it will be quite dry there.' He paused and studied the trunk once more. 'It wasn't the fact that you'd brought it with you but its appearance that caused me some surprise. You've travelled, I see.' His gaze took in the tatty, obscure labels, most of which Olivia had deliberately pulled off, leaving only oblong ghosts to remind her of the past.

'It belonged first to my father.'

'I see. You spoke of digs. For some reason I assumed that your home was here in Rotheringham—your family home, I mean.'

'No. I have no family.' She smiled faintly. 'You find that hard to believe?'

'Finding my own, which is on the large side, sometimes insufferably overpowering, your lonely state has a certain appeal. But I cannot believe that you are completely on your own. No boy-friend?' He glanced at her bare hand.

'I have friends, good friends ... but they don't take the place of family.'

Matthew Raynor strolled over and picked up the frame from the chest. Olivia, knowing every detail of it by heart, knew that the faces, like all photographs, did not give a complete picture. Her mother, looking fragile and very feminine, was giving a shy smile, illuminating a sweet face. Her father, his large, dark eyes staring out of a pale face, was looking serious and slightly soulful.

'My mother, according to Father, was most enamoured of that picture because it portrayed everything she wanted to be and was not. Circumstances insisted she be strong and resourceful. My father was very rarely sad, which he looks there —he was one of the most optimistic people I know. My mother died when I was six, my father just over two years ago.'

Matthew Raynor nodded and replaced the photograph.

'You appear to have inherited both your mother's resource-fulness and your father's optimism,' he remarked evenly, and grasping the empty trunk with both hands he left the room.

Olivia closed the door behind him and took a deep breath. How silly of her to be lulled into a false sense of security, and how clever Matthew Raynor was to get her talking. She crossed to the chest and repositioned the frame.

Harriet had set two places on the long wooden table with its white scrubbed top when Olivia rejoined her downstairs.

'Hope you don't mind eating in the kitchen, it saves time and now that the rain has stopped we can enjoy the sun while it's on this side of the house.'

Olivia laughed. 'Please, don't remind me of that rain.' She looked appreciatively round her. 'What a lovely big kitchen.'

Harriet nodded her head complacently. 'I can't stand modern kitchens, all streamlined and cold. Of course, I like labour-saving equipment, I'd be a fool not to, but I like a bit of atmosphere and individuality—and comfort. I was brought up on a farm and I suppose this is as near to a farmhouse kitchen as I can make it.' Harriet poured soup into bowls and placed them carefully. 'Charles is in the study with a tray, he doesn't want to stop working—which augurs well for the future. Matt's gone to the theatre, he'll probably have something there, and Paul is still on his rounds.'

Olivia's soup spoon remained poised. 'Matthew's gone to . . .?'

'The theatre. Didn't you know? Oh, that will please him. I'm afraid over the years we've become so used to folk wangling their way into our lives for one motive or another that we see bogey men everywhere. The things people get up to you'd never imagine!'

'What,' asked Olivia faintly, 'does he do there?'

'Directs, and very good he is too. The Royal's always had a good reputation, mind, but that didn't save it nearly being knocked down to make way for a supermarket.' She snorted. 'Planners! They've no soul. Anyway, a petition was formed and it was saved. Charles found some backers and he asked Matthew to get it back on to its feet. He's been here a year now and gradually we're being noticed in the national press.' She beamed proudly. 'We've got Anthea Beresford at the moment and she's proving a wonderful draw, capacity audiences, and Matt's commissioned plays specifically for the Royal. Remember Tom Lovell's *Cloven Tongues*? Well, he wrote it for us and it had its premiere here before transferring to London. More soup, Olivia? No? Apple tart, cheese and biscuits and coffee. Hope that'll do until this evening?'

'It sounds delicious,' answered Olivia, trying to adjust to this piece of news. So Matthew Raynor was also connected with the theatre. A director. Well, she thought, I'm not really surprised; instinct had told her she knew the breed. Aloud she said: 'Does he act?'

'Not often now. Used to, but he said living up to his father was too much effort. Reckons three actors in the family is two too many. He prefers to direct.'

Yes, thought Olivia dryly, he'd sooner tell people what to do than accept orders from others. 'You said three actors?' she prompted in some puzzlement.

Harriet smiled and folded her arms comfortably on the table.

'I'd better tell you about the family. Charles has three sons, Paul, Matthew and Julian. Paul's the eldest and is a doctor.' She frowned, thinking deeply. 'He must be all of thirty-six now. He's a mixture of Charles and Eve—Eve Holland she was, a beautiful woman and a wonderful actress. She died, oh, must be over ten years ago now. How time flies!' Harriet was silent for a moment, drinking her coffee pensively, then she continued briskly: 'Paul lives here permanently, with his son, Toby. His wife died in childbirth and they thought they'd lose the baby too, but they managed to save him. What a thing to happen these days, but it did, even with the best men available.' Harriet's voice became clipped as if remembering still hurt.

'How old is Toby?' asked Olivia softly.

'Six. He's away for half-term with his other grandparents. Paul's bringing him back at the weekend.' She poured another cup of coffee for them both. 'Paul's a good doctor. He ought to take a partner, the practice is getting too big for one man to cope with, but he's like all the Raynors—pig-headed and stubborn.'

Olivia smiled. 'And you love them all.'

'Oh, well, they're all the family I've had for over thirty

24

years,' Harriet chuckled, 'and I'm the only one I allow to criticise them.'

'Surely Charles Raynor doesn't have the chance to stay here very often?'

'Not as much as he would like. Cressida House is the family home and available to the family whenever they want it. The next three months the three of them were to have worked together at the Royal, but this accident's messed those plans. Still, mustn't grumble, just thank God he wasn't killed.'

'Is Matthew the middle son?' Olivia felt slightly guilty at pumping Harriet for information, but if she became too inquisitive she was sure Harriet would put her firmly in her place.

'Yes, he's thirty-four ... very much like Eve ... she was a dear friend of mine. Julian is the baby of the family, twenty-nine, and a second Charles in looks and temperament.' Harriet collected their used crockery and stacked them in the sink and Olivia followed, taking a tea towel from the rail.

'Are either Matthew or Julian married?'

'No!' Harriet laughed. 'Julian's having too good a time to tie himself down with one girl, and Matthew ... well, there's been one or two I've thought he might settle with, but nothing's come of it. The trouble is the only women he seems to come into contact with are actresses, and I wouldn't trust half of them further than I could throw 'em. They see him as a convenient step-ladder to their career!' Harriet sighed. 'Matt's always been the odd one out, but they say the middle one of three often is. You never can tell what Matt's thinking, he's a cool one.' She shrugged. 'If it hadn't been for his father's accident and knowing how pleased Charles was to have them all under the same roof for a time ...' Harriet dried her hands, confidences were over. 'Thank you, love, for helping. Charles told me to tell you that he won't have anything for you until tomorrow, so you can please yourself what you do this afternoon.'

'So long as you keep out of my way,' added Olivia with a smile.

'Exactly,' agreed Harriet imperturbably.

Olivia decided to explore the garden. As she had never been in one place long enough to put anything into the ground and be there when it came up, gardens for her were what other people had, although this didn't stop her having a love of flowers. The garden of Cressida House was L-shaped, the part nearest to the house devoted to lawn, flower beds and fruit trees and the bottom half to vegetables and fruit bushes. She sat for a while savouring the sun and then decided to climb the stone wall separating the garden from the Castle grounds and explore the Castle. It was further than she at first thought and because of the earlier rain the ground underfoot was soft and heavy going, but the visit was well worth it.

The Castle was a semi-ruin set on a hill, and climbing the battlements Olivia shaded her eyes and looked across the gently undulating park to a small herd of deer grazing quietly in the young bracken by the edge of one of the many deep pools. A horse and rider passed along the bridle path on the perimeter and for a moment the deer stood immobile, ready to gain the sanctuary of a small copse nearby, but as the rider passed they relaxed and resumed their grazing. Olivia breathed a deep sigh of contentment. The day might not have started off too well, but she hadn't any complaints for the way things had worked out. Only Matthew Raynor seemed to be the fly in the ointment and with any luck she would keep out of his way as much as possible. As for Charles Raynor ... she could still hardly believe it! A cloud passed over the sun and she shivered slightly. It was time to go back. The return was quicker, being downhill, and Olivia was quite breathless by the time she reached the garden wall. Climbing it from the Castle side was harder because of the differing levels of ground, but she was determined to make it and after a struggle gained the top, sitting astride one of the flatter rocks which made up the stone wall. About to bring her other leg over, she paused and froze. Very, very slowly she turned her head and out of the corner of her eye she saw a huge Alsatian dog watching her intently.

He was truly a magnificent animal, but for all his beauty Olivia wished he were elsewhere at this present moment. The look in his eye declared openly that this was his territory, and by golly, she thought, I'm in no position to argue! Dogs, like gardens, were something that Olivia also had never possessed, and although she wasn't scared of them under normal circumstances, this, she conceded, was definitely not normal!

The Alsatian was obviously a Raynor possession and as no

one in the family had thought to introduce her, so far as he was concerned she was a stranger and therefore not to be trusted. More than a stranger—a trespasser.

Saying in a cheerful voice: 'Hello, dog. Good boy,' she moved cautiously, only to hear a small, warning rumble in his throat. They eyed each other for a few moments and then he lay down, head between paws, brown eyes never wavering.

'Hell!' Olivia peered anxiously across the garden, but the house was hidden by trees. 'I would like you to know, old fellow, that my rear is beginning to ache and a jagged end of stone is doing its best to maim me for life!' Once again she tried to move and once again the faint rumbling could be heard, although the animal was so sure who was boss he didn't change his position. How humiliating to have to shout for help! Olivia bit her lip ... there was nothing else to do, but really, she did feel a fool. At her first attempt his head shot up, but she averted her eyes and yelled again and gradually the beautiful head sank between his paws once more. Olivia began to feel cold. She was only wearing a short-sleeved jumper and skirt, and considering that she had been thoroughly drenched that morning the chances of ending up a patient of Doctor Paul seemed to be multiplying by the minute. In between shouts of 'help!' she sang, but even that palled after a time and she was just considering whether to throw herself off the wall on to the Castle side and risk the fall and/or the possibility that the Alsatian would follow when she heard a shout and thankfully saw a man appear from behind the trees. The Alsatian leapt to his feet and bounded over, tail wagging, to greet the newcomer and then raced back to sit in exactly the same spot, eyes ever watchful.

'Well, well, some people have fairies at the bottom of their garden, but we appear to have ...?' and his voice lifted in question.

'Not Livingstone nor Stanley,' said Olivia crossly, for she felt ridiculously trembly now that a rescuer had at last appeared on the scene. 'You are Doctor Raynor, I presume? I'm Olivia Darcy, and will you please call off your beautiful beast?'

'Caliban, here!' It was an order and the dog immediately crossed and stood patiently by his side. 'I'm sorry, Miss Darcy. Now you can get down.'

'I don't think I can,' said Olivia calmly, 'I've gone numb.'

'In that case ...' Paul Raynor lifted her off and gently lowered her to the ground. Olivia immediately collapsed on to the grass, a mass of excruciating pain. Ignoring her pleas to leave her alone, he walked her up and down, until gradually the cramp subsided. Olivia pulled a face.

'I suppose it's a good plan to have a doctor to the rescue. Thank you.'

'I thought at first you were another of our usual trespassers,' and seeing her blank look, he added: 'autograph and job-hunters. My dear girl, how long have you been stuck up there?'

Olivia shook her head. 'I've no idea. It seems like three weeks, but I don't suppose it is.'

'Come along. Hot sweet tea should do the trick,' and putting a hand beneath her arm Paul Raynor led her up to the house and into the kitchen, Caliban padding softly at their heels. He sat her in the chintz-covered chair and began to prepare the tea. Olivia studied him, liking what she saw. He was dressed in riding kit and was probably the horseman she had seen earlier. He was as tall but broader than Matthew and had the squarer features of their father. His hair was light brown and he had his father's intense blue eyes. His whole countenance was pleasant and his physique rugged and strong; a man, Olivia reflected, who would immediately instil confidence into his patients purely on his warm, calm smile.

'And what is your conclusion, Miss Darcy?'

Olivia blushed. 'I was just thinking it strange that you should be a doctor, surrounded as you are by so many theatricals,' she improvised hastily.

He pursed his lips and placed a cup of tea before her, taking one for himself and sitting opposite. Regarding her over the brim, he smiled.

'I suppose it does seem strange unless you know that my paternal grandfather was a doctor. I used to love staying with him in the holidays and he would let me help him mix the more simple medicines. He used to dispense most of his own in those days. It was he who encouraged me to take it further as my career.'

'Did you never act, even as a child?'

'Oh, I was dragged into things. It took me quite a while to convince the drama masters at school that I was not another Charles, and then when Matthew followed me they finally gave me up. I did one or two revues at medical school, but the acting gene is sadly lacking, I'm afraid.'

'Was your father disappointed?' she asked.

'Good lord, no. He would never have tried to persuade any of us into the theatre. No career for the half-hearted ... total commitment, he always tells would-be students.' He poured out another cup for them both. 'I love watching it, but just can't do it. The other two—well, they've more than made up for one dissenter.' He smiled and said with amusement, 'So ... you are our new prop.'

'New what?'

'Prop. Seems whenever we have a crisis we obtain a prop. Harry was the first and we've had a succession coming and going ever since. You're our latest.'

'Thank you very much,' said Olivia dryly. 'I've been called some things in my time, but never a prop!'

'I should have thought,' said a voice from the door, 'that you could have shown rather more imagination than that, Paul.'

'Ah, Matt, doctors are not encouraged to use imagination, only facts. We leave imagination to actors,' Paul grinned. 'Come and have tea, I think we've left you some in the pot.' He looked at his watch and grimaced. 'I'll have to go and change, nearly surgery time.'

'Laura, as usual, has everything under control,' Matthew announced, collecting a cup and pouring himself some tea.

'Laura,' explained Paul with a smile, 'is another of our props. An invaluable nurse-cum-receptionist-cum-child-minder. I'd be lost without her. Well, Matt, I congratulate you on finding Miss Darcy. She's just what Charles needs.'

Olivia choked on her tea and suffered Matthew to thump her on the back, which he did with unnecessary fervour.

'You think so?' Matthew returned, when peace had been restored.

'Definitely.' Paul turned to Olivia. 'After the accident it was important that Father should rest, but he's never been a particularly restful person ...'

'Only on stage,' broke in Olivia, 'on stage he commands by his very stillness.'

'I see we have another worshipper,' groaned Paul, getting to

29

his feet. 'See you both later,' and with a wave of the hand he left them.

There was a prickly silence for a moment and then:

'And what has Miss Darcy been doing with herself this afternoon?'

'Miss Darcy has been exploring the garden and the Castle and getting to know Caliban.' She rose and smoothed her skirt, flicking him a quick look from behind her fall of hair. 'Perhaps you would be good enough to tell me who is my actual employer?'

'My father.'

'Then should he inquire how I spend my free time I shall be happy to tell him.'

Matthew Raynor raised his brows and smiled faintly, but any further conversation was stopped by the arrival of Harriet, her colour high and exasperation showing in her voice.

'As if I didn't have enough to do without fobbing off silly women who ought to know better! That newspaper article about the accident and the fact that you're all working at the Royal is a darned nuisance.'

'It will all die down in a couple of days, Harry.' Matthew laid his hand on Caliban's neck, the Alsatian leaning contentedly against his thigh.

'And a good thing too,' she retorted crossly. 'Now, what was I doing before that dratted phone rang? Oh, yes, laying the table.'

'Can I do that for you while you do something else?' offered Olivia.

'Bless you, girl. The cloth is in the left-hand drawer of the sideboard and the cutlery is in the right. There's only five of us today. Lay for Paul, although it depends on how large the surgery is as to whether he'll eat with us.'

Olivia was conscious of thoughtful grey eyes following her out of the kitchen.

When she came down the stairs later she heard Charles Raynor saying:

'Don't fuss, Harry, I can manage quite well, thank you,' and Harriet, passing the foot of the stairs, raised her eyes in a gesture of resignation. Olivia stood on the bottom step feeling rather nervous.

'Good evening, Mr Raynor.'

'Olivia, my dear, how delightful you look, and how clever of you to choose that particular shade of green. Come and have a sherry before dinner.' He allowed her to open the sitting room door and she preceded him in, cheeks prettily flushed with the compliment, which had done much for her morale; this first meal with the Raynor ménage was looming up as something of an ordeal.

Matthew was already seated in one of the deep armchairs, a glass in his hand, a manuscript on his lap. He looked up when they entered and her heightened colour was greeted with a sardonic look. He uncurled his long body and walked un-hurriedly to the drinks table.

'Your usual, Father? And you, Miss Darcy?' and he indi-cated the choice, his hand hovering over the sweet sherry.

'Dry, please,' she said firmly, ignoring the gleam in the grey eyes.

'I do feel that "Miss Darcy" is a little formal, Matt. I sug-gest you call her Olivia. After all, it's such a pretty name.' Charles turned to her, smiling. 'We shall, of course, expect the informality to be reciprocated.'

'I'm not at all sure I can promise you that,' answered Olivia quickly. 'It's going to take me all my time getting used to the idea of working for you without the presumption of calling you Charles!'

'Very prettily said,' murmured Matthew as he handed her a glass.

Charles was enjoying himself. 'I think we were very clever to find Olivia, Matt. Shall we drink to our good fortune?'

Matthew followed his father's gesture obediently enough, but Olivia dared not catch his eye.

'To your quick return to the theatre,' she offered quietly.

'I'll drink to that,' said Paul, coming into the room. 'I en-visage a stormy few weeks to come with Father frothing at the bit. You, Olivia, will have to bear the brunt, I'm afraid.'

'Nonsense,' said his father emphatically. 'You'll be giving Olivia a completely false impression of me before she's even begun.'

'I suspect Miss Darcy's spectacles are of the rose-coloured kind,' suggested Matthew dryly.

'And a good job too,' announced Charles Raynor, giving her

his famous smile. 'Is that the new Bennett play, Matt? What's it like?'

'Exciting theatrically, a few snags on production side, but I think we can cope.'

'How are you feeling, Olivia, after your ordeal with Caliban?' asked Paul, coming over to her.

'A bit stiff,' Olivia admitted with a grin.

'Do you realise that your wretched dog kept Olivia at bay on top of the boundary wall this afternoon, Matt?' demanded Paul, obviously gratified by the attention his question received. Olivia, though touched by his kindly concern, wished the incident could have died a natural death. 'I've told you before about introducing the brute to house-guests,' and Paul went on to explain how he had found her. Olivia laughingly related how she had got herself into the predicament in the first place and managed to turn the whole thing into a joke against herself.

Charles, although joining in the laughter, was concerned. 'My dear girl, I'm so sorry that you should have spent such a disastrous first afternoon with us, but I can see you've come out of it with flying colours. Matthew, you'll have to find some way of making it up to Olivia.'

'That's not necessary,' broke in Olivia, a shade too quickly.

'I apologise on behalf of Caliban, Miss Darcy, but he was only showing his natural mistrust of strangers.'

Like master, like dog, thought Olivia, accepting his apology with a quiet, 'That's all right, it wasn't the dog's fault.'

'There's Harry calling,' said Paul. 'Come along, Father, I know you like to be independent, but it will be much easier and quicker in this instance if you'll allow me to push you.'

'Oh, very well,' agreed Charles Raynor with exaggerated resignation. 'If this wretched body of mine doesn't heal quickly you'll have to find me a play with a meaty part for a man in a wheelchair, Matt.'

'If he can't he'll write you one,' promised Paul.

'Olivia, dare I ask? Do you play chess?' Charles Raynor demanded over his shoulder as Paul manoeuvred him through the doorway.

'Why, yes,' exclaimed Olivia. 'Only I haven't played for some time.'

'He'll be pleased you're rusty,' said Paul with a studiously poker face. '*We* can all beat him!'

They laughed and Charles Raynor could be heard grumbling goodnaturedly as he was pushed down the corridor. Olivia replaced her empty glass on the tray and found Matthew waiting for her to precede him. She paused.

'Why do you look at me like that?'

'Don't you think it gives me pleasure to look at you?' he asked mockingly, eyeing her up and down.

'No, I do not.' Olivia's eyes flashed angrily. 'I surely know the difference between ...' She flushed and bit her lip. 'What on earth do you think I am?' she demanded crossly.

'A very clever woman, Miss Darcy,' he replied suavely. 'But don't forget—I shall have my eye on you.'

'Have a care that your motives aren't misconstrued!' she retorted, and giving a contemptuous flick of her long hair she swept past him. But she was not allowed to have the last word.

'Your timing and delivery of an exit line is quite exceptional, Miss Darcy, although slightly overplayed,' and face inscrutable, he followed her into the dining room.

CHAPTER TWO

'Conceal me what I am.'

'Do you mean to tell me,' Rosemary asked incredulously, her eyes wide with astonishment, 'that he thinks you're trying to hook his father?'

'That's right,' affirmed Olivia succinctly.

While Rosemary Mason digested this somewhat surprising piece of news, Olivia stretched contentedly out on the studio couch and gazed with satisfaction at her surroundings. Part of her contentment was the array of family paraphernalia adorning the room—nappies airing by the fire, Jamie's box of toys, the desk with Tom's school books waiting to be marked and the furniture, each piece carefully chosen from auctions and second-hand shops and lovingly renovated. The other part of her contentment lay in the friendship of the small, slightly plump girl sitting on the chair opposite, who was sewing, and who now rested the garment on her lap and inquired in an indignant tone:

'Is the man an idiot?'

Olivia grinned at her loyalty. 'Dear me, no! Far from it. Very astute is our Matthew. And to be fair, from what I can gather, they have this trouble quite regularly—besotted females either wanting to make it on the stage or make it to the altar. I think Charles just breezes along in his charming, captivating way and Matthew has to clear up after him. Anyway, he prejudged me as being in either category,' and remembering the ill-fated interview and the barely disguised antagonism since, Olivia grimaced.

'But why? I mean, what reasons has he on which to base his suspicions?' Rosemary shot a keen look at her friend. 'I know you, Noll, and I wouldn't put it past you to play up to him,' and breaking off the length of cotton, she surveyed with satisfaction the patch she had just stitched on to her young son's dungarees. Olivia sat up, tucking her legs beneath her.

'Rose, I behaved beautifully.' She laughed at the sceptical

34

look given her. 'Considering I looked like a drowned rat I didn't expect to bowl him over with my immaculate personal appearance, but he didn't even ask for my references, just took a long, penetrating look at me down his aristocratic nose and said I wasn't suitable.'

'There must have been something,' insisted Rosemary with a smile.

'If there was, apart from the first devastating impression I gave, then he kept it to himself. On my honour—I just stood there, steam rising gently from all parts, answering politely,' and at the image these words painted the two girls collapsed in a heap of laughter. When she could control her voice, Olivia went on: 'I did lose my temper towards the end, hadn't anything else to lose, and with a disdainful raise of the brow and curl of the lip he says "You're not suitable" and off he stalks to get a taxi. Was it my fault his father comes in and takes over? I mean, I could understand if Matthew Raynor had decided against me later, when he saw how well his father and I were getting on, that at least would make sense. Or if he was annoyed that it had all been settled behind his back—but, Rose, he was anti-Olivia before his father had even seen me, let alone taken a liking to me ...'

At this point Rosemary raised her eyebrows and Olivia shrugged. 'We naturally talked and Charles Raynor found out that I wasn't a complete ignoramus regarding the theatre ... in fact, my delight rather carried me away and maybe I did allow my admiration and respect for him to show—he'd not have been human, let alone an actor, if he hadn't responded!'

'Presumably *he* was willing to take the risk of you being the latest in a line of besotted females,' put in Rosemary, beginning to fold the nappies from the clothes-horse.

'Presumably *he* could see how sensible and stable I am,' retorted Olivia, ignoring the hoot of laughter this brought forth, 'and I don't think he's aware of half of what goes on with Matthew and Harriet guarding him.'

'You mean Charles Raynor took one look at your adoring face and snapped you up?'

'You put things so beautifully, Rosie, old thing.' Olivia paused and added thoughtfully: 'He might not have done but for the fact that Matthew had tried to palm a couple of old dragons on to him before I appeared on the scene—I think

Charles grabbed me like a drowning man.' She tilted her pixie face impudently. 'You note, Rose, the assured way in which I say "Charles"? It's taken me all of these six weeks to convince myself that an ordinary mortal such as I is allowed to. I still "Mr Raynor" him to his face, though.'

Rosemary folded the last nappy and pushed them into an already overflowing cupboard, shutting the door with a practised thump. 'We'll not wait for Tom, heaven knows when he'll be home, he has a parents' evening on tonight. Who'd be married to a teacher!'

'You would be,' Olivia stretched happily. 'I do love your house, Rose, it's so cosy and ... homely.'

Rosemary grinned. 'That's not the word Tom would use. Actually it's rather tidier than normal; knowing you were coming I made an effort and cleared up when the horror went to bed.'

'Do not call my godson a horror, and I'm not talking about it being tidy. It's the atmosphere.'

'We like it. I'm glad we decided on buying old property. Some of these new housing estates would drive me mad, everyone keeping up with their neighbours! Come and help me prepare supper. I've got mushrooms for the omelette.'

'Mm ... sounds delicious.' Olivia followed her into the kitchen and for a few moments the two girls were silent as they worked. Rosemary, whisking eggs in a basin, frowned slightly.

'I can't see why you didn't tell Matthew Raynor about yourself in the first place, Noll. It makes everything so complicated.'

'It needn't be complicated,' insisted Olivia, cutting the onions with reckless abandon, eyes streaming. 'Oh, well ... I admit I'm not too happy about it, but the whole affair was a mess from start to finish. He just rubbed me up the wrong way—and anyway, I didn't really lie.'

'Huh!'

'I didn't, Rose. In all fairness, I'm not, at this moment in time, connected with the theatre. The fact that I *used* to be is irrelevant.'

'Do you think Matthew Raynor would think so?'

'No.'

'Well, then.' Rosemary flipped the omelette over expertly and scooped it on to a plate. 'Start yours, mine won't be a

36

minute. I still think you could have mentioned it ... casually ... passing.'

Olivia snorted. 'If he'd been at all decent in the beginning I'd have told him my life history, blood group, the lot—but one icy look, together with his Gestapo manner, put me right off. And as for mentioning it casually——! If I'd told him about my year away from the theatre I bet he wouldn't have believed me.' She produced a bottle of wine from her duffle bag, like a conjuror producing a white rabbit from a hat, and placed it with a flourish on to the table. 'Abracadabra!'

'Oh, Noll, you shouldn't have.'

'Oh, Rose, I have,' mimicked Olivia. 'I brought it for to-morrow's meal, but there's enough for a tipple tonight. Rosé for Rose—Rose for Rosé! Mm ... it all looks good. Where are the glasses, girl? Let's eat, I'm starving!'

'You always are,' grumbled Rosemary, eyeing her slim friend enviously as she brought her plate to the table.

'Never mind, love, Tom likes his women plump and cuddly. How's he getting on at the new school?'

They chatted amicably over their meal and later, sitting by the fire drinking cocoa, Rosemary returned to the subject that had not been far from her thoughts all the evening.

'Your year's nearly up, isn't it?'

Olivia nodded and sipped her drink appreciatively, continuing thoughtfully: 'I know you were dubious about it, Rose, but economically I was down to rock bottom. I'd battled on while Dad was alive and as you know, had one or two lucky breaks, but then he became ill and the year after his death it was hell getting work.'

'I know,' agreed Rosemary sympathetically. 'I just thought, emotionally, the time wasn't right for making such an important decision. You'd barely got over nursing your father and then you go and get appendicitis. You were bound to be feeling low.'

'Especially when I'd just landed the first decent part that had come my way in months. It's not often Madam Fate gives you a second chance.'

'You could have come and stayed with us, used us as your base.'

'I know, and it was grand of you both, but I've always been independent and this year away from acting was something I'd

37

got to do, for my own peace of mind. The fact remains that as a typist I haven't been out of work for longer than three days during the past nine months.'

'And have you loved every minute of your work?' asked Rosemary slyly.

'I've loved having a wage packet every week,' answered Olivia rather bitterly.

'I think it's so unfair,' burst out Rosemary, her dark curls bobbing angrily. 'You have talent: Yes, you can laugh. I know all the spiel about wondering whether you only went into acting because you knew your father wanted you to ... that's rubbish! Okay, so your father was a comedian on the Halls and had ambitions for his daughter on the legitimate stage, but you wouldn't have got as far as you did without talent.'

'Oh, as for talent, Rose, that's not particularly necessary for getting work, only for getting to the top. For work, luck's the thing. Being in the right place at the right time; having the right face, height, voice, fitting the image the director has of the part.'

'Exactly!' exclaimed Rosemary eagerly. 'You're in the right place now,' she added triumphantly, and seeing the incomprehension on her friend's face said impatiently: 'You say Charles Raynor has taken to you—ask him to help.'

Olivia frowned. 'I can't, Rose, I ... just can't.'

Rosemary, having allowed her crusading spirit to swamp and overtake her knowledge of Olivia's character, knew she was wasting her breath, but having gone this far decided to take things to their obvious conclusion. 'Why not?'

Olivia shrugged helplessly. 'I couldn't take advantage of his kindness. He's been wonderful to me, Rosie, I ... couldn't spoil it.' Her voice hardened. 'And I couldn't allow Matthew Raynor to be proved right!'

'Noll, you're hopeless. You've too much integrity—you're not tough enough.'

'Maybe, but I went into the Raynor household as a typist and I'll leave as a typist; it's as pure and simple as that.'

'You mean *you* are,' conceded Rosemary indulgently. 'What's the Great Man like?'

Olivia stared into the fire, considering for a moment. 'You've seen him on stage, Rose, heard his voice, felt his magnetism—

well, it's all there, off stage too.' She wrinkled her nose. 'Charm is such an abused word, but that's the only way I can describe what he has. He's physically attractive, of course, and I could listen to him reading the telephone directory, let alone poetry or prose, but he has the power to ... capture people, mentally as well as physically. He has a tremendous sense of purpose, a wicked sense of humour and the power to make you feel important to him.'

'Mm ... I have a smattering of sympathy for Matthew Raynor.'

'So have I, Rose! Charles must be hell to live with at times, I concede all that. I haven't met the younger son, Julian, but this Raynor charm—Paul has it to a lesser degree, even Matthew—although it's never been directed at me, but then he's not my type anyway. He's too devious and decidedly too domineering. No, I like my men more straightforward and less cynical.'

'Like brother Paul?' suggested Rosemary blandly.

Olivia grinned. 'Easy-going, companionable, always friendly. Yes, if I were on the look-out for a husband, I reckon Paul would be a good candidate. I've seen Matthew giving us some side looks. It might be worth giving him food for thought.'

'You mind you don't get into deeper water than you already are,' cautioned her friend, remembering the many escapades Olivia had inveigled her into during the eighteen months they had shared the same school before Olivia had moved on. But her warning went unheeded as Olivia leant forward, chin on hands, eyes aglow.

'Rose, can you imagine—Charles is doing some recordings of famous speeches and he let me go with him to the studio. Anthea Beresford has joined him on one or two. I just sat back and let it all flow over me, they were both marvellous.'

'Don't get too carried away, will you, Noll?' asked Rosemary, slightly perturbed.

'I know the job can't go on for ever, if that's what you mean. Charles is improving daily and when he's out of the wheelchair it won't be long before he's back on stage.' Her face became pensive. 'But until that happens I'm savouring every minute.'

'And when the job's finished?' asked Rosemary tentatively.

'Then I'm going back. Yes, I thought that would please you.

39

I made a decision and stuck to it, right or wrong, but when Charles Raynor walked into that room it was like a physical blow. For nine months I'd put theatre completely behind me, thought I'd settled down into a new way of life ... but when he quoted those lines from *Twelfth Night* I thought I was going to make an idiot of myself.'

'I knew you wouldn't be able to stay away, I just knew it.'

'No half measures, I'd decided, a complete break, and then fate steps in and sends me to the Raynors! All the old longings have stirred up again. I'm like a starved person, hungrily over-eating! Forgotten are the gloomy digs, rotten food, lack of money, the bitchiness and squabbling, temperamental producers, lecherous casting directors, costumes that never fit and the parts you never get but desperately want. Instead I remember the part I wanted and did get—Isobel in *Innocents* at the Cheltenham Festival, it's the best thing I've ever done— was I sorry when that was over, I loved it. I remember the comforting feeling when the stage door closes behind you and the theatre atmosphere enfolds you like an old friend; the thrill of the curtain music; the anticipated murmuring of the audience; the not knowing whether they'll be for you or against you; the silence when you know they're for you and the burst of applause at the end.' Olivia had been pacing the floor, her whole being alive and animated, her face alight with so much enthusiasm that Rosemary wanted to imprint the scene on her memory so that she could tell Tom later. Olivia turned and caught sight of the smile on Rosemary's face and she grinned.

'Wow, that was some soliloquy! But you see what I mean?'

'In a way I do. Although I've been sitting here rather envying you your experiences. All I ever achieved were the minor traumas of an accountant's office!'

'You are an idiot, Rose. You wouldn't swop your gorgeous Tom and young Jamie for all my experiences, you know you wouldn't.' Olivia threw herself lengthwise on the settee and settled her hands behind her head. 'Mm ... just talking about the old days makes me feel like changing my mind and throwing myself at Charles Raynor's feet, pleading for his patronage—then I remember "poker face Matt" and the feeling dies a sudden death.'

'I'm sure you're exaggerating, Noll. *I* feel sorry for the poor bloke. What's he like, apart from being objectionable and prejudiced?'

'To look at or general aura?'

'Both.'

'I recognise the breed, not from rep days—he's a touch above the producers I worked for—but from drama school days. Very self-assured and remote, like a miniature god! Harriet has a series of scrapbooks which I've browsed through, and reading the reviews Matthew's good at his job.' She grinned. 'Harriet swore me to secrecy—said he'd burn them if ever he found out. Perhaps I'm judging him on very limited knowledge, for I hardly know him, and thank goodness, rarely see him. Toby adores him and children are usually discerning ... oh, Matthew and I just don't get on, and that's all there is to it. I mean, how can you when there's no trust? To look at ...' she paused and pursed her lips.

'Well ... attractive—if you like that sort. Tall, slim but quite powerfully built. Cavernous face, dark hair, thick and curly, the lucky devil, and rather beautiful teeth whenever he cracks his face, which isn't often in my presence. He ought to do it more, makes him look almost human. Nice voice, I suppose, although I'm usually battling with what he isn't saying, if you know what I mean, rather than how he's saying it, but if he were kindly disposed to you, I'll concede it's pleasant. Dresses soberly but expensively. Overall impression is one of quiet, determined self-confidence. Nothing seems to daunt him. I reckon that's what bugs me. I'd love to see him rocked off his poise. The only thing about him that appeals is his choice of car—a Lotus Europa!'

'My God! You must dislike the man! That's an incentive for anything!'

'Don't kid yourself, chum,' shrugged Olivia, 'the dislike is mutual and I can't see myself getting the chance to wash the damn thing ... let alone drive it!'

'Well, he sounds a dangerous type to hoodwink, Noll. Don't needle him unnecessarily. More cocoa?'

Olivia yawned and shook her head. 'No, thanks, and I'll heed your dire warnings.' She frowned and swung herself into a sitting position. 'Rose, what do you know about a man called

41

Adam Carlyon? Does the name ring a bell with you? I'm sure I've heard it from somewhere.'

'What does he do?'

'Directs, but I don't think that's the connection.'

'Adam Carlyon ... no, I don't think ... no, the name means nothing to me. Why?'

'His name was mentioned the other day and it's annoying me that I can't remember where I've seen or heard it before. Oh, well, it'll come to me no doubt in time. I think I'll go to bed now, Rose.'

'I'm coming up too. Before we had Jamie I used to wait up, but not any longer, not with him waking at six-thirty in the morning!' Rosemary looked at the clock and grinned. 'Looks like they've had to resort to liquid refreshment to revive themselves—I've never heard of parents' evenings going on this long! You go first, I'll just lock up and see to the fire.'

'Goodnight, Rosie—and thanks,' said Olivia.

'Thanks? For what?'

'For letting me come now and again.'

Rosemary hastily put down the cups and crossed the room to give her a fierce hug. 'Noll, you know we love having you.'

'That's a good job, because you're stuck with me,' Olivia answered cockily, her flippancy deceiving neither of them.

Relaxed and content after her weekend with the Masons, Olivia returned to Cressida House late on the Sunday evening to find two strange cars in the drive. She stood for a moment outside the softly lit front lounge windows taking in the scene. Charles was in his wheelchair talking to Anthea Beresford. The actress, Olivia guessed, was in her mid-fifties but looked much younger, her dark hair coiled attractively in a chignon and her whole appearance one of poised sophistication. Paul was softly playing the piano, the music being turned over for him by a vivacious redhead, who was keeping only one half of her attention on her job, the other half being directed at Matthew who was in full view facing the window, talking to someone seated on the window seat, her back to Olivia. To complete the group, Harriet was handing a cup of coffee to a tall, dark-haired man who was conspicuous for his very tanned face and who, at that moment, carried the cup over to the woman on the window seat. Olivia shrank back further into the shadows guiltily. He had seemed to look out of the window straight at her, but she knew it was impossible for him to see anything and, cross with herself for having peeped in the first place, she hurried round to the back.

Having no intention of proclaiming her presence, she walked quietly along the hall and mounted the stairs. Four steps up and the lounge door opened, the volume of voices suddenly increasing and then dying as the door closed once more, stopping her in her tracks. She gave a guilty start, then felt annoyed and in consequence when she turned and found Matthew watching her from the hall below this annoyance was transposed to him, and her voice was offhand and cool.

'Oh, hello, Matthew.'

'Good evening, Olivia. I heard Caliban and came to investigate, although I thought it was you. Won't you come and join us?' He moved slightly and rested a hand on the banister. She had never seen him in evening dress before and remembering the scene she had just witnessed and all the splendour that adorned the gathering, thought her sweater and jeans would make a good contrast. And she had to admit, looking at him now, that Matthew could do his fair share of contributing to that splendour—good food, drink and convivial company making him seem more human than usual and the formal dress accentuating his dark good looks ... if you liked that sort of thing. She involuntarily looked down at herself. Matthew's lips twitched and for once the grey eyes were amused.

'You're welcome to meet our guests. I wouldn't have thought that the redoubtable Miss Darcy would have bothered about how she was dressed.'

Olivia was surprised at his perceptiveness. To minimise the risk of her deception being found out she had decided on staying in the background as much as she could. 'It's rather late. Another time, perhaps?'

He nodded. 'Very well. Did you have an enjoyable weekend?'

'Yes, thank you. Well ... goodnight.'

'Olivia.' His voice stopped her ascent. 'I understand your reluctance to announce your return by intruding on our guests, but I rather think we shall have to devise some system of communication. My father is inclined to worry over you—or

43

didn't you know?' Matthew's face and voice gave nothing away.

'Oh! I . . .' A rush of emotion cut off her words.

'A note left on the memo pad, perhaps?'

'Of course.'

'Rather old-fashioned of him, I'm afraid, but with you living under his roof he feels responsible. You'll find it irksome, no doubt.'

Olivia turned and gazed at him steadily.

'I don't mind in the least. It's a long time since . . . someone felt responsible. It's rather a comforting feeling. Goodnight, Matthew,' and she continued her way up the stairs, conscious of Matthew's thoughtful eyes following her.

'Livia!'

She was past the half-opened bedroom door, but hearing her name she hesitated and then walked back.

'What are you doing awake, Toby?' Olivia crossed to the bed.

'I've been asleep, but I just woke up. I've got a tickle in my throat.'

'That's rotten,' she sympathised, brushing back the lock of hair that insisted on falling across his forehead. 'I'll fetch a drink of water and we'll see how it is then.' She smiled and left the room, returning with a glass. Toby sat up and drank deeply, his eyes never wavering over the rim of the glass. He gave a deep sigh when it was finished.

'You *were* thirsty!' exclaimed Olivia, tucking him back into bed.

'I'm not a bit tired, Livia, stay and talk.'

'You may not be, but I am!' Seeing his face she relented. 'Oh, very well, you little wretch! What shall we talk about?'

Toby grinned and snuggled down the bed. 'Grandpa's friends. Did you see the pretty lady with the curly hair? What do you call that colour, Livia?'

'Auburn, and yes, I did catch a peep at her.'

'I think she's Uncle Matt's friend really. Grandpa let me stay up past my usual bedtime.' He leant forward conspiratorially. 'He let me have a sip of his wine! I wish you'd been there too, Livia. Why weren't you?'

'You mustn't forget that I only work for your grandpa, Toby. That doesn't mean that I'm included in family dinner parties.'

44

'That's what Uncle Matt said when Daddy asked where you were. Uncle Matt said that it would be asking for trouble.' He turned a puzzled face to her. 'How can you do that, Livia?'

It is the perverseness of human nature that when someone reaches the same conclusions as oneself but for different reasons, contrariness can set in. Olivia now wished that she had contrived to be present that evening.

'We'll not worry our heads about silly grown-ups' talk,' she replied cheerfully. 'Now, shall I tell you where I've been this weekend?'

She talked softly for about ten minutes, hearing the noise of departing guests in the background. When Toby's eyelids could stay open no longer she began to ease herself gently off the edge of the bed. A shadow crossed the open doorway and putting a finger to her lips, Olivia crept out and after a moment Paul followed her, his brows raised in question. Olivia explained what had happened.

Paul smiled his slow smile. 'Don't let that son of mine take advantage of your soft heart, Olivia.'

Olivia returned his smile and shook her head, then with a whispered 'goodnight' went to her room. Lying in bed, she heard the house gradually settling for the night, but although she was tired she couldn't drop off. She kept remembering Toby's words and the quick, stupid stab of hurt she had felt; kept seeing Matthew leaning indolently at the foot of the stairs, amusement in his eyes. Unexpected, therefore unnerving and difficult to cope with ... having been used to cool indifference. This redhead must have a mellowing effect, she mused, turning over to find a more comfortable position. But it won't last.

Her thoughts turned to Paul, the calm, dependable friendliness in his blue eyes, and something more? Something else she couldn't cope with? At least there were no complications about Toby ... now. She thought back to their first meeting and the shy smile that Toby had given her. Olivia's heart had immediately been won, but she soon realised that his friendship had to be taken at his own pace. For here was no noisy, exuberant six-year-old, filling the house with his chums and alternating between angel and devil. Rather a boy too quiet and self-contained for his years, giving the impression of remaining aloof, withholding approval until cautiousness could

45

be set aside and the business of making demands could safely begin. In fact, a stranger to the house could easily mistake Toby for Matthew's son rather than Paul's, for apart from the eyes he had the promise of his uncle's angular face and slim build and already possessed his air of singlemindedness.

For the first few weeks, therefore, Olivia had had to contend with blue as well as grey eyes carefully observing her every move, but fortunately the blue ones gradually lost their wariness and with tentative overtures on both sides, her relationship with Toby showed signs of blossoming. The barriers finally came down when Toby found that Olivia was prepared to read to him. Olivia, although having no experience of six-year-old boys, soon perceived that Toby had an insatiable appetite for books. She had always enjoyed reading aloud, and the well-thumbed selection of children's classics in the library of Cressida House she renewed acquaintance with a pleasure equal to his own.

It became a habit, therefore, for Toby to come down after his evening bath and curl up beside her on the huge sofa for a further instalment of whichever book they were reading.

'Are you sure this child of mine isn't becoming a nuisance, Olivia?' Paul stood at the door, taking in the scene. 'I'm sure there must be other things you'd rather be doing.'

'No,' asserted Olivia with a smile. 'I'm renewing my delight in the adventures of Ratty, Mole and Toad. I enjoy this half-hour as much as Toby,' and she ruffled the boy's hair.

'Don't expect it as your right, lad,' Paul told his son, and Toby shook his head solemnly. 'Would you like to come with me to the Royal on Thursday, Olivia? I haven't managed to see the current play and it comes off at the end of the week.'

'I'd love to, Paul, thank you,' was her spontaneous reply.

'Good. We'll go and eat afterwards,' and lifting Toby into his arms Paul said: 'Goodnight, son,' and gave him a kiss before replacing him on to the sofa where the child nestled up to Olivia, waiting expectantly, his eyes on the book. Paul laughed. 'I'll go. I know when I'm not wanted!'

Olivia continued to read *The Wind in the Willows*, pushing Paul's invitation to the back of her mind, together with the niggling doubt as to whether or not she should have accepted it. Would it only complicate matters? Would Matthew ...? Bother Matthew! Right on cue Matthew strolled in to collect a pile of manuscripts he had left on a nearby chair. Toby's innocent, 'You've stopped making the voices, Livia,' made her jump, and a glance at Matthew's face as he left the room told her nothing, but she was sure that the fact that she read the narrative in her own voice and changed it for the dialogue of the different animals was not lost on him.

The following afternoon she remarked the fact to Rosemary, who was positioning the pram out of the wind prior to feeding the ducks on the park. Rosemary began to toss pieces of bread on to the water.

'I think you're too sensitive. Lots of people act when they're reading aloud, makes it more interesting. You've got a guilty conscience, that's your trouble.'

'You could be right,' agreed Olivia. 'Oh, look, Jamie, the sparrows want some too.'

'How are things generally and Matthew in particular?'

'Things generally are fine. The job is everything I could wish it to be, Charles continues to be super, Harriet's taken me under her wing and clucks like a mother hen, Paul is very kind and Toby is a darling.' She took a quick look at the pram. 'Hey, Rose, should your offspring be eating the bread?' and laughing, she rescued the ducks' tea from Jamie's eager hands. 'Matthew in particular? ... well, not much change really, although I have a glimpse of another side of him when he's with Toby and gets lulled into a false sense of security.'

'Can't you ignore him?'

'None of the Raynors are easily ignored, Rose!'

Olivia remembered this conversation the following morning when Paul confirmed their theatre visit during breakfast. The family very rarely sat down together to eat breakfast, but on this particular day the three Raynor men were present. Charles lowered his paper and smiled his approval while Matthew, pausing momentarily to shoot first his brother and then herself a quick, penetrating glance, continued to open his mail without comment.

Olivia, knowing she was safe while Charles was in her company, felt anger rising, for what could be more innocuous than an invitation to the theatre? Any doubts she had previously had over accepting disappeared and turning to Paul she skilfully drew him out on one of his schemes to help the elderly living alone. The fact that Paul was so dedicated made his enthusiasm infectious and Olivia was able to ease her conscience in using him by the interest she found in the subject. Matthew was called from the table to take a telephone call and did not reappear, but by the look on his face Olivia thought that perhaps she was not his most favourite person, and tried to kid herself that she didn't care.

The trouble is, she grumbled to herself as she began to work, that I want everything to be perfect, and as perfection is hard to come by I'm in for a disappointment. I shall have to try to stop wanting to be liked. She frowned over this weakness, trying to justify it, shrugging it off with a—for heaven's sake, he's an interesting and intelligent man and I should like to have his respect, but since he has some bee in his bonnet about me and I can't have it, that's his affair and to hell with him! I shall not allow him to undermine my contentment here. And she thrust Matthew Raynor from her mind and concentrated on the job in hand.

Later in the morning Charles wheeled himself into the study, a letter in his hand.

'Olivia, give the local radio station a ring, will you, and make an appointment for one afternoon next week? They've invited me to speak about the theatre in their *Controversy on the Arts* programme.'

'Very well, Mr Raynor.' Olivia took the letter from him and made a note on her pad. For quite some time now she had moved her typewriter into the study on Charles's request. For a while they worked in silence, Olivia reading his notes prior to typing them out.

'Have you ever considered writing your autobiography, Mr Raynor?' she asked, chuckling quietly over an amusing anecdote, enjoying his lively style and complete control over words and situations. He answered her with a gravity belied by the expression in his blue eyes.

'My dear child, no! That will have to be left until I'm not around to bear the repercussions. We in the profession are terribly touchy and thin-skinned,' he gave a quick smile, 'and I'm having to sieve through and select those stories I think suitable for this lecture tour, otherwise I shall find myself in trouble.'

They shared a smile and after a while, sensing his scrutiny,

Olivia looked up again, her eyes questioning, and found him considering her thoughtfully.

'Olivia, I want to tell you how pleased I am with our working partnership. You're an intelligent girl—you must have realised that I engaged you ... no, not on mere impulse, that wouldn't be a fair assumption, but rather on instinct which happily has exceeded my expectations and more than paid off. The motivation, I'm afraid, was a completely unwarranted desire to get under ... someone's skin.' He paused and after a moment continued pensively: 'Indeed, Matthew did not deserve such treatment and I can only plead, much to my shame, chronic distemper due to the accident and a subsequent inability to come to terms with my enforced inactivity.' He pursed his lips and the blue eyes were penetrating. 'Unfortunately, I cannot help noticing that this has caused a certain amount of constraint between the two of you, and this I regret.'

Olivia said with some difficulty: 'I don't think you should feel it your fault, Mr Raynor. I must share some of the blame. You see, Matthew had already interviewed me and said that ... I wasn't quite suited ... before you ever saw me. I ought to have told you. I'm sorry.'

'Mm ... I see.' A flicker of amusement crossed his face, but his voice remained bland. 'I would ask you to forgive Matthew for his reservations. They are partly my fault for forcing his hand and partly because he has had to contend with some rather embarrassing and painful situations over the years, both on my account and on his own, and this has made him untrusting and slightly cynical. He used not to be so, although he has never been as outgoing as his brothers. You're not seeing him at his best, I'm afraid.'

'Please don't worry about me, Mr Raynor,' said Olivia quickly, unexpectedly embarrassed at the proud and lofty Matthew being cut up and fed to her in small pieces, 'and I quite understand and sympathise about your son.' She hesitated and said shyly, 'I'm very happy here ... and love working for you.'

He smiled. 'Good. To have your interest and enthusiasm has helped me enormously. I'd go so far as to say that you've probably kept me going—stimulated the creative drive.'

Olivia was so delighted at this accolade that she wanted to

shout out loud or dance a jig, but repressing both of these wild urges she consoled herself with an idiotically inane smile and hoped that Charles Raynor would realise what his words meant to her. She rather thought that he did.

'You are an extremely good listener, Olivia. I'm afraid once an actor always an actor. We are never so happy as when there is an audience before us, even a captive audience of one, especially if it's such an appreciative and attractive one.' He broke off and looked beyond her to the door. 'You would agree, Matthew?'

'Olivia doesn't need me to endorse your views, Father. I'm sure they carry much more weight with her than mine.' Matthew closed the door.

'Nonsense,' said Charles, giving her a wicked side glance. 'Every woman needs to be told she's attractive, and the more who tell her the better.'

'I don't think anything I say now would mean very much. Do you, Olivia?' Matthew raised his dark brows mockingly. 'It would seem too dutiful, surely?'

Olivia, aware of her employer's silent amusement, parried smoothly:

'Even as a child I liked the anticipation of a treat almost as much as the treat itself. Perhaps you could save it up for another time, Matthew? It will give me something to look forward to.'

'I think that would be a good idea,' he replied evenly, grey eyes narrowing so that Olivia wondered whether it was wise to do battle with Matthew Raynor and decided that indifference ought to be her plan for the future.

'Sorry to interrupt, Father, but Carlyon will be at the Royal tomorrow afternoon. Any chance of you coming down? If so we'll call a meeting.'

'Every chance.' Charles turned to Olivia. 'You shall come too, Olivia. You'll be seeing one half of the theatre tonight with Paul and tomorrow you'll be able to see the other half. It's time you had a look around, it will interest you.' He reached out to place the book he was holding on to the table and stopped, face contorted with pain. 'It's all right,' he growled, as both Matthew and Olivia leapt to his side. 'Just a twinge, nothing to worry about.'

Olivia fetched a glass of water from the tray on the desk

50

and Matthew, lips tight, strode over to the communicating door between the study and his father's bedroom. Putting his head round the door, he surveyed the room briefly before returning, his face grim.

'If Paul finds out that you've been trying those damned crutches, you'll be in for trouble.'

'He won't find out, unless you tell him.' Charles sipped the water and breathed carefully, the colour gradually returning to his face.

'Olivia, if you see your employer putting so much as a toe to the ground,' Matthew went on, 'I want you to go to Paul immediately, do you understand?'

Olivia, one look at the concern on his face, nodded acquiescence. Charles smiled ruefully.

'You see how I'm treated, Olivia. Can't call my soul my own!'

'I should think not.' Matthew's voice was brusque. 'You're too much of an investment.' He looked down at his father repressively: 'If you're not feeling up to it tomorrow we'll cancel the idea of a meeting.'

'I shall be perfectly all right when I've had a rest.'

'We'll see. If you're no better this evening Paul had better look you over.' Matthew turned the chair and wheeled it through into the bedroom. 'I know how hard it is for you, Father, and if it gives you any pleasure, you weigh heavily on my conscience.'

Olivia heard Charles say 'Rubbish!' before the communicating door closed.

So that Toby would not miss his evening read, Olivia suggested that he had his bath earlier than usual and this was accepted eagerly. When the customary chapter was finished, Toby asked shyly:

'Will you come in to see me, Olivia, when you have your pretty dress on?'

'Of course I shall,' replied Olivia indignantly. 'I shall tuck you up in all my finery. Off you go, and mind you don't fall asleep until I come.'

Although Olivia still had mixed feelings about the evening before her, nevertheless, it was pleasant to be taken out, and she surveyed herself critically in the mirror. Not too bad, she

51

decided. The rich burgundy dress was one she had always liked and felt comfortable in; the cowl neck and long sleeves giving it a sophisticated elegance without being too dressy. She slipped on some silver shoes, dabbed a finger of perfume behind each ear and collecting her evening bag and cape she hurried along to Toby's bedroom. With a flourish of arms, a couple of twirls culminating in a Garbo pose against the door, she asked gaily:

'There! What do you think?'

'Doesn't she look pretty, Uncle Matt?' Toby's words brought Olivia's head round with a startled jerk to the direction of the bed and she found Matthew sitting on it, a derisive look on his face. Toby gazed at her in admiration.

'Doesn't she?' insisted Toby, weighting his question with tugs to his uncle's sleeve.

'This seems to be my day for having words thrust into my mouth,' drawled Matthew. 'Yes, Toby, Olivia does indeed look pretty ... I envy your papa.'

'You can take her another time,' offered Toby kindly, and Olivia hastily crossed the room and gave him a quick kiss on the cheek, ignoring the mocking glint in Matthew's eyes.

'Sleep tight, Toby. I'll tell you all about it tomorrow.'

'I do like your hair on the top like that, Livia. It makes you look like a princess,' he said gravely.

Olivia curtsied, 'Thank you kindly,' and blowing him another kiss she escaped from the room. Paul was waiting for her in the library and his face echoed his son's in admiration.

'Has Toby been allowed to see you first? I hope so. He wanted to be one up on me.'

Olivia smiled and affirmed that Toby had passed judgment. 'How is your father, Paul?'

'Seems better, but I've ordered a stay of bed.' Paul frowned and shook his head. 'I can't understand why he should have had this trouble; he'll have to have further X-rays if it persists.' He helped her on with her cape. 'I'll just let Harriet know we're off.'

As Olivia followed him out into the hall Matthew came slowly down the stairs. He stood on the bottom step, leaning easily against the banister. Olivia ignored him and considered herself in the hall mirror, tweaking a piece of hair unnecessarily into place. After a moment she lifted her eyes and met his through the glass. Suddenly she was sickened of the whole thing. Without pausing to think, her voice low and intense, she said:

'What would you say, Matthew, if I offered to hand in my resignation to your father? I will ... if that's what you want me to do.' Watching his face through the reflection, she could see no visible reaction to her words. Turning slowly, she suffered his eyes to rake her up and down, only a glint in her green eyes and slightly heightened colour betraying her feelings. 'Well?'

'I would reiterate my original estimation of you, and say that you're a very clever woman, Miss Olivia Darcy.' His voice hardened. 'Your sense of timing, once again, is perfect. Hand in your notice indeed! With my father having a sudden relapse? Just what reason would you give at this inauspicious time?'

'Well, I ...' Olivia bit her lip.

'Exactly! We are all well aware of your lack of family to provide a pressing reason to go home. We are also aware of your so-called affection for your employer, and now you talk of leaving! Yes, you're very clever, Olivia.'

'Just don't forget that I offered,' ground out Olivia.

'Knowing exactly what the outcome would be.' Matthew smiled thinly, his stare, cold and ruthless, holding her own.

'I think you're insufferable, Matthew Raynor!'

'Good. Anything else would be merely play-acting.'

Olivia turned quickly away and fumbled in her bag for her gloves. Paul reappeared, saying as he strode down the hall:

'I can't find Harriet anywhere, Matt. Will you tell her I've rung the exchange, so the emergency number is in operation? You know where I am for the first half of the evening if I'm needed urgently, but,' he smiled down at Olivia, taking her arm, 'I sincerely hope the need won't arise. We're going on to the Lancers afterwards.'

'Are you indeed?' Matthew's tone made Paul grin.

'Sorry, I had the idea first, little brother! Goodnight.'

'Goodnight ... and have fun,' was Matthew's mocking rejoinder.

Driving into the city, Paul said suddenly:

'I hope you'll like this play. Matt never discusses his productions beforehand, so I know nothing about it.'

53

'Even if the play doesn't appeal, I shall enjoy going to the theatre. There's always something to appreciate and I'd like to see one of Matthew's productions.'

Paul shot her a quick look. 'You don't get on with Matthew, do you?'

Olivia was startled and more than a little troubled. 'That's not really true. I just find him difficult to fathom. I ... don't think he altogether approves of me.'

'You're far out there,' Paul said emphatically. 'We're all delighted how well you get on with Father and pleased with the progress being made with this tour programme. For believe me, had there been the slightest excuse Father would have abandoned it and then we should have had to think of something else to keep him out of mischief. As it is, things have worked out far better than we dared hope.' He swung into the theatre car park. 'You mustn't let Matthew throw you. He takes some getting to know, doesn't give all of himself in one go, he hands a piece out, a bit at a time. And don't let that aloof façade fool you. He's one in a million to have around when you're going through a tough patch.' Paul's voice had become grim and the unspoken words 'as I well know' lay heavily between them.

Rotheringham Theatre Royal had great similarity to many other theatres built around the turn of the century, and as Paul led her through the foyer and into the rapidly filling auditorium Olivia felt she was greeting an old friend and she viewed the ornate scrolls and smiling cherubs with sentimental affection.

Three hours later they were sitting in the Lancers Hotel and Olivia was now aware of the reason for Matthew's raised brows ... unobtrusive luxury were two good words to describe it.

'This has been quite an evening for me. A good play, a beautiful companion and an excellent meal—what more could a man ask?' and Paul smiled across the table.

Olivia laughed. 'I'd agree the first and last, but the rest! ... and that's not fishing for a compliment! To be truthful, Paul, it's quite a while since I've enjoyed myself so much.'

'Then I'm content. You enjoyed the play?'

'Yes, indeed. The Company has a high standard, but that doesn't really come as a surprise, for anything your father is 'involved with must be above average.' She paused. 'The production was interesting, full of subtleties. In different circumstances I should like to w ...' She very nearly said 'work' and hurriedly changed it to 'watch Matthew work.'

'I should imagine that could be arranged. Are you ready for coffee?'

Olivia nodded and Paul's hand came down over hers and imprisoned it, his thumb lying gently across her wrist. He smiled slightly and raised a brow.

'Mmm ... pulse rate high—I wonder why?'

Because I very nearly said something I shouldn't, thought Olivia wryly, saying with a teasing quality in her voice: 'Your magnetic personality, or perhaps the introduction of wine into the bloodstream?'

'I hope the first but strongly suspect the second. Drink up your coffee and dilute the alcohol!'

'Yes, doctor,' submitted Olivia demurely, 'I will, when I can have my hand back.'

On the journey home Paul surprised her by saying: 'When my father has no further need of your services, Olivia, you won't be doing anything silly like disappearing out of our lives for ever, will you?'

Olivia was thankful of the darkness. 'I ... haven't thought that far, Paul. I'm enjoying the work so much that I'm afraid I just batten down all thought of the future. You're spoiling me, you see.'

'Excellent. I like that idea. I rather fancy that you've not had your fair share of being spoilt.' His voice was grave.

'Oh, I haven't done so badly,' Olivia said heartily, his gentleness touching a raw spot.

'It's not good for anyone to have no family at all. I give you leave to have a share of ours.'

'Super! May I? Let me see ...' Finger on lip, Olivia thought deeply. 'I think I'll choose a slice of Harriet's fussing, your father's voice saying ... oh, anything! but preferably poetry; Toby's hand in mine, your kind smile—I haven't met Julian yet so I can't make a choice—what can he give me?'

'Fun,' answered Paul promptly. 'And what about Matthew?'

'I'll admit Matthew needs to be considered carefully ...' Frowning slightly, her face quickly cleared and with a smile Olivia said: 'I know! I'll have a share of his Lotus—which is pure wishful thinking, isn't it? I doubt whether he would allow a mere female to drive his beautiful new car.'

'Poor Matt hasn't been too lucky with cars just lately, so he may be forgiven,' offered Paul, swinging into Cressida's drive. When the engine note died Olivia turned in her seat and said softly:

'Thank you for a lovely evening, Paul.'

He took her face in both hands and looked at her steadily for a moment.

'The thanks are all on my side, Olivia.' His kiss was gentle and undemanding. Giving her a whimsical smile, he said: 'Run along in and get that beauty sleep, my dear. Goodnight.' He left his seat and walked round to open her door.

'Goodnight, Paul.' Olivia was thankful of the front porch light, for the night was a particularly black one. She had just gained the step when she heard Paul say:

'Hello, Caliban, old fellow. Having your bedtime constitutional? That you, Matt?'

Olivia heard the crunch of gravel and turned, making out a dark shape coming up the drive to join Paul by the side of the car, their soft murmuring just indistinguishable. Caliban's cold nose touched her hand and made her jump. Giving him an absent-minded pat, Olivia went in.

Even though it was a moonless night Matthew couldn't have failed to see their embrace, for the headlights had been reflected off the garage doors.

Olivia smiled with satisfaction. Good. It would give him something to think about.

CHAPTER THREE

'I beseech you, what manner of man is he?'

A FEW spots of rain appeared haphazardly on the windscreen and Olivia flicked the wiper switch, easing her foot off the accelerator as the glass blurred momentarily.

'There are no rehearsals scheduled for this afternoon, Olivia, so you'll be able to wander around wherever you wish. I shall be interested to see what you make of the place.' Charles's voice took on an indulgent tone. 'Of course, we have a soft spot for the Royal. She's our "baby". We know her weaknesses and limitations but contrive to rise above them, and succeed, I think. I've played in all kinds of theatres in my time, and there's something to be said for the small, intimate ones like the Royal. Do you agree?'

Olivia nodded, concentrating on the flow of traffic. Charles glanced sideways at her and smiled. 'There's really no need for the frown and the biting of the bottom lip, my dear. You're doing very well.'

'Thank you, but if I'd known, when you asked if I could drive, that your car was a Jaguar I'd have said I couldn't!'

'I don't see why. It's a car, like any other, a means of getting from one place to another.'

'Not quite like any other. It's large, beautiful and very expensive,' retorted Olivia, braking hard to avoid a cyclist.

'Turn left here, Olivia, and then first right.'

'Is Rotheringham a theatre-minded city?' asked Olivia, obeying his instructions. Charles considered for a moment.

'Yes, I would say it is. The university has its own theatre and there are a number of thriving amateur societies. Then there's the old Palace, we pass it in a minute.' He sensed a reaction from her and added: 'You know it?'

'Not this particular one, but my father introduced me to Variety many years ago.'

'You speak as though you're in your dotage, child. There's certainly been a revival in that direction during the last few years, although it's slightly more sophisticated than in the past. Television has made its demands, I'm afraid. I played an interesting fellow a couple of years ago in a play called *The Entertainer* . . .'

'Archie Rice?' broke in Olivia without thinking.

'Ah, you know the play. In that case, you'll know what I mean when I say that the stand-up comic is one of the hardest forms of entertainment there is . . . a very lonely life up there on your own.'

You can say that again, thought Olivia grimly to herself.

'This is the turn, isn't it?' She drove the sleek, grey Jaguar through the gateway. 'Does it matter where I park?'

'Next to the Lotus, if you will. There! That was excellent.'

'If you say so, but I've a feeling you're being kind. The journey wasn't as smooth as I would have wanted it to be.' Olivia pulled a face. 'I feel like a wet rag and my left leg is numb.'

'You'll soon get used to the pedals. Is this Matthew?'

Olivia followed his gaze and saw a familiar figure rounding the corner of the building, hands in pockets.

'Yes, it is.' She began to gather together handbag and gloves. 'How long will your meeting be, Mr Raynor?'

Charles pursed his lips. 'No telling, but don't worry. If we finish first we'll soon find you.'

Matthew said: 'So you made it,' as he opened the door for Olivia to get out. She was slightly nettled.

'Of course. Did you think I wouldn't?' she asked over her shoulder as she went to the boot and unlocked it. Matthew lifted out the wheelchair and opened it up, giving her a sharp sideways look.

'Not really. I have every faith in your ability to make yourself useful, even to driving automatic Jags.'

Olivia swallowed hard and said shortly: 'I don't think your father ought to have come.'

'Neither do I, but he has a mind of his own.' Matthew left her to re-lock the boot and when she joined him Charles was already transferred to the wheelchair.

'I see Carlyon has arrived—that is his car, Matt, isn't it? If you'll hand me my briefcase, Olivia? Thank you. Off you go. I won't be needing you. Through the stage door over there, down the corridor, up the stone steps and you'll be backstage.'

'I don't think you'll get lost, do you, Olivia?'

'I shouldn't think so,' she replied calmly, ignoring the challenge in Matthew's question. 'The place doesn't look big enough, but if I do, I'll sit down and wait for you to rescue me,' and giving her employer a quick smile and his son a sickly flutter of her lashes, she walked towards the stage door, making a conscious effort to appear relaxed.

If Olivia had felt a spark of recognition the previous evening when she had entered the front of house with Paul, what she felt for the next hour backstage could only be described as a minor explosion.

How many times in the past had she walked comparable narrow corridors? Sat in the same small, crowded dressing rooms before cracked, mottled mirrors over which hung innumerable faded notices? The recognition was so strong it almost hurt and she breathed in the familiar atmosphere, smiling in remembrance of Charles's words to her at their first meeting—that he would be visiting the Royal to revitalise himself—and undergoing a fellow feeling. She wandered around, noting that although it was cramped and manned with old equipment, the place seemed to be run efficiently, a quality one would expect from a Company headed by Matthew Raynor.

Leaving the best until last, Olivia pushed open the heavy soundproofed door and stepped on to the stage.

The set for the evening performance was waiting in readiness; everywhere was quiet and still. Olivia walked to centre stage. The only light came from a triangular shaft from the door through which she had just entered. This shaft filtered between the end flat and the proscenium arch and by it Olivia could discern the seating in the auditorium stretching out before her. There's something rather forlorn about rows and rows of empty seats, she thought, almost as if they're silently reproachful. She frowned and closed her eyes, imagining the empty seats full of expectant patrons. Tentatively at first, gradually gaining confidence and volume, she launched into some of her favourite pieces.

Almost from the beginning of this private performance a man had entered and had stood at the back of the auditorium watching the tall, slender girl, arms hanging loosely by her side, legs slightly apart, head thrown back allowing thick brown

59

hair to fall freely down her back—and automatically assessed her professionally. Her performance, small though it was, pleased him.

'."He is dead and gone, lady, He is dead and gone; At his head a grass-green turf, At the heels a stone . . ." '

As the plaintive notes died away the onlooker thought it time to proclaim his presence.

'Miss Darcy?'

The quiet voice brought Olivia back to her surroundings with a start. Shielding her eyes, she peered into the darkness and with a hesitant, 'Yes?' walked uncertainly to the edge of the forestage.

'I'm sorry to have to bring you back from Elsinore so abruptly.' The man smiled up at her, white teeth gleaming in a tanned face; dark eyes alert and interested.

'Er . . . I thought I was alone.' Olivia felt foolish and slightly alarmed. How long had he been in the auditorium? How much had he heard? Who, in fact, was he? 'Perhaps I shouldn't be on the stage?'

'I don't see why not.' He reached his hand and helped her down. 'You've played Ophelia?'

'Oh . . . yes, only at school,' and Olivia was thankful that she had never been in *Hamlet* professionally. She wouldn't like to have to convince this man that she was a typist, not if he had heard all of it; he didn't look the type to be hoodwinked easily. They began to walk back through the auditorium and she eyed him covertly from beneath lowered lashes. Tall, distinguished, intelligent face, he was the man she had seen through the window at Cressida House on Sunday evening. He spoke and walked as a man who was used to authority.

'Does Mr Raynor want me?' she asked at last.

'Charles, no, but Matthew would like to have a word.' He looked at her closely. 'You're Charles's . . . secretary?'

'Yes,' affirmed Olivia with a conviction she didn't feel. Now was the time for him to show surprise, to pass some comment, but he only nodded.

'Adam Carlyon,' and her hand was grasped in a firm grip.

The name caused her stride to falter slightly. Adam Carlyon! The more she surreptitiously studied his face the more she knew she had never met him before, and yet the name was so familiar—but from where?

'Do you work here, Mr Carlyon?' she inquired, hoping he would give her a clue.

'On occasions. Do you like working for Charles?'

'Very much.'

'He's an interesting man,' Adam Carlyon remarked mildly.

'Ah, you've found her, Adam—good.' Matthew came round the corner, glancing back the way they had come. 'You were on stage . . .?'

Olivia tensed. Wait for it—here it comes. The perfect cue for Adam Carlyon to say, yes, I found her spouting *Macbeth*, *The Dream* and *Hamlet*! What an impression that would give to the already suspicious Matthew!

'Yes, it was most interesting,' she answered feebly, and threw a quick look at Adam Carlyon, but he showed no signs of any further information. He considered her briefly and then turned to Matthew.

'Now that I've found Miss Darcy, have you decided what to do, Matt?'

'I think so. Will you go in to him, Adam, and keep the meeting going? Then it won't look as though there's been collusion between us.'

'Of course,' and with a smile at Olivia, Adam Carlyon left them. What a lovely, lovely man, she thought with relief.

Matthew's brows were pulled together by a deep frown. 'Olivia, I need your assistance. My father is in pain, but he'll not admit it, especially to me, and anything I suggest by way of getting him home he'd regard with deep suspicion, so I want you to try.' He gave an exasperated sigh. 'He really is a stubborn man. He should never have come today, but he insisted he was well enough. Now, in front of all the committee members, he certainly won't admit he was wrong,' and he rubbed his forehead irritably.

Olivia felt a stab of sympathy for Matthew. Always pale, his face was drawn and he looked very tired. Her voice was full of concern. 'What did Paul say? I thought he was going to give him a look over this morning?'

'Paul?' He lifted a brow sardonically. 'Paul is seeing the world through a haze of benevolent optimism at the moment. He must have had a good night out last night.'

The stab of sympathy died a quick death. 'What do you

want me to do?' she asked coldly, 'although I honestly don't think I'll be more able than you to ...'

'Oh, come, Olivia!' he said impatiently. 'You do yourself an injustice. You surely know how to use those green eyes and sweet smile to the best advantage.'

Resisting the temptation to wipe the cynical look off his face with the palm of her hand, she repeated her question curtly: 'What do you want me to do?'

'I thought you could produce a headache and ask if you may go home. That would give a legitimate excuse for him to leave with you.' He took her arm and led her to the office door. 'Wait here. I'll go in and pass on your request. With any luck I'll be able to bring him out with me.' He paused. 'I'm sure you'll be able to act up the headache, Olivia.'

'Five minutes in your company and it's quite easy,' she retorted.

He smiled. 'I'm sure Paul will be only too delighted to treat it for you.'

When the door swung to behind him Olivia let out a deep breath. On the day she walked out of this job she would have great pleasure in telling Mr Matthew Sarcasm Raynor exactly what she thought of him! A few minutes later the door reopened and Matthew manoeuvred the wheelchair out smoothly. Olivia was dismayed to see how drawn Charles Raynor looked, but was careful not to show it. She stepped forward apologetically.

'I'm awfully sorry, Charles, to be such a nuisance. Has Matthew explained about my headache?'

'Yes, my dear, we'll have you home in next to no time.'

'Oh ... but surely there's no need for us both to leave? I can easily catch a bus.'

Standing behind his father, Matthew frowned.

'Nonsense,' Charles said brusquely. 'The meeting's virtually over. Adam can cope with what's left. Matthew shall drive us home.'

Matthew's frown disappeared. 'Home it is, then,' he announced calmly.

The journey home was taken in near silence. As Charles preceded Olivia down the hall he asked:

'Have you something for that headache, Olivia?'

'Yes, thank you, Mr Raynor.'

62

'Oh dear! What a pity . . .' Charles gave a wry smile. 'We're back to "Mr Raynor" again. You said Charles quite naturally at the theatre.' His eyes were kind. 'I insist on being humoured.'

'I'm sure Olivia will be only too happy to humour you, Father,' came the dry observation from behind her.

'Thank you . . . Charles,' replied Olivia, all sweet obedience, and watched him give a satisfied nod before wheeling himself into his room.

'There, that wasn't so difficult, was it?' murmured Matthew as he followed his father in. Lips tight, Olivia went to her room.

It wasn't until much later that Olivia realised her employer's briefcase was still in the Jaguar. The car was parked in the drive where they had left it and as she emerged from the back, briefcase in hand, the sound of another car swinging into the drive attracted her attention and looking up, she saw the Lotus, gravel spurting in all directions, pull up immediately behind. The engine note died abruptly and Matthew eased himself out and strolled towards her. Olivia closed the Jag's door and turned to go, pausing reluctantly when he called her name. He stood, hands on hips, looking down at her.

'Thank you for your help, Olivia, this afternoon.'

She raised her brows. 'I do hope it wasn't too painful. Having to thank me, I mean.' She met his gaze steadily although her heart began to thump, as it always did whenever she engaged in verbal combat with him. Matthew considered her thoughtfully.

'You misjudge me. My thanks were sincere. However, I will admit that being beholden to you is a feeling I do not wish to have repeated too often.'

She bit her lip in chagrin. He never gave an inch, did he! She shrugged.

'It's all in the day's work, Matthew. He who pays the piper calls the tune.'

His jaw tightened. 'Unfortunately, that's not quite true and you know it. My father's dependence on you ties my hands.'

'Ah, well, you can't win them all.'

His eyes narrowed. 'You interest me deeply, Miss Olivia Darcy—and not, I hasten to add, in a way that need alarm your admiring swains . . .'

'You flatter yourself!'

'... although those flashing green eyes could perhaps prove an incentive in other circumstances, you're well aware of how to use your assets to their best advantage.' His tone was all insult.

'I can't win with you, can I?' she snapped. 'You were quite prepared for me to use them this afternoon. Come to the point.'

'The point, Olivia, is your position in this household. I've come to the conclusion that you're either too good to be true or else ... very ingenuous.'

'You say the sweetest things! What exactly are you getting at?'

He lazily leant an arm on the roof of the Jaguar, blocking her path.

'We know so little about you, but I'm willing to bet you know practically everything about the Raynor family. We do know, of course, how useful you are, how indispensable ...'

'That's my job. I'm only doing my job,' she protested vehemently.

'In which you are efficient and amenable, your youth, energy and enthusiasm making Charles feel young again ...'

'You should be pleased instead of ...'

'But it's not only my father, is it? Harriet enthuses about what a "good lass" you are and how you're absolutely "no trouble".' He gave a short laugh. 'If Harriet had any perception she would see you as "trouble" with capital letters, but she's a trusting soul at heart. Then there's Paul. Well, Paul has woken up to the fact that there are other things in life than a dead wife's memory and healing hands. Not a bad thing so far as it goes and so long as it goes no further. And Toby,' his voice hardened, 'for the first time in his young life is being allowed a glimpse of what it must be like to have a mother, to love and cherish. Take especial care over Toby, Olivia, and see that he comes to no harm through any cause of yours. You haven't met Julian yet ...'

'But that won't stop you from giving an opinion, surely?' interjected Olivia scornfully.

Matthew smiled. 'Julian can take care of himself.'

'And you, Matthew?' she managed, her knuckles white as

they clenched the briefcase hard against herself. 'Can you take care of yourself?'

'Oh, I think so, Olivia,' he drawled. 'There was a time when it would have amused me to take you on, but I'm getting too old for skirmishes of that nature. To me you're an irritating problem which at this particular moment I could well do without.'

'For some unknown reason you saw me as a problem the minute you set eyes on me.'

'Ah, the fateful interview. Yes ... I ought to have put my foot down there and then, but it seemed more important at the time that my father should be settled into a routine as quickly as possible, so ...'—he shrugged—'... you've become a problem. But problems have to be tackled and you're quite a challenge—I never refuse a challenge.'

'How brave of you—but what have you to lose?' Olivia turned away, trying to regain her composure, determined he should not see the angry tears threatening to spill over.

'Exactly! But you give so little away, Olivia,' Matthew continued reproachfully. 'Even the redoubtable ladies, Shawcross and Turnbull, couldn't tell me much about you—just your previous address.'

Olivia was horrified. How dared he spy on her—how dared he! She rounded on him furiously. 'You've been to the agency? There was absolutely no need for you to do that. I would have told you where I lived myself had you asked!'

'Of that I'm sure, especially as you knew I'd be able to find out anyway.'

Olivia controlled her voice with an effort. 'What did you think of number twenty-five Columbine Terrace?'

'I thought the name the best thing about the place.'

'For once we're in complete agreement.'

'You appear slightly put out that I've been investigating you, Olivia, but I think when you've calmed down, you will admit that what I've done is normal under the circumstances. Consider. We take you into our house, treat you as one of the family and yet we know little more of you now than the day you first entered it.'

The fact that there was truth in what he said did not help.

'It all seems very reasonable, put like that,' retorted Olivia bitterly, 'but what impression did you give the agency, with your Gestapo methods? Have you forgotten that I've got to go back there for another job when your father returns to the stage? But people in your exalted position forget little things like that! What hardship have *you* ever had to face, brought up in a family like this? I can hardly suppose that you've had to worry about being out of work in your life!'

'It's not my life that's under discussion, and you can rest easy regarding the agency. I exerted all my natural charms and the information was offered without the lady realising she was giving it.' He gave her a searching look and added softly: 'You do anticipate going back to the agency?'

'Of course I ...' Olivia broke off abruptly and a flicker showed in his eyes. She continued deliberately, 'Unless something more interesting or ... more profitable turns up.' She steeled herself against the sudden contempt on his face and smiled. 'I have one or two plans in the offing, any one of them may come off. It's always as well to have more than one string to the bow, don't you think?' One look at his face told her she had gone too far.

'What I think, Miss Olivia Darcy,' said Matthew grimly, 'you are already aware.'

'The feeling,' retaliated Olivia, 'is mutual.'

'I shan't grieve for that, my back is broad, but there are others more vulnerable. The first signs of stepping outside your legitimate job and you'll go, is that understood? I'm warning you, Olivia—any mischief and you can expect no mercy from me.'

Olivia, smarting from the injustice of it all and the arrogance of the man, curled her lip. 'You be warned too, Mr God Almighty Raynor! For the last time, I repeat that I came to this house in ignorance of who lived here, needing the job offered, knowing I was fully capable of doing it and accepting it with no other motive. I find you distinctly disagreeable, offensive, dictatorial and conceited. If you think that I'll leave because of your beastliness to me, I'm sorry to disappoint you. I know I offered yesterday, but that was a moment of weakness. It's a pity you didn't accept, but you like to control things, don't you? You want to be the one to say go.' She took a much-needed breath, chin jutting angrily. 'Will you kindly let me pass?'

'Not bad ... not bad at all,' he marvelled unpleasantly. 'I

66

particularly liked the haughty tone at the end. Of course, what would be the culminating triumph of that impassioned speech ...' He broke off and peered towards her. 'Ah! You have not failed me, Miss Darcy—tears! There's a definite pearl just about to drop from your most exquisite lashes. The final artistic touch!'

Olivia thrust the briefcase at him and pushed past, staggering as her heel caught the stone edging of the shrubbery, bringing her down heavily. The front door opened a few yards to their left and Harriet's voice called uncertainly:

'Matt? Are you there? Telephone!'

Olivia's action had taken Matthew by surprise. He cursed under his breath, threw out a hand to save her, but was hindered by the briefcase and being off balance. She struck his hand away and thrust herself up, a sharp branch whipping back and scraping her face, catching her hair. With a sob she tore herself free and fled round the side of the house. Matthew stood for a moment, watching her go, then hearing Harriet call once more, he walked slowly to the house, his face grim.

'Olivia?' Harriet's voice was anxious as she tapped on the bedroom door. 'Olivia, are you all right?'

Olivia sat up and composed her voice. 'Yes, thank you, Harriet.'

'You didn't come down for dinner.'

'No, I had a headache.' She gave a laugh. 'Serves me right for pretending this afternoon, doesn't it? I've taken something for it and I'll have an early night. I'm not hungry, honestly, Harry.' She willed Harriet to accept her explanation and to her relief heard her say doubtfully:

'If you're sure ... I'll leave something on a tray in case you change your mind. I'm off to the hospital now, it's my W.V.S. stint tonight. Goodnight, Olivia.'

'Goodnight.' Olivia waited and then crossed and turned the key in the lock. Sighing, she walked over to the tallboy and picked up the hand mirror, eyeing herself gloomily.

'What a mess I look!' she muttered, taking in the red, swollen eyes, the pale, tear-smudged face and the angry scratch down the side of her cheek. There was a similar scratch across the back of her hand, both were extremely sore, and as her right knee was swollen and throbbing painfully, she considered she had every excuse for wallowing in a few moments of self-pity. But it really got you nowhere. It served her right for letting that man get under her skin. Had she accepted his thanks and not taken the conversation further all this would not have happened. She pulled a face. Don't kid yourself, chum. It had been brewing for some time. She crossed to the small wash-hand basin and holding a flannel under the cold tap, squeezed it out and laid it soothingly across her cheek. She repeated this a few times, alternating hand and face and taking in eyes for good measure. She then carefully pulled up the leg of her pyjamas and bathed her knee. You'll have a lovely bruise tomorrow, my girl, she mused, and drying herself off she limped over to the bed.

' "Oh, what a tangled web we weave!" '

She lay back and tried to get things into perspective, but soon realised that she was too committed to do so. The trouble was that things had got out of control. All she had wanted to do was to get on with her job to the best of her ability and leave when it was over. Instead of which, she had been drawn deeper and deeper into the family confidences and way of life, almost without being aware of it, until ... she had grown so fond of them that the very idea of being accused of having an ulterior motive, of betraying their trust, horrified her. And that was how it would look, she realised miserably, if Matthew ever found out that she was a professional actress. The evidence was too damning and she had been a fool not to have seen what a ridiculous idea it was. If *only* she had told Charles ... but if she had, she wouldn't have been given the job. You might have, a niggling doubt voiced itself, and think how much happier things would have been with everything open and above board.

Olivia thumped the pillow crossly. It was all very well saying 'might'. How did she know? It was always easy to be clever with hindsight, and what if she hadn't got the job? She thumped the pillow again, wishing it were Matthew Raynor receiving the blows. She had heard the Lotus leaving not long after reaching her room, the telephone call summoning him, presumably.

Her one aim now was to finish the job quietly and without any more upsets and then fade out of their lives gracefully. In that way only could she justify herself. She frowned pensively.

Matthew Raynor had probably done her a service. She hadn't been so angry for a long time. The past year she had been in an almost somnolent state and he had woken her up. She grinned reluctantly. She bet she had woken him up too! she thought with relish. 'I have one or two plans in the offing, any one of them could come off.' Wow! Well, it was his own fault for putting the idea into her head in the first place with his nasty, suspicious mind.

Olivia dozed fitfully, the pain of both flesh and thoughts keeping her from dropping completely off to sleep. A sharp rap at the door brought her sitting up in bed, wide awake. Cautiously, she asked:

'Yes? Who is it?'

'Matthew. May I see you for a moment?' His voice was low but determined. Olivia looked at the clock incredulously—a quarter to twelve! How dared he come at this time, demanding to see her! Forgetful of all newly made resolutions, she answered:

'No. Go away,' quite pleased how disinterested her voice sounded. There was silence for a moment and then the handle turned and she smiled with satisfaction. So he would have just walked in without a please and thank you, would he? As if he could read her mind, Matthew continued:

'Olivia, open the door—please.' That 'please' must have choked him, she thought smugly. 'Olivia. Can you hear me?' The level of his voice was raised.

'Yes, and the whole house will soon. I don't want to see or speak to you. Will you please go away and leave me alone? Or are you considering breaking the door down?' Even as she said it Olivia thought what a corny script she was using. Evidently Matthew thought the same, for his voice took on a dry note.

'I don't think that will be necessary. I've only to make enough noise to wake the rest of the household and then we shall have to indulge in one or two explanations—won't we?'

Olivia bit her lip in frustration, coming to the reluctant conclusion that he would do just that. She threw back the covers and paced angrily across the room, turned the key and strode back to bed, where she threw herself in and drew the covers over her head. Matthew crossed to the bed.

'I've never been enamoured of caveman tactics, Olivia, and

69

the thought of breaking down your door doesn't appeal to me. Equally, wrenching back the covers seems a mite too hammy, but unless you sit up and give me your full attention, that's what I shall be forced to do.'

Olivia considered the situation and finally drew back the covers, but continued to keep her injured cheek to the pillow, her eyes closed.

'Thank you.' His voice was clipped.

'There seems to be no privacy in this house,' she snapped. 'What do you want, Matthew? I'm tired and want to sleep.'

'You're not the only one. I've had one hell of a day and ...' He stopped short and said more calmly: 'I gather that's your dinner downstairs.'

'I wasn't hungry,' she muttered.

'Harry said you had a headache. Was that true?'

Her eyes flew open. 'Why should you suspect otherwise? I've already told you that you're a permanent headache so far as I'm concerned.'

'If you do battle then you must be prepared for the consequences,' he said bitingly. 'I apologise for the lateness, but I've only just got back and I saw that your light was on. Did you hurt yourself this evening when you fell?'

'My God!' Olivia sat up incredulously. 'Can this be true? Showing concern for my welfare, Matthew? I can't believe it! You'd better be careful—it might be misconstrued. I might take advantage of the fact that you're visiting my room in the middle of the night and put you in a compromising position!'

'Quite right,' he agreed silkily, 'but I feel that you are more compromised than I and should you use the situation, as you suggest, then I would remind you that it works both ways ...' he smiled and said softly: '... and I would make a very demanding lover.'

Olivia felt the blood rush to her cheeks. What was required was a disdainful lift of the brows and a bored 'Indeed?' Instead of which she blushed like a silly teenager! He had made her suddenly conscious of the intimacy of the whole proceedings, her physical vulnerability especially so, for she was clothed in only the thinnest of pyjamas, the top button of which was undone, and after the recent dramatic entry beneath the bedclothes and subsequent outraged bounce back, her night attire could only be described as disarranged! Under Matthew Raynor's all-enveloping, satirical gaze her blush seemed to start from the tip of her toes to the top of her head, but she was damned if she was going to give him the satisfaction of buttoning up. Tossing back her hair, she said indifferently:

'Your concern for my health is gratifying but unnecessary. As you see, I'm perfectly well. Now, will you please go?'

It had been a mistake to sit up. She might have known his gimlet eyes wouldn't miss a thing, even in subdued lighting. As she was about to retreat back beneath the covers, his hand shot out and grasped her arm, holding it high so that the sleeve fell aside to reveal the angry welt. Olivia winced at his grip and when his other hand forced her face round she gave a protesting sigh.

'So ... you're perfectly well?' he quoted brusquely. 'You're a little fool. These need to be treated.' He took her dressing gown from where it was lying on the bedside chair and threw it on the bed. 'Put this on and sit here.' He then left the room.

'Do this, do that,' muttered Olivia, hastily doing up the offending button and slipping her good arm into the gown, leaving the injured one free. She had barely finished when Matthew returned, a tray of food in one hand, first aid equipment in the other.

'This will sting,' he told her, voice matter-of-fact, but his hands were careful enough. He was quite right. Olivia, determined to be stoical, couldn't help a small gasp escaping from between compressed lips and her hand jumped nervously. 'The pain will go off in a moment, but the soreness will last.' Holding her head to one side, he treated the weal on her cheek similarly.

His face was so close that Olivia could feel warm breath on her cheek. It really was quite remarkable how thick his lashes were, she thought, and there was a tiny brown mole just below his eye which she had never noticed before. Suddenly the dark lashes lifted and for a moment all she could see was an expanse of grey, not the cold grey of winter seas but soft pearl grey, warm and questioning. She dropped her eyes immediately and fervently hoped that her red face would be put down to reaction from the liniment.

'There, I think that will do for this evening. Tomorrow

you'll have to see Paul and he'll give you an anti-tetanus jab.'

'Oh, but I don't need that!' Olivia objected in some dismay.

'Oh, but you do, my girl,' mimicked Matthew. 'That was Mother Earth you were grovelling in and no chances must be taken.' He went to the basin and rinsed his hands, turning to study her as he dried them.

'Does it hurt?' She nodded. He folded the towel and replaced it carefully. 'You really are an impetuous young woman, aren't you?'

'You made me angry,' she muttered.

'So you didn't mean what you said?' he asked suavely.

Olivia opened her mouth and shut it again. 'A few scratches don't alter anything,' she managed at last. 'I can't imagine that your opinion of me has changed in the last hour, and mine of you certainly hasn't.' He continued to regard her and suddenly she could no longer stand the continual battle of personalities that always seemed to happen whenever they were together. She rose to her feet, only to falter when she put weight upon her injured knee. Matthew caught and steadied her.

'What's the matter?' he asked sharply.

'I bruised my knee, but the skin didn't break. I expect it stiffened up while I was sitting. It doesn't need looking at, truly.' Matthew frowned, accepting what she said with a brief nod. A good job too, thought Olivia. I'm blowed if I'm baring my legs to him as well!

Matthew crossed to the door, pausing before opening it. 'I've seen your appetite and know it's healthy. Eat up that food and stop being pig-headed. Have you anything you can take if you can't sleep?' Olivia nodded. 'I'll say goodnight, then.'

'Goodnight ... and Matthew? Thank you for ... well, thanks.'

'Not at all.' He eyed her narrowly. 'What will you tell Charles?'

She regarded him in some surprise. 'Why, that I fell in the shrubbery.'

'Not that it was my fault?' He wasn't concerned, merely curious.

'But it wasn't your fault,' she answered irritably. 'You didn't push me down and personally scratch my hands and

72

face, did you? Besides, running to Charles would be the last thing I'd do.'

'I wish I could make you out, Olivia Darcy,' he said softly.

'You'll not do that, Matthew Raynor,' she replied with great firmness, 'not in a month of Sundays!'

He raised one dark brow and with a dry 'We'll see' left the room.

Laura Swann, Paul's receptionist/nurse, was a shy girl who lived with her widowed mother. She had left school and taken a special course of training and had applied to work for Paul and had been doing so ever since, a period of five years. Olivia liked her quiet, calm manner, and if it wasn't for the fact that she didn't want to get involved in an exchange of confidences, would have sought her company more often.

Laura said she would let Olivia know when Paul was free and in consequence, later the next morning, Olivia tentatively tapped on the door of the surgery. The light above switched to 'Enter'.

'Olivia, good morning.' Paul rose from his chair and came round the desk to her. 'I don't believe I've seen you today so far, have I? Are you here as friend or patient?'

'Both, I hope. Actually, Paul, I stupidly managed to fall in the shrubbery yesterday and scratched myself. I bathed and put something on the scratches but didn't think I should ignore it in case grisly things happened.'

'You're quite right. Let me see.' Olivia offered her hand and he took it in his own large capable one, making hers look ridiculously small and fragile. She was aware of the strength yet gentleness of his touch. How calm and strong and secure he was, she thought.

'Mm ... seems to be mending well. I don't think there's any problem, but to be on the safe side I'll give you a jab.' He left her to get the necessary equipment, returning to give his slow smile. 'This won't hurt. I know that's the stock phrase, but ... there, I was right, wasn't I?' Paul sat back on the edge of the desk, arms folded, a quizzical look on his face. 'It all sounds rather intriguing, Olivia—falling in the shrubbery?'

Olivia grinned and said airily: 'There's nothing sinister about it, I can assure you.' She held out her hand and examined it, saying with mock seriousness: 'Will you be able to save it, doctor, or will it have to be ... amputation?'

Eyes twinkling, Paul replied with equal gravity: 'I hope not, Miss Darcy. Seriously, if you have any further trouble, come back.'

'I will,' she promised. 'Do you think it will scar?'

'I don't think so. Last night's prompt attention will prove beneficial.' He touched her cheek thoughtfully. 'No, I'm sure it won't. You have good, healing skin. It would be a pity to spoil such a pretty face.'

'I wasn't fishing for compliments,' scolded Olivia, eyes glowing nevertheless. Paul opened the door for her.

'I believe I have to thank you for the flowers that have been appearing with pleasing regularity on my desk?'

'Oh,' Olivia stopped in some confusion. 'I pick some for your father and thought ... you don't mind?' she asked anxiously. 'I knew you couldn't do with a huge bowl of flowers, but I thought perhaps a small posy would be acceptable.'

'Indeed it is. I must also thank you for all you're doing for Toby.' Paul's voice was suddenly brusque. 'I realise he's a difficult child to get to know. Spends too much time among adults, that's the trouble. He appears to have taken to you—his whole conversation seems to be "Olivia says", and I just want to make sure he doesn't become a nuisance. After all, you didn't come here to look after Toby and I don't want him to monopolise you ...'

'I don't mind, Paul, really,' Olivia broke in quickly. 'He's a lovely, intelligent boy and you must be very proud of him.'

His voice was teasing. 'I wasn't fishing for compliments, either.'

Harriet tut-tutted over the accident but didn't seem to connect it with Olivia's non-appearance for dinner. Charles showed concern and touched her by fussing. He was much improved himself, but continued taking things easy and insisted that Olivia did too. Toby was most upset and gave an almost professional examination of her wounds, and Olivia wondered if he would eventually follow his father into medicine. Matthew she did not see.

The rest of the week continued smoothly, mainly because Olivia kept out of Matthew's way, which was easy as he seemed to be spending odd nights out of town. She spent an enjoyable and relaxing weekend with Rosemary and Tom and kept right off the subject of the inmates of Cressida House.

On the Tuesday of the following week, Charles sent Olivia into Rotheringham for a reference book out of the main library. She refused his offer of the Jaguar most firmly, saying it would be easier and safer for her to use the bus. On her return, laden with four large books and a packed shopping basket, she was standing rather wearily, lost in thought, in the bus queue, when the woman behind nudged her sharply and muttered:

'I think someone wants to give you a lift.'

Startled, Olivia looked up to find the Lotus had pulled up alongside. The rest of the queue was taking a decided interest in the whole proceedings and her neighbour, taking a proprietorial hold of Olivia's arm, said suspiciously:

'You be careful, love. Do you know him?'

'Yes, oh yes, thank you.'

Matthew leant across the passenger seat and said smoothly: 'May I give you a lift, Olivia?'

There was an audible response from the onlookers. Matthew had obviously passed the test with flying colours and their verbal approval brought a tinge of pink to Olivia's cheeks as she was almost pushed, by the now indulgent neighbour, into the car. Glancing back, Olivia smiled as the Lotus moved away and nearly burst out laughing at the encouraging smiles given in return. As she tried to control the fit of giggles threatening to overcome her Matthew, who had been concentrating on getting the car back into the line of traffic and had at last succeeded, said with amusement in his voice:

'Did they think I was absconding with you?'

'I think so,' spluttered Olivia helplessly. 'They were rather sweet but hopelessly influenced. It only needed one look at your immaculate suit and the sound of your voice to reassure them.'

Matthew smiled, and Olivia caught her breath. Yes, he was very nice when he smiled, his eyes had a way of crinkling. No wonder the queue was swayed by it. What a pity she personally didn't see it more often.

'How wrong can they be,' observed Matthew wryly. 'A good suit and a posh accent is no criterion for a decent upright citizen. Many a murderer sports the same disguise.'

'Do you mind!' replied Olivia in mock alarm. She considered his words for a moment and then mused: 'We all have

75

our own disguises, though, don't we? It fascinates me ...'
She stopped short.

'Yes?' prompted Matthew, and Olivia could have kicked herself. Unthinkingly she had started this conversation and it was rather too near her present predicament for comfort.

'Well ... we all subconsciously react differently according to the person we're with, don't we? What is expected of us, I mean.'

'Until you find the person with whom you can be completely yourself.'

'Do you think that's ever truly possible?'

He gave her a quick look. 'Cynicism, Olivia?'

'No, I don't think so ... realism.' She turned earnestly to him. 'Sometimes I wonder if it's ever possible to know *ourselves* completely—without expecting someone else to.'

'It can happen conversely—self-analysis is too painful a pastime for some.'

The journey continued in silence for a while, but not a constrained one. Olivia was turning over that last observation and finding that it caused some heart-searchings which needed to be put away for the present and be brought out again when she could give them her full attention.

'Did you enjoy the play?' asked Matthew suddenly.

Olivia and Harriet had been to the opening of *Consent to Murder* the night before and she now realised that this was the first time she had seen Matthew since.

'I *am* sorry: I ought to have said. Yes, I did enjoy it.' She smiled. 'It was a good, old-fashioned, edge-of-seat thriller and I'm sure you'll do good business with it.'

'Yes, I think we will.' There was amusement again in his voice. 'You don't have to apologise for not mentioning it.'

'Well, I did mean to say how good it was and wish I'd done so without being prompted. I mean it too. I can't abide people who gush in public and gripe in private,' she added ingenuously.

'Mm ... thank you, I'll accept your compliment gracefully. It remains to be seen whether the theatre critic agrees with you. If he does, we shall do extra good business.'

'Do you find the newspaper write-up influences the public?'

'Not our regulars—they come rain or shine, Ibsen or

Christie, but it influences those who only go to the theatre for an occasional night out.'

'When do you think your father will be joining you at the Royal?' She lightened her voice deliberately.

'He'll be coming down to rehearsals quite soon now that he's spending time on the crutches. I'm starting him off in a fairly static role, one undemanding physically.'

'Have you ever directed your father and brother together before? I imagine ... oh!' Olivia gasped, Matthew swore under his breath and braked violently as a car shot out of a side road in front of them.

'It's all right, Olivia, I'd got my eye on him ... he seemed to be coming a mite too fast.'

'What idiots some drivers are!' she exclaimed fervently. 'I wasn't worried,' she added, slightly surprised that she wasn't.

'Your faith in me is touching but misplaced,' he replied, voice rather harsh. 'Has no one told you that I was driving the car in which my father sustained his injuries?'

Consternation written all over her face, Olivia breathed:

'No ... oh, Matthew, how awful for you! What happened?'

'Almost exactly what happened then. Some fool shooting out and crashing into the passenger side.'

'It wasn't your fault.'

'Theoretically not, but I can't help asking myself whether or not I could have anticipated it.'

'Were you hurt?' she asked.

'A bump on the head, minor cuts and bruises, nothing serious.' He smiled rather grimly. 'Has your faith in me diminished?'

'No.'

'Well, you could hardly be expected to say anything less,' he replied with a short laugh, braking the Lotus gently by the side of the house.

'It's the truth,' Olivia said indignantly, 'whether you want to believe it or not. When I'm with you I feel safe,' and then realising the ambiguity of that sweeping statement, she trailed off with, 'when you're driving.'

The ensuing quietness made the interior of the Lotus seem suddenly too intimate for comfort.

'Do you always tell the truth, Olivia?' asked Matthew, voice non-committal.

'Whenever possible,' she replied, with even deliberation, and opened the door. 'Thank you for the lift, Matthew.'

At twelve o'clock that night Olivia decided to give up all plans of sleep and began to read a book. Gradually, as she had hoped, her eyelids became heavier and heavier and, yawning, she put aside her book and reached out to switch off the bedside lamp. Hand outstretched, she heard a splatter of noise against the window. Startled, she listened intently and heard the sound again. Slipping out of bed, she drew back the curtains and looked out. Someone was standing on the terrace, arms akimbo, head thrown back, gazing up at the window.

Afterwards she wondered why she knew it was perfectly in order to flick the catch and open the window.

'About time,' a voice floated up to her. 'I thought you'd never come.'

Olivia reached back for her dressing gown and thrust it on, and as she leant over the sill, the moon came out from behind a cloud.

'I say, old man, get a move on—good lord! Not Matthew?' She could hear the delight in his voice. 'Definitely not Matthew! Well, well ... the old rascal!'

The implications were obvious and Olivia was just about to open her mouth to protest when he threw out his arm theatrically and in soulful accent said:

' "But soft! What light through yonder window breaks? It is the east, and Juliet is the sun." '

'Shush!' ordered Olivia. 'You'll wake the whole house!'

'Shush?' he repeated disgustedly, and she could just make out the pained expression on his face. 'I speak the immortal words of the Bard, the moon comes out on cue, the scene is set to perfection for one of the most famous love scenes in history—and all you can say is "Shush"?'

Olivia collapsed into helpless, suppressed laughter.

' "O, speak again, bright angel," but not,' he added darkly, 'if all you've got to offer is "Shush"!'

Olivia couldn't resist it.

' "What man art thou, that, thus bescreen'd in night, So stumbles on my counsel?" ' There was an astonished pause and then:

' "By a name I know not how to tell thee who I am." '

'Well, I wish you would,' answered Olivia prosaically. 'If

we were in the middle of a heatwave I wouldn't mind going on, but it's rather chilly.'

'Have you no soul, woman?'

'No, and if you don't keep your voice down I'll have no job either. Anyway, I rather think you've chosen the wrong play.'

'You intrigue me. Wouldn't you say that the scene was set admirably?'

'Oh, yes, the scene ... but not the characters. You see, I'm not Juliet—I'm Olivia.'

There was silence while this piece of information was digested and then she saw the gleam of white teeth as he smiled up at her.

'Then, girl dear, I would agree with you ... most remiss of me. "O, when mine eyes did see Olivia first!" So you are Olivia?'

'Yes. And who, may I ask, are you?' although she had already guessed.

The smile flashed again.

'Me? Oh ... I'm Sebastian.'

CHAPTER FOUR

'I warrant thou art a merry fellow and car'st for nothing.'

'COME off it,' demanded Olivia as she closed the back door behind him. 'You're letting your artistic imagination run away with you. Sebastian indeed!'

He stood smiling at her while Caliban circled excitedly. Not so tall as his brothers, this third son was every inch a Raynor. Hair the colour of corn, a luxuriant beard to match, tanned glowing skin, laughing blue eyes and a beaming smile. No wonder Matthew had said that Julian could take care of himself. She realised, with some amusement, that he was sizing her up too, and wondered what he thought of the old dressing-gown and hair fashioned into one thick plait. By the look in his eyes he wasn't deterred, and she hastily held out her hand and said in a voice that brooked no argument:

'You *must* be Julian—you're so like your father, at least, from what I can make out, under all that hair!'

'So I'm told, although it's difficult to see in oneself, apart from the obvious similarity in colouring.' He grinned. 'And I really am Sebastian—Julian Sebastian for my sins. I kept it quiet at school. We've all been lumbered equally disastrously. Very few people know mine, so you're honoured.' He held out his hand.

'I shall not breathe a word,' promised Olivia solemnly, giving her own.

'Olivia ...' He lingered over the name very reminiscent of his father. 'Sebastian and Olivia—now how's that for co-incidence?' and Julian's blue eyes gleamed wickedly.

'If I were to meet a Sebastian anywhere, I suppose it's more likely to be here, surrounded as I am by theatre people.' She kept her voice matter-of-fact, but despite herself she couldn't help responding to his outrageous audacity and smiled back. 'My hand?'

Julian regretfully let it go. 'What are you doing in Matt's bed?' He threw himself into the comfortable chintz armchair, one of a pair, and gave her a wicked glance. 'I take it he's not in there with you?'

'You take it right,' she replied swiftly, and although well used to this type of teasing raillery normally, felt the colour suffuse her cheeks and added airily: 'I didn't even realise I was in your brother's room, no one told me.' She eyed him suspiciously. 'You're pulling my leg.'

Julian raised his hands in protest. 'Certainly not. That was always the room that Matt used whenever he visited.' He paused, studying her intently, face straight but eyes dancing. 'Mm ... you're not really Matt's type—he usually goes for the small, feminine, helpless sort that need protecting.'

'Really? I'm not quite sure whether to take that as a compliment or not. I've never considered myself an Amazon before.'

Julian grinned. 'Oh no, definitely not an Amazon, and I strongly suspect you have a mind of your own. So ... no Matthew. Ah well, I'm glad I didn't interrupt anything.'

'I hope he bullied you as a child,' remarked Olivia pleasantly.

Julian threw back his head and laughed. 'My dear Olivia, you obviously don't know Matt. Nothing so straightforward! M. B. Raynor, Esq. is far more devious and clever at getting results. What do you think of him?'

'That he's used to having stones flung up at his window,' parried Olivia smoothly.

'Not only intelligent and beautiful but reticent too! Perhaps the kind and gentle doctor is more to your liking?'

'You're talking nonsense ...'

'Yes, I know, I do frequently.' He smiled disarmingly. 'You're not going to desert me, Olivia, are you?'

'Having done my good deed for the day I think I'd better go back to ...' She found herself being led persuasively across the kitchen.

'Olivia, be an angel, stay and talk while I find something to eat—better still, stay and share with me. I've not had anything since mid-morning and I'm famished. We'll have a grand midnight feast.' Julian released her and flung open the door of the fridge, passing out a bottle of milk to an amused but resigned Olivia. 'Get two glasses and start pouring.' He peered inside. 'Ah! Beef!'

'I hope we're not taking tomorrow's dinner,' Olivia ventured, 'although I strongly suspect that you can do no wrong in Harriet's eyes, so I'll put all the blame on your shoulders.'

Julian stopped slicing the meat and put hand to heart. 'You do that, girl dear—I'll always shoulder the blame for you.'

'Such gallantry,' mocked Olivia, finding that she was expected to make up the sandwiches.

'We'll share the plate,' Julian announced blandly, 'it's cosier.'

'We'll not share the chair,' said Olivia firmly, settling herself on a small stool near his chair and tucking into a sandwich of the doorstep variety. When his hunger had been assuaged, Julian leant back with a satisfied sigh.

'That's much better. You know I'm really very grateful to you, Olivia, for coming to my rescue. It's nice to know I can depend on you.'

She eyed him warily. 'I hope that doesn't mean what I think it means. I'm normally a deep sleeper, so don't depend too much, will you? Tonight you were lucky.'

'Not to worry,' he replied cheerfully. 'As a last resort your window's handy via the conservatory roof—although glass is tricky stuff.'

Olivia choked. 'You dare!' she managed at last, then couldn't help laughing at the devilment on his face.

'I enjoyed our balcony scene.' Julian lighted a cigarette and drew on it deeply, leaning back in the chair as though settled for the night. 'I thought we were rather good.'

'Modest too!'

'Of course, with practice we would be better.'

Cautiously, Olivia answered: 'You think so?'

'Tell me, what are you doing here? I supposed at first that you were one of the parent's lame ducks—although we've not had one quite like you before, they're mostly younger and sillier or older and ghastly pathetic.' His blue eyes narrowed. 'But now I don't believe you're anyone's lame duck—so that means you're at the Royal too.' He grinned at her startled expression. 'Didn't you know you'd have to put up with all the Raynors down there? I hope I'm not the final straw as we'll probably be playing opposite each other. What has Matt offered you?'

'Your brother wouldn't offer me anything, and certainly not

a part in one of his plays,' broke in Olivia at long last, unable to keep the acidity out of her voice. 'And if he did, I'd refuse, even if he went down on his bended knees—and he's not likely to do that!'

'I've always been of the opinion that kneeling is damned uncomfortable and more than a little ludicrous,' said a dry voice from the door, 'and rather dated, don't you think?' There was a stunned silence and then:

'Speak of the devil,' countered Julian lazily, giving Olivia a raised brows glance before turning to face their unexpected visitor. 'Well, brother?'

'Very well, Julian, thank you,' replied Matthew, strolling over to the other armchair, clasping Julian's shoulder briefly in passing. 'Good evening, Olivia. I see there's no need for me to introduce you to each other.'

Olivia, who had been trying to make herself as small and as inconspicuous as possible, saw the glint in the grey eyes and sat up straight. Now was not the time to retreat.

'Hello, Matthew,' she replied evenly, thankful when his steady gaze passed from her to his brother.

'I must say you're looking revoltingly fit, Julian. Chichester must have agreed with you.'

'Chichester was fine and the Tom Lowry most successful —it's a definite possibility for us here.' Julian paused and added straight-faced: 'Rather late to be up and about, Matt, isn't it?'

Matthew smiled faintly, allowing his eyes to pass from Olivia, to the remains of their feast and finally to his brother, who was enjoying himself immensely.

'I could say the same. I see you are still indulging in your habit of losing your key, Julian. I was all ready to come to the rescue, but Olivia has, most happily, beaten me to it.' His voice was smooth. 'Are you going to tell Julian why he won't be acting with you at the Royal, Olivia ... or shall I?'

Olivia, who had taken cover behind her glass of milk, now stopped drinking. She removed the creamy moustache with the tip of her tongue and said brightly:

'We hadn't got around to personal details, had we?' She turned to Julian, unaware of how earnestly her green eyes were fixed upon him. 'I'm here to do some typing for your father,' and not waiting to see his reaction, she delivered a steadfast gaze at Matthew. She felt quite calm, although her heart was thumping more rapidly than usual. If this was to be the show-down then so be it. Had she been given a choice this present moment would not have been her ideal one. Scrubbed shiny face, her hair in a plait, old woolly dressing-gown and bare feet which she was trying to hide did nothing for a girl's morale!

'So our illustrious parent is writing his memoirs at long last,' said Julian with nothing more than amusement tinging his voice. 'I thought he was leaving that to you, Matt?'

'Not his book, Julian,' answered Matthew gently, eyes still on Olivia. 'He's collating material for a lecture programme in the States.'

'Is he now?' Julian smiled at her. 'And the fair Olivia is assisting him—lucky Charles!'

Olivia returned the smile, hoping the relief she felt was not apparent. Not by the flicker of an eyelid had Julian revealed his surprise that his father's typist was capable of spouting Shakespeare out of the blue. She allowed the brothers' con-versation to wash over her, brooding over the mess she was in. This was the second time she had been lucky—first with Adam Carlyon and now with Julian. How ridiculous she had been to think that she could sink her identity with the theatre completely in such an environment. It was so truly part of her and her upbringing that she could no more subdue it than she could give it up. Julian had only to quote one line from *Romeo and Juliet* and there she was—quoting back without a second thought. It seemed that the only person she was completely on her guard with was Matthew. Lifting her eyes, she found him regarding her, a fleeting expression of . . . well, what it was she couldn't discern, for he leant over and passed an ash tray to Julian and his face became hidden.

How totally different they were! Matthew was now lying with his head against the chair back, eyes half closed, listening with a smile on his face, his attitude very much that of elder brother indulging younger. By his appearance, which was im-maculate, he had obviously been wining and dining—with the gorgeous redhead? Olivia wondered. Julian, on the other hand, in an open neck shirt and well worn cords, was leaning for-ward, elbow on knee, face bright with enthusiasm, as alive and vibrant as his brother was indolent and languid. Don't be a fool, Olivia Darcy, she told herself sharply as she downed the last dregs of milk. That indolence and languor is pure façade. He's lying there as relaxed and lazy as a cat, but if he wanted he could pounce with the speed and sureness of a tiger. Considering that leaving now would not look as if she were running away, she rose when there was a convenient pause in the conversation and murmured:

'I'll say goodnight. I'll not be able to keep my eyes open tomorrow.'

'Today, you mean,' yawned Julian. 'I hope my bed's made up, Matt?'

'Since we understood you to be leaving Chichester five days ago, and knowing Harriet, need you ask?' Matthew eyed him speculatively, adding dryly: 'Mm ... five days ... you look rather hollow-eyed, Julian. I hope whatever it was that kept you from us was worth it.'

'She was, brother, she was,' replied Julian, unabashed.

'You realise you'll have to rid yourself of all this fungus?' Matthew pulled at the beard, smiling.

'I know, I know, but not yet awhile, surely?' Julian sauntered to the back door. 'I'll fetch my case, I left it in the car. 'Night, Olivia. Thanks for coming to my rescue.'

'Goodnight, Julian,' she answered, and then she was alone with Matthew. Walking rather self-consciously across the kitchen, her bare feet making no noise, she murmured a 'goodnight, Matthew', as she passed his chair. Caliban was in his favourite position, head resting on his master's knee, quivering with pleasure as the long, slender fingers gently stroked his back.

'Goodnight, Olivia,' Matthew replied, without looking up.

'I understand you've met my youngest son, Olivia?' Charles turned a smug face in her direction as Olivia entered the study. 'Even in this day and age it is possible, you see, for an Olivia to meet a Sebastian.'

Olivia eyed him indignantly. 'I think, Charles Raynor, that you're a teasing, unscrupulous man. You might have warned me!'

He laughed and held out his hand, taking Olivia's and looking at her with affection. 'Forgive me, my dear. The coincidence was too good to be true. I'm only sorry I wasn't

85

able to introduce him to you myself, but I'm sure Julian was equal to the occasion. What do you think of him, eh? Not a bad-looking lad, is he?'

'Since you must know that he's the image of yourself when young, aren't you being a little presumptuous?' she teased in return.

'Not at all,' came the emphatic reply. 'I know the value of my face and I should hope Julian does too. No good apologising for the gifts the gods give, use them, and anyone who tells you different is a fool. The danger lies when the value of outward appearance becomes distorted. Any conceit Julian has is not, I'm sure, for his looks.' He lifted a brow.

Olivia said gently: 'Julian appears to be as charming and as likeable as his father ... who knows exactly what I think of him.'

'This girl is quite delightful,' Charles said to Matthew, who had appeared at the open doorway in time to hear her speech. 'We shall have to think of some reason to persuade her to stay with us indefinitely, Matt.' He patted her hand before releasing it.

Matthew glanced at her briefly. 'Olivia may have plans of her own.' He dropped a manuscript on to his father's lap. 'Here's the Bennett play. Read it and see what you think. We've sorted out the difficulties.'

'Good. I have high hopes of Bennett. Do you think I'll be fit in time?' Charles asked, voice even and unemotional. Olivia, who had busied herself opening the morning post, inwardly fuming over the icy look Matthew had delivered to her, was not deceived. Neither, it seemed, was Matthew.

'Yes, if you don't do anything stupid.' Matthew's voice softened. 'You must have patience, Father.'

Charles stared out of the window. 'Yes, you're right, of course. At least I'm down to a stick—those damned crutches nearly drove me mad.' He gave an impatient sigh. 'It's because Julian's home—I want to make plans.' He frowned and peered at his son. 'You're looking tired, Matt. You're doing too much.'

'You're merely contrasting me to Julian, Father,' Matthew remarked dryly. He walked to the door, pausing briefly. 'I'll be ready to take you in to rehearsals in,' he looked at his watch, 'ten minutes.'

'How's life at Cressida House these days?' Rosemary asked, studying the menu with interest. 'I say, Noll, it's a bit expensive here.'

'Oh, Rose, honestly! All the times I come over to your place and now, when I want to take you out to lunch ... Shut up about the cost and choose.'

'On your head be it. Half the delight is not knowing which scrumptious dish to finally decide upon, but I generally end up choosing the same one.'

'In other words, the prawn cocktail and then the steak,' prompted Olivia with a grin.

'How well you know me! Yes, please. I'd better have salad with the steak.' Rosemary waited while their order was taken and then said, 'You didn't answer my question.'

'Life at Cressida House is mostly satisfying and would be completely so if it weren't for you know who. We now have our full complement of sons with the advent of Julian Sebastian,' and Olivia proceeded to relate the episode of his arrival.

'Mm ...' Rosemary nibbled a prawn thoughtfully. 'He sounds like dynamite to me.'

'He's a veritable Adonis,' said Olivia with relish.

'That's what I mean—dynamite! I've met the type. Good-looking, goodnatured, charming and virile. Beware! How much longer have you to be subjected to the fascinating Raynors?'

'Not long now,' answered Olivia, unaware of how dismal she sounded. 'Charles is rehearsing full time at the theatre and when the play opens I'll finish.'

And wishing you were opening too, thought Rosemary, giving her friend a quick look.

'Has Julian said anything about mistaking you for an actress?'

'Not a thing—unlike his dear brother, who would love to find an excuse to reveal all and throw me out, even if it happened to be on my last day!'

'To be fair, you can't compare Julian and Matthew in the same light,' intervened Rosemary quickly. 'Julian has no axe to grind, but Matthew's the man in charge down at the Royal. If you had been out to get a foot in, using his father as a lever, then it would be Matthew in the unenviable position ...'

'Oh, yes, let's be fair,' interrupted Olivia grumpily. 'I quite realise the man's problems, I just resent being typecast.' She shrugged. 'Anyway, the job's nearly over and I think, with a bit of luck, I might be able to leave in an orthodox manner without histrionics.'

'I wish I could meet these Raynors before you leave. Does Matthew have any fears that you might get your claws into Julian?'

'Dear me, no. I rather think he feels I may have met my match in Julian. In actual fact, Julian and I get on very well. We both know the rules of the game and so long as we stick to them and don't expect anything more, then things are fine. Julian gives the impression of not having a care in the world, but there's more to him than that. He's amusing and great fun, but I suspect he has his own scars and this banter is a cover-up.'

'Who knows, being the son of a famous actor could have its disadvantages?' suggested Rosemary dryly.

'Could be,' agreed Olivia with a grin, 'but I'd swop those disadvantages for a few of my own any day. I really can't make up my mind whether to fall for Julian or Paul. My first choice still favours Charles.'

'That's purely father image,' retorted Rosemary. 'Goodness, just look at this steak!'

'I've got something else for you to look at, Rose.' Olivia lowered her voice. 'You said just now that you'd like to meet the Raynors. Well, one of them is sitting ... don't look now, idiot, wait a minute and then glance across the room to the right. At the table in the corner is dear Matthew, and the redhead with him is Philippa Markham, an actress from the Royal.'

Rosemary's eyes widened in anticipation and after attacking her steak appreciatively for a few moments she then dropped her napkin and bending to pick it up gave a swift, but intent look in the direction Olivia had indicated. Back in an upright position, she raised her brows in surprise.

'He's not a bit how I imagined him to be. Can I have another peep?'

'No, you can't, I don't want to attract his attention. What do you think of his lady friend?'

'I only gave her a cursory glance, I was more interested in him. She's pretty ... what's she like as an actress?'

'She must have something to be a member of the Raynor company. Without sounding full of sour grapes I'd say competent but not inspired.' Olivia nudged Rosemary's knee. 'You can turn round now, they're leaving.'

Rosemary didn't need a second invitation. 'She looks like a cat who's been at the cream. No one should look that sure of any man. Are they wooing?'

'I have no idea, I'm not in Matthew's confidence. According to Julian Matthew likes women who bring out the protective instinct.'

'Well, that redhead looks as though she needs as much protection as a boa-constrictor!' Rosemary continued to watch until Matthew held the door for his companion and they disappeared out of sight. 'How you can say he's not attractive, Noll! Those eyes ... that smile!'

'I didn't say he wasn't attractive, I just said he wasn't my sort – and it's all very well to go into raptures,' Olivia said crossly. 'So far as I'm concerned those eyes are usually as cold as a wintry day, and that smile—well, I think if he smiled at me like that I'd pass out on the spot in surprise!' She grinned. 'Now, stop waxing lyrical over Matthew Raynor and let's decide which of these delicious concoctions we should eat—and to hell with the calories.'

'Ah well,' sighed Rosemary, philosophically helping herself to a thick wedge of coffee gateau, 'I can always start my diet tomorrow.'

'You need exercise, my girl. Why not take up horse riding— like me?' Olivia awaited results. They were not long in coming. Rosemary gasped:

'You? On a horse?'

Olivia raised her brows. 'Your incredulous tone wounds me deeply, Rose. I did actually have a few lessons as a child during one of our more affluent periods. Those lessons,' she continued airily, 'have come in most useful. As long as the horse doesn't get any wild ideas of doing anything fancy I quite enjoy it. When in Rome, etcetera ... There's a good riding school near Cressida House and a bridle path runs through the Castle parkland. I usually go with Julian, who chooses a nice gentle beast for me. Paul joins us sometimes. Needless to say, the whole family are very equestrian.'

'There's something rather sensual about men on large, snorting horses,' said Rosemary dreamily. 'Does the gorgeous Matthew join in the fun and games?'

'Not when I've been, thank goodness. Now that would put me off. I hardly see him these days. Charles thinks he's working too hard and I must admit sometimes he looks positively haggard, although he seemed all right today, didn't he? Probably benefiting from Miss Markham's company. Once or twice I've noticed his light on very late.' She saw Rosemary's knowing look and grinned. 'Julian's taken me out dancing a couple of times.'

'And you got back "quite late".'

'Don't worry, Rosie, everything's under control.'

'I'm very glad you think so,' said Rosemary sceptically.

'Olivia, what are you doing that for?' Charles asked, walking quietly into the lounge.

'Harry doesn't mind,' Olivia replied, looking up with a smile.

'Of course she doesn't. She's always hated arranging flowers and is only too glad for you to do it, the same as Paul is only too glad when you stand in for Laura. We all take you for granted, child. Has Matthew ever thanked you for the tray you leave in the library when he's late from the theatre?'

'No,' said Olivia, 'and there's no need for him to do so.'

'Mm ... I suppose I ought to be glad you're going out more.' His voice became matter-of-fact. 'I thought you'd get on well with Sebastian.'

'You can take that smile off your face, Charles,' Olivia said calmly. 'If Julian knew what you were thinking ...' Or Matthew, she added silently.

'Oh, Julian knows.'

'You're terrible!' gasped Olivia, laughing despite herself.

Charles walked slowly to the huge sofa and sat down, watching her thoughtfully.

'Olivia, have you any plans when you leave us?'

The laughter stuck in Olivia's throat and she swallowed hard before saying fairly evenly:

'I shall go to the Agency, something always turns up.' She concentrated fiercely on the foliage of the flower arrangement, her back to him. 'I'm sorry, of course, that my job is nearly over. I've been happy, you know that, and you've been very

90

kind to treat me as one of the family and I ... I want to thank you most sincerely.' There was silence and then Charles said quietly:

'My dear, have things been so bad for you in the past?' The compassion in his voice was nearly her undoing and she said with an effort:

'Oh, no. I've been lucky really.'

'I haven't wanted to probe into your affairs, but I understand from Harry that you have no family. I don't like to think of you so alone in the world ... I've become very fond of you, you know.'

Olivia nodded, not trusting herself to speak.

'Come here, my dear, there's something I want to say to you.' Charles patted the cushion by his side and after a moment's hesitation Olivia did as she was bidden. He took her hand. 'There's no reason why we should lose sight of you just because your job here has finished. I want you to wait before going to the Agency.'

Olivia turned a puzzled face to him. 'You mean you know someone who needs a typist?'

'I mean that I don't want you to spend your last few days here worrying about the future. There isn't much more work for you to do and I don't want you to have a guilt complex about having too much spare time.' Charles's voice deepened. 'There's something I want you to promise me.' He rose and walked over to the window, standing hands in pockets, purposefully avoiding looking at her directly. He said abruptly: 'I've always wanted a daughter ... you are as I imagine she might have been. I want you to promise me that if ever you need help or advice you will come to me. If I'm not available then go to Matt, he'll know where to find me. Will you?'

'You're very kind,' stammered Olivia, knowing she could never follow his request through but wishing from the bottom of her heart that she could.

'Good. That's settled, then.' He leaned forward, looking out of the window. 'Here they are with the horses and you aren't ready yet. Run along and change. I'll tell them you're coming.'

Olivia crossed quickly and took his hand, holding it briefly to her cheek before rushing out of the room. Straight into Matthew's arms.

'Oh!' she exclaimed tremulously. The cool grey eyes noted her flushed cheeks and flicking a glance at his father talking to Julian through the open window, Matthew released her with deliberation.

'I'm sorry, I didn't notice the time ... I've been doing the flowers,' she babbled incoherently. She was halfway up the stairs, thoughts in a tumult, when he said:

'I'll tell them to go on ahead and we'll catch them up.'

'Oh ... yes, very well,' Olivia replied uneasily, for the last thing she wanted was a jolly twosome canter with Matthew, but there was nothing she could do about it. Passing the landing window she saw Matthew join his brothers and the two other girls at the entrance to the drive, and after a few minutes' consultation the others trotted off down the road, leaving Matthew with two of the horses. Suddenly conscious of wasting time, Olivia ran to her room.

'I won't look so grand as Philippa Markham, that's for sure,' she muttered, grabbing jeans and shirt and quickly working her hair into one thick plait. 'At least Laura's outfit looked old even though it's authentic.' Olivia was thankful that Laura was one of the party; from the little she had seen of Philippa she had deduced that they would never be soulmates! Allowing herself a hurried glance in the mirror, she hurried down the stairs, grabbing the hat she hired from the stables from the hall table. Pulling the front door behind her, she heard Matthew's impatient, 'At last' and said:

'I was as quick as I ... oh!'

'What's the matter?' Matthew demanded, steadying her horse and helping her to mount.

'Er ... nothing.' Olivia clutched the reins and suffered Matthew's assistance as he checked the girth before springing easily into the saddle of his own mount and leading the way down the drive.

But there was something most definitely the matter. Where was the docile brown mare that she was used to? What was she doing perched up here on a large black beast whose eye was decidedly not docile? She looked at Matthew confidently riding the huge piebald ahead and tried to control the nervous flutterings in her stomach. Someone had once told her that animals always know when a person is nervous and she made herself relax. What a way to spend a beautiful sunny Sunday!

And with Matthew, who was probably fed up with being foisted with her company anyway.

When they reached the bridle path there was no sign of the other four riders, and Matthew began to canter in the direction they were to have taken. Olivia followed, and gradually her unease lessened and she even began to enjoy herself. At least the black seemed well schooled, and perhaps she had imagined the wicked glint in his eye? They rode for about ten minutes and then Matthew reined and scanned the park. He turned and called back to Olivia.

'I think they must be over there. Must have taken a different path. If we go this way we'll be able to rejoin them higher up.'

Olivia nodded breathlessly and obediently followed, and before she knew what was happening Matthew and the piebald had sailed effortlessly over a small stone wall and with horror she realised that the black had every intention of following.

Not having reached the illustrious stage of jumping over obstacles in her childhood lessons, Olivia knew it was totally useless to try and remember any instructions that could have come back to her in her moment of stress. Instead, frantically praying for dear life, she shut her eyes and bellowed 'Matthew!' at the top of her voice.

The black jumped beautifully and landed with precision and dignity the other side of the wall. Olivia also landed with precision but not much else on the other side of the wall—unfortunately not in the saddle but in an ignominious heap among the bracken and ferns. When soft flesh met hard earth her shout was cut off in mid-stream as the breath was knocked out of her body.

She lay, hat over one eye, mouth full of foliage, gasping for that lost breath, and couldn't tell if the thundering noise she could hear was the horse about to crush her to death or her panic-stricken heart working overtime. The undergrowth was urgently trampled down and two dusty brown boots appeared in her line of vision. She groaned and rolled over on to her back. Overhead Matthew began a quiet string of colourful swearing, undergoing the emotions of a man who had just passed from the horror of what he might have found to the furious relief at what he had.

'Do you think anything's broken?' he demanded at last, and

Olivia shook her head weakly. 'Lie still,' he rapped. 'I want to catch your horse,' and disappeared through the waist-high bracken.

'I don't believe it—I just don't believe it,' Olivia addressed the pale blue sky. 'He's gone to get that damned horse and left me here, dying for all he knows!' and spitting out the last of the good free earth she concentrated on ignoring the persistent pain shooting through her left shoulder and watched a butterfly quivering delicately on a frond of fern. After a while the ground began to reverberate again and the bracken swished and crackled and the brown boots were with her once more. Olivia removed her regard of the butterfly to that of her companion. The black-as-thunder look had been diluted slightly, although the grey eyes still glittered and there was an ominous whiteness round the grim mouth.

'I can't catch the damned brute, he keeps shying away, but at least he's keeping us in view.' His eyes flashed. 'What the devil do you mean by jumping when it's quite obvious you can't? You could have killed yourself! It would have taken only a few extra minutes to use the gate, you little fool!'

'Matthew Raynor, don't you shout at me like that! What choice did I have in the matter? Did you ask? No. You just charged, and so did that damned horse, and the next thing I know I'm flying through the air!'

'You've been riding almost daily with Julian—how was I to know ...'

'Well, you know now. I can't jump. I never have. I never will. I may never jump again—and I don't mean on a horse either!'

'Stop being dramatic. Where does it hurt?' Matthew knelt by her side.

She gave a bitter laugh. 'My goodness, don't come showing the old concern, if you please! I quite realise you're more worried about the horse than me. Why don't you catch him and see if he's all right and ...'

'And why don't you try shutting up? Hell, woman, I didn't want him joining up with the others and worrying them, or going back to the school for that matter. In either case it would alarm folk unnecessarily and ...'

'Oh, really? Well, it would be nice to have someone around here who was worried about me ...'

94

'They'll have cause for concern if you don't lie still and be quiet for two minutes so that I can check that there's nothing seriously wrong with you!'

Olivia clamped her lips tightly and glared up at him. Systematically Matthew checked all her limbs and giving a satisfied grunt sat back on his haunches.

'You're a very lucky young woman. That shoulder took the brunt of your fall. Come on, you'd better get up.'

'I'm quite happy where I am, thank you.'

'Don't be ridiculous. You can't stay here all day.'

'I don't see why not, it's far safer than where I was before. Mother Earth received me to her bosom and I'm quite sure . . .' She looked suspiciously at him. 'Don't you dare laugh, Matthew Raynor, or I'll . . . I'll . . .'

'I'm sorry, Olivia,' and Matthew stretched out in the bracken by her side and began to laugh. Olivia turned her head cautiously and looked on with deep interest. This surely couldn't be the dour-faced, sarcastic Matthew Raynor she had been forced to do battle with over the past few weeks? Yet it was—beautifully transformed. He really was quite delightful to watch, almost worth falling off a horse for. When the last gasp died down Matthew gave a long groan and rolled over on his side. Olivia blinked rapidly as the grey eyes observed hers from a space of six inches. She wet her lips with the tip of her tongue and smiled tentatively, surprised at the weight of disappointment that came over her when there was no answering response. Matthew's face suddenly seemed wiped of all expression and was curiously still for a fleeting moment, then he sat up slowly and shook his head, saying with dangerous calm:

'You scare the pants off me like that again, Olivia, and I'll tan your backside!'

She grinned. 'If I ever do anything like that again, Matthew, I'll turn over and let you.' She sat up cautiously, and to Matthew's inquiry of 'what hurts?' she replied emotionally: 'Everything!'

Matthew stood up and held out his hands. 'Come along— up!'

'If you insist,' groaned Olivia. He hoisted her up easily and when she would have staggered held her firmly in his arms while she tested her legs. What an extraordinary day, she reflected, as Matthew led her carefully to the grassy bank near the offending wall and deposited her gently on to the turf. He knelt beside her, a slight frown on his face, and Olivia turned her attention from the smell of his tweed jacket and the faint, lingering whiff of after-shave, to the question he had just asked.

'I . . . think I'm all right—the sky's stopped spinning.'

'Good. Sit here while I catch your animal.'

Olivia sat back dreamily, feeling the sun on her face, a curious lethargy creeping over her. The piebald, tethered nearby, blew through his nose and stomped a hoof impatiently as Matthew returned, leading the black.

'Right, let's be on our way.'

Olivia stared, an awful suspicion rearing its ugly head. 'On our way?' she repeated slowly.

Matthew looked at his watch. 'Yes, of course. I want my tea even if you don't. We planned to picnic in Old Nick's Hollow, and that's only five minutes away at the most.'

'We could have planned to picnic at Buckingham Palace for all I care,' she replied calmly, and Matthew, about to untie the piebald, paused.

'You don't stand a hope in hell's chance of picnicking at Buckingham Palace, but Old Nick's Hollow is readily available.'

'Then go, by all means, and avail yourself of Old Nick's charms, but I . . . I am going to walk sedately back from whence I came and find the nearest bath, soak for about three days and then I might . . .'

'You,' said Matthew firmly, looming above her and hauling her unceremoniously to her feet, 'are getting on to the black and riding with me to rejoin the others.'

'Like hell I am,' said Olivia with relish.

'Like hell it may be,' he retorted, plonking her hat firmly on her head and leading her to the black, 'but ride you will.'

They eyed each other, Matthew unwaveringly relentless and Olivia mutinously stubborn. She decided to change her tactics and smiled beseechingly.

'Matthew, I can't, honestly. I'm one large bruise, and quite frankly the animal frightens me to death.'

'Exactly,' agreed Matthew, fully aware of the not too subtle strategy. 'That's why you must mount and ride him now or

96

else you'll find it extremely difficult when you next want to ride again.'

'I'll never want to ride again,' predicted Olivia fervently, removing her arm from his grasp. Matthew said calmly:

'Keep your voice down, Olivia, you're frightening the horse.'

'I'm frightening . . .' she stopped and whispered furiously, 'I'm frightening the horse? You must be mad! That brute isn't one bit frightened. It's me that's frightened, and I am not going on that horse!' The last words were spaced out with deliberation and rose in an ever-increasing crescendo.

'Look here, Olivia,' Matthew faced her, voice studiously patient but just edged with enough steel to make her listen. 'I know what I'm talking about. It is most important that you get up on that horse, now, this minute.'

'Important to whom? You? The horse? Or me?' Olivia's green eyes flashed. 'I don't know about you, or the horse, but *me* . . . I'm walking!' Thrusting past, she staggered through the long grass. His voice followed her, casually.

'I thought you'd more guts than that, Olivia, but it seems . . .' He sounded regretful and out of the corner of her eye she saw him give a disappointed shrug. There was a long silence broken only by the sound of the two horses cropping the grass and an aeroplane droning high up. Olivia slowly retraced her steps to stand a yard away from him. His face was devoid of expression.

'You really are a cunning devil, Matthew Raynor.'

'Yes.'

'I'm not really the hearty, out-of-door type.'

'I know.'

'But I thought riding . . . might be fun.'

'It is,' he replied gently.

'Mostly.'

'Mostly.'

She peeped up from under her lashes. 'It is rather a long way to walk home.' He nodded, lips twitching very slightly. She eyed the black, who returned her look disdainfully. 'What were you going to do if I'd kept on walking?' she asked with interest.

'Let you.'

'Oh.' Olivia considered this for a moment. 'Not dragged me

back by the hair and heaved me up like a sack of potatoes?'

His face lighted up with one of his rare smiles. 'You do have a vivid imagination, woman. No. I'm a believer of using brute force solely as a last resort and then only when the occasion demands it. This is something you have to do yourself.'

Olivia nodded and walked over to the black, gritted her teeth and collected the reins.

'Up you go.' Matthew gave her a lift up and she was astride. The black side-stepped nervously. 'Whoa, boy ... easy!' Matthew quietened the horse and looked up at her. 'Good girl! Now we'll take it very steady. There's no difficulties ahead.' He fetched the piebald and mounted.

Who does he think he is? thought Olivia, resigned to her fate. A prophet? But his 'good girl' had sent a quiver of pleasure through her, and squaring her shoulders she smiled and off they went.

They found the others already picnicking and Julian passed a few ribald comments about their lateness, adding slyly that if they must roll about in the bracken it was always as well to remove the evidence from one's clothing. Olivia braced herself for the inevitable explanation and was amazed when Matthew calmly told him to mind his own business, and while she was thankful that her inexpertise was not to be made common knowledge, she couldn't help but be aware of the murderous look in Philippa's eyes.

Later, the horses walking sedately on the final stretch home, Julian came alongside Olivia and wagged an admonishing finger.

'Tut-tut, whatever next, you hussy!'

Olivia glared. 'You are dreadful, Julian. Why did you say that?'

'To needle Miss Markham. She annoys me—and Matt didn't seem to mind. Perhaps he wished it were true?' His eyes danced.

'So you knew darned well what had happened!'

He grinned. 'I gather you parted company with the black. Glad you came to no harm.'

'No harm? I'm bruised from head to toe. What were you doing, to allow them to put me up on this?'

'I'm sorry, dear, sweet Olivia, but it was arranged before I

98

arrived on the scene. I thought that if you were nervous of riding him you would have told Matt.'

'Oh, did you? Well, I have some pride, you know.'

He raised his brows. 'But only where Matt's concerned, evidently,' and giving her an enigmatic look he dropped behind to ride with Laura and Paul took his place. They chatted amicably for a while and then Paul said:

'I'll give you something to put in the bath tonight, Olivia,' and his eyes twinkled.

'I might just as well have let Matthew proclaim it to the world,' she said in disgust. 'We didn't fool anyone.'

'Oh, you did. The girls didn't realise what had happened.' Paul smiled.

'Well, at least I kept my dignity intact so far as they were concerned.' She eyed him with pursed lips. 'Why didn't we fool you, Paul? Was the idea of Matthew and me frolicking in the bracken too incredible to swallow?' The words came out more harshly than she intended and she saw his look of surprise.

'Not incredible, merely out of character for the surroundings,' Paul said gently, adding with a wry smile, 'I'm a doctor, my dear, trained to observe. You couldn't use your left arm and that bruise will soon be showing on your forehead. I hope Matt looked after you properly?'

Olivia grinned. 'Yes, after giving me his repertoire of distinguished oaths.'

Paul laughed. 'Well, he would never have forgiven himself if anything had happened to you while you were a guest under our roof.'

Olivia nodded. 'Oh, yes ... yes, I quite realise ...' She hesitated. 'I wouldn't like to have caused trouble between Matthew and Philippa because of Julian's teasing, though.'

'I shouldn't worry about that,' said Paul easily. He looked back over his shoulder. 'They seem happy enough now.' Olivia followed his gaze and nodded absently. 'If Matt had wanted to explain, he would have done so.'

'Yes, he would, wouldn't he?' replied Olivia.

CHAPTER FIVE

'Give me now leave to leave thee.'

'WELL?' demanded Julian. 'What do you think?' and he stood in the doorway, legs astride, hands on hips, a challenge in his blue eyes.

'My goodness,' exclaimed Olivia with a laugh, 'you've shaved it off!' She walked over and rubbed his chin teasingly. 'You look very nice.'

'Mm ... with all your dark insinuations as to what I was hiding beneath my beautiful beard it's reassuring to find that you think I look "very nice".'

'Julian Raynor,' mocked Olivia, 'you surely hadn't forgotten what you looked like?'

He grinned and rubbed his chin speculatively. 'I must admit I feel curiously indecent. We're having photographs taken tomorrow, so it had to go. You are coming to the opening, aren't you, Olivia?'

'Of course. You don't suppose I'd miss the chance of seeing the celebrated Charles Raynor and Anthea Beresford, do you?' She frowned in concentration. 'Oh, yes, and there's a new bloke too, but I can't remember his name.'

'Wretch!'

'Will it be good? Is Matthew pleased with it?'

'I think so.' He shook his head wonderingly. 'I have to remind myself that it's only brother Matt, who gets claustrophobia in lifts, is allergic to cats and cried buckets when he read *Beau Geste*, just to keep things in perspective, he is such a good director. Getting John Bennett's *Pilgrimage* is a feather in his cap too.' Julian looked at his watch. 'I have to call in at the theatre this evening for a fitting, one of my suits needs slight alteration. Like to come with me? We could go somewhere afterwards.'

'That would be lovely,' Olivia said with enthusiasm.

'I'll get the T.R. out, won't be a minute.'

Olivia nodded and watched him go with amusement. It

would be like going out with a stranger—Julian minus beard. It made him look younger, more like Charles. Perhaps I'd better fetch a jacket, she decided, and made for the stairs, almost colliding with Harriet who was descending looking rather harassed.

'Oh, Olivia, there you are. I'm rather worried about Toby. He's got a temperature and Paul's out on call and it's my night at the hospital. Mrs Peters has just phoned to say she can't come and baby-sit and everyone else seems to . . .'

'Not to worry, Harriet,' said Olivia, following her into the kitchen. 'I'll stay with Toby.' Harriet turned to her in relief.

'Olivia, would you?'

'Of course. What do you think is the matter with him?'

Harriet frowned. 'He's not been himself for the last couple of days, but I put it down to the start of a head cold. I know he's not a noisy lad, but even so he's been very quiet.'

Olivia bit her bottom lip. 'Yes. I know he's upset because I'm leaving.'

'Oh, my dear, are you?' Harriet looked surprised. 'I thought Charles was going to try and persuade you to stay on for a while? Why don't you, Olivia?'

'I can't stay here indefinitely, Harry.'

'No, but you could look round for another job at your leisure.' Harriet lifted her head and listened. 'There's Julian with his car. Was he taking you . . .?'

'Now don't fuss.'. Olivia took her arm and led her to the door. 'Off you go and get ready or else your friend will be arriving to pick you up and you'll keep her waiting.'

'But Julian . . .'

'Nothing had been arranged definitely for tonight, and I'll be glad to sit with Toby.'

'Bless you, love.' Harriet smiled gratefully. 'There's no need to sit with him—at least, he'd like you to for a while, I expect, but if he drops off there's no need to stay.' She looked at her watch, gave an exclamation and hurried out.

'What's Harry flapping over?' asked Julian. 'I've just passed her muttering about lemon drinks and temperatures.'

'Crisis, Julian. Toby's not well and as it's Harry's WVS night I've said I'll stay with him.'

'Blast! What's happened to Mrs Whatsit who usually sits in on this sort of thing?'

'Mrs Whatsit has had one of her turns.' She smiled appeasingly. 'I'm sorry to spoil our evening, Julian.'

He put his arm round her shoulders. 'Oh, well, can't be helped. I am going to miss you when you leave us.' He gave her a side glance. 'Don't forget to leave your address with us. I shall want to send on those photographs we took on that fateful horse-riding picnic. How're the bruises?'

Olivia pulled a face. 'Not too bad. I didn't think I could go so many different colours in the space of so short a time.'

'Olivia? I'm just off,' called Harriet from the hall.

'Yes, Harry—'bye.' Olivia slipped from the circle of his arm and went to the door. 'I must go to Toby.'

Julian followed her to the foot of the stairs. 'What's the matter with the brat?'

'We don't know. Could be the first signs of anything.'

'Shall I come up and have a chat with him?'

'Heavens!' Olivia was horrified. 'Definitely not. Whatever would Matthew say if I allowed his juvenile lead to come into contact with germs? Off you go,' she said firmly, adding with a grin, 'He'd sooner have me, anyway.'

'Very true. He's got sense, has young Toby.' He pulled her to him. 'You really are very sweet, Olivia, aren't you?'

'Yes, I believe I am,' she answered demurely. Julian laid his chin against her cheek consideringly.

'With or without beard?'

'Oh, I can't decide,' said Olivia, eyes dancing, 'until I've had a little more time to sample ... no, Julian ... please! Toby ...'

'Very well.' He released her reluctantly and as Olivia escaped gave her a resounding spank. 'And that, young woman, is for "juvenile lead"!'

She laughed and ran upstairs to Toby, whom she found flushed and fretful. Wishing she knew more about childhood complaints, she wiped his face with a cool flannel and gave him a drink of lemon, then sat and read a chapter from one of his favourite books. When she finished he asked:

'When are you going away, Livia?' in a sad little voice.

She answered matter-of-factly: 'Tuesday, I think. I shall write to you, of course. Tobias P. Raynor, I shall put on the envelope. There are so many Raynors in this house that it must be made clear.' She smoothed the hair from his forehead. 'Now close your eyes and try to sleep. I'll stay with you until you do.' The droopy lids closed obediently and Olivia relaxed back in her chair.

How difficult it all was! If only she could pack up and go, without any fuss and bother. Now that the end was near she wanted to go, not prolong the leavetaking, but she was committed to the opening night on Monday and the party afterwards, being given to celebrate Charles's recovery and return. That meant four more days to get through. Where to go then? Tomorrow she could scan the evening paper for a room. She would get herself established and then do the rounds of the theatrical agencies. It would be hard at first to leave the safety of the typing pool, but she was determined to have another go. Rotheringham was out, of course, but Queensbridge was only twenty miles away and boasted a beautiful new and thriving theatre. She sighed. It would be better when she had left Cressida House. There were too many conflicting emotions involved and when she had gone, perhaps this tight knot inside her would unravel itself.

She glanced at Toby and realised that his breathing had become regular and he was asleep. Drawing the sheet gently over his outstretched arm, she left the bedroom and walked down the stairs just as the front door opened and Paul entered. She quickly explained the situation and while he went upstairs to look at Toby she went to the kitchen and made a pot of tea. When she returned with the tray Paul was lying back in the armchair, eyes closed, but he sat up when he heard her.

'Tea! Manna from heaven.'

Olivia placed the tray on a low table and knelt to pour.

'What do you think is wrong with Toby?' she asked.

'No telling at this stage. He definitely has a temperature, but we'll just have to wait and see what develops—if anything. There's one or two things floating around the schools at the moment. Don't look so worried, Olivia.'

'One feels so helpless ...' and she broke off, suddenly remembering how helpless Paul must have felt six years ago when his wife died. 'Sugar?'

Paul nodded and reached for his cup. He eyed her thoughtfully.

'It was good of you to stay in this evening, Olivia.'

'I was glad to.'

'So ... Julian went out and left you.'

'Your voice sounds recriminating, Paul, and it shouldn't be,' replied Olivia calmly. 'To use a well-worn cliché, Julian and I are good friends but nothing more, so you see, any indignation on your part would be unwarranted.'

Paul nodded, 'I see. I wouldn't want you to be hurt. Julian's a rascal but a very likeable one, and I thought ... Well, his loss tonight is my gain—emergency calls apart. Shall we have some music?' He rose and selected a record and then rejoined Olivia on the sofa, tucking her arm companionably through his own. 'You're determined to leave us next week?' She nodded, avoiding his eyes. He was silent and then: 'I have the feeling that if we're not careful you will just walk out of the door and we'll not see you again.'

As this was exactly what Olivia intended she moved uneasily.

'Paul, you've only known me for three months ...'

'We may be extroverts and gregarious, but we're very clever at getting rid of unwelcome guests and hangers-on. Therefore you must take our words of friendship at their face value.'

'But you don't really know me,' she protested helplessly.

'Rubbish. Three months' close contact with you has told us that you're honest, reliable and conscientious, soft-hearted and kind, an amusing companion and a good listener—the last always essential where actors are concerned—and you must just accept that the Raynor family have taken you to their hearts and will not relinquish you without a battle. We're all going to miss you, especially Toby, and if I thought it your intention to disappear completely from our lives, then I should have to find some way of keeping you here,' and he smiled at her, eyes teasing.

'I'll not ask for the grisly details.' Olivia lightened her voice deliberately, his words making her heart sink deeper and deeper. Honest! She swallowed hard. 'When I'm settled somewhere, I'll write, I promise.'

Paul gave a satisfied grunt and gave his attention to the music. After a while Olivia was sure that he had dropped off to sleep and she was glad not to have to make conversation. So engrossed was she over the innumerable and imponderable thoughts that were darting about inside her head that when the main light was abruptly switched on and Matthew stood staring at them from the doorway, she gave a startled jump.

'I'm so sorry,' Matthew said drily. 'I thought the record player had been put on and forgotten.'

'Do put that damned light off, Matt. If you feel the necessity for one, use the table lamp,' Paul demanded calmly, eyes still closed.

Matthew obeyed. 'I thought you were asleep, brother.'

'Well, I wasn't. We didn't need a light for what we were doing, did we, Olivia?' and Paul gazed at her cheerfully. Olivia smiled back, but felt a curious reluctance to give the wrong impression to Matthew. Relations had improved between them since the horse episode the previous weekend ... nothing stupendous, but a lessening of tension, an easing of constraint, and with only four days to go she would like to say goodbye to him feeling that she had gained some degree of ... friendship? Hardly that—tolerance, perhaps. At the beginning she couldn't give a damn what he thought of her, but now ... she rather wanted his respect, and she understood the situation here now, could see the pressures. Yes, it would be nice to give those grey eyes a friendly look and perhaps take away with her the impression of one of his too infrequent smiles. On those thoughts she excused herself, sleepily, and went to bed.

With the advent of spots and the diagnosis of the measles Toby filled Olivia's four days and the time passed quicker than expected.

During Monday morning she brought him downstairs and he lay on the sofa wrapped in a blanket. He was an easy child to amuse and was frowning with concentration over a birthday card he was making for Harriet's birthday which was two weeks away. Olivia, seated in a chair opposite, was also engrossed in a similar pursuit, although hers was for Toby.

'There,' she exclaimed with satisfaction. 'Finished. I'll just print GET WELL SOON in red letters here and sign my name ... here ... and now I can deliver it,' and she handed the card over with a smile. Toby took one look and chuckled helplessly.

'Oh, it is funny, Livia. That's me, isn't it, sitting up in bed? I'm sure I haven't that many spots.'

'Don't you believe it,' replied Olivia darkly. Toby stood his card on the table and gave a deep sigh.

'I wish you weren't going, Livia,' he muttered at last. 'It won't be such fun without you.'

'I know, but things change all the time, Toby.'

He dropped his gaze and continued colouring, giving her a quick look beneath lowered lashes before asking tentatively: 'Couldn't you marry Uncle Matt, Olivia?'

Olivia stared blankly at him for a moment and then said gravely:

'Why ... why do you ask, Toby?'

He squirmed irresolutely and then blurted out: 'Uncle Julian was talking to Uncle Matt and I heard him say that you would make someone a marvellous wife and it was time Uncle Matt got married.'

'And what did your Uncle Matthew say to that?'

'Nothing, because they saw me. Uncle Julian was laughing and Uncle Matt looked cross. Will you marry Uncle Matt, Livia?'

Olivia struggled for the right words. 'Toby darling, before I marry someone I must know him very well. I've only been here for three months and that's not really long enough to get to know Uncle Matthew well enough.'

Toby shrugged. 'It was just an idea.'

You can say that again! thought Olivia, wishing she could hit the incorrigible Julian over the head with his bright ideas.

That evening, dressing for the opening night and the party afterwards, Olivia took pains to make sure she looked her best. Tonight was to be her swan-song and she needed every bit of artifice to help see her through. She considered herself in the mirror and was pleased with the results. Her hair was coiled high on her head, a switch hanging down the back. The effect was slightly Grecian, which suited her dress which was flame-coloured chiffon, long and flowing. She frowned, wondering if perhaps it was too striking, but a glance at her watch showed that it was too late to do anything about it now, and hastily grabbing her faithful long black cape she hurried out of her room to join Paul and Harriet.

Sitting in the auditorium watching the seats fill up with a smiling, chattering audience dressed specially for the occasion, Olivia suddenly spotted Adam Carlyon sitting further forward on their left. Paul, following her gaze, said:

'You haven't met Adam's wife, Elizabeth, yet, have you,

Olivia? She's two along from him, just out of view. I don't know whether they'll be staying on afterwards or not. John Bennett who wrote tonight's play is next to her.' Paul gave a swift but searching look around the theatre. 'I can see at least two London critics and one local one, so the newspapers are represented. I nipped backstage, by the way, to wish them all luck.'

'Oh, good, how are they?'

'Quiet or chatty, depending on how nerves take them.'

They exchanged a smile as the house lights dimmed and the audience gradually quietened. Music swelled and filled the auditorium, fading gently as the curtain rose and the first performance of *Pilgrimage* by John Bennett began.

As Paul and Olivia fought their way to the bar during the interval Olivia kept an eye open for Matthew, but could see no sign of him.

'What do you think so far?' asked Paul, trying to squash his rather broad frame into a narrow space as he handed Olivia her drink.

'Good. Very good, in fact. Your father hasn't lost his touch, has he?'

Paul nodded in agreement and then smiled at someone behind her and, turning, she saw Adam Carlyon pushing his way towards them through the crowd.

'Hello, Miss Darcy, Paul.' Adam Carlyon emerged triumphant and they chatted for the rest of the interval about the play. When the bell rang indicating the start of the second act Paul said as they made their way back to the seats:

'Where's Elizabeth, Adam?'

'She didn't fancy the crush and went in search of fresh air.'

'Are you staying later?'

'We hope to, if Elizabeth is feeling up to it, and if I know Elizabeth, she'll make sure she is. I go this way. I'll see you later, no doubt?' Carlyon asked Olivia. She smiled her reply. There was something about this quietly spoken man with the dark expressive eyes that appealed to her.

'Is his wife ill?' she asked Paul when they were on their own.

'Quite the reverse. Very fit and blooming with health. She's having a baby,' replied Paul, guiding her to her seat.

The enthusiastic applause at the end of the play augured well for box office returns for the remainder of its run. As they made for the exit Olivia asked Paul curiously:

'In one word, how would you describe that play?'

'You don't ask much, do you?' He thought hard. 'Personal failure.'

'That's two, but I'll allow it.' Olivia replied kindly, and then gave the matter her consideration. 'Non-communication,' she decided at last, 'and that's hyphenated,' she added with a grin.

'I expect if we asked half a dozen people they would come up with different words, all with a central link. I wonder if Matt's feeling better now.'

'Has he been ill?' Olivia asked in surprise.

'Looked rough this afternoon but refused all offers of help ... and it's no good looking at me like that, Olivia. Matt is a grown man, quite capable of knowing when he needs a doctor. Come along, the crowd's thinning out now, we'll make our way to where the "king" is holding his gathering.'

'You mustn't talk of your father like that,' scolded a laughing Olivia. 'He may be forgiven celebrating his welcome return to the stage, he's a super actor, is your papa.'

'He is, isn't he? And young Julian's good too.'

'You sound like his grandfather,' teased Olivia.

'Sometimes I feel like it. Here we are, let's go in and see who's arrived.' Paul pushed open the door and as the volume of noise greeted them, turned back his head and gave a wry smile: 'Looks as though everyone has!'

The party was being held in the largest rehearsal room, made slightly larger by a dividing partition being folded back and another room leading off was converted into a bar. A space was cleared for dancing and tables and chairs were available for those that wanted them.

'I see Harry looking worried about the catering,' said Paul with a smile. 'Father always gets carried away with his invitations and Harry always takes that into account, but still she worries. Come and be introduced to John Bennett.'

It was quite some time before she bumped into Julian, who gave her a warm embrace and exclaimed:

'Olivia! Light of my life!'

'Julian, I did enjoy the play ... it was very good.'

'I hope you've spread your praises around?'

'I have,' replied Olivia promptly, accepting a glass of wine from him. 'I told Charles how wonderful I thought you all, and he introduced me to Anthea Beresford and we sat round and filled ourselves with delicious food—have you had any yet?' Olivia sipped her drink, eyes sparkling. 'Isn't Anthea a honey? No one would believe she was a successful actress at the top of her profession. She has no affectations and is very friendly.'

'When you're at the top you can afford to be, Olivia.'

'Don't be cynical, Julian, it doesn't suit you, and you know full well that there are plenty of people at the top who make you well aware of the fact. When you're way up there, with your name in lights, make sure the same can't be said of you.'

'You think I'll get there?' he queried.

'I do.'

'You may join the fan club, darling. Drink up.'

Olivia obeyed him, amused eyes above her glass.

'What an old fraud you are, Julian.'

'Yes, I'm afraid I am, love,' he lowered his voice, 'but the fewer who know the better—so bad for the image . . .'

'And it would never do for people to realise that all those high spirits are merely a façade for a serious, dedicated actor.'

He looked round nervously. 'Olivia, please! You'll ruin me,' and giving her a grin he asked: 'Have you met our play-writer yet?'

'Yes. He seems rather shy. Obviously more garrulous with the written word than the spoken.'

'You have been getting around this evening, haven't you? I can't imagine how I missed you, especially as you look so beautiful.'

'I bet you say that to all the girls,' mocked Olivia. 'You must understand, Julian, that when compliments are your stock in trade, they do tend to be diminished.'

'I see,' said Julian, eyes gleaming. 'So that if . . . if say Adam Carlyon or John Bennett were to tell you how beautiful you look, you would believe them?'

Olivia laughed. 'Yes, I suppose so . . . although I can't imagine either of . . .'

'Or someone you know better but who isn't given to flowery phrases?'

'Well, yes, but I . . .'

He grasped her arm and led her round the room, stopping

every now and then to exchange a brief word to those guests he knew, introducing Olivia, and then making his way determinedly to some hidden goal.

'Julian! What are you doing?' hissed a bewildered Olivia, and then in dawning horror, she whispered frantically: 'Don't you dare! You villain!'

'Matthew,' declared the irrepressible Julian, 'here is Olivia.'

Matthew raised his brows: 'So I see. I don't believe we've met so far this evening, Olivia.' He passed a cool gaze over Julian's hand round her wrist and added reflectively: 'And Julian has very kindly rectified the omission.'

'Julian,' retorted Olivia, freeing her arm and glaring at her kidnapper, 'should have been severely spanked as a child—hard and often. I'll be much obliged, Matthew, if you would take not the slightest bit of notice of him.'

'That is my normal procedure,' admitted Matthew, 'where Julian is concerned.'

Julian grinned, 'I know when I'm not wanted,' adding unrepentantly, 'and I bet you'd believe Matt,' before disappearing among the guests.

'I won't embarrass you by asking what that was all about,' said Matthew. 'Perhaps you would like a drink, Olivia?'

'I don't think I'd better,' answered Olivia gravely. 'I think I've had too much already, thank you.' There was silence as Matthew continued to regard her and she found herself blushing like a schoolgirl and frantically thinking of something to say. Her memory saved her. 'Paul said you were not well this afternoon. I hope you're feeling better now, Matthew?'

He smiled. 'Thank you, yes. Headaches are rather a taboo subject between us, I think.'

Confused, Olivia said desperately: 'I think I will have that drink after all, thank you,' and while she waited for Matthew to return she realised that this was only a temporary breathing space. But they had the Bennett play as common ground and spent the next ten minutes discussing it. When the drink was finished and Matthew took the empty glass from her, he asked quietly:

'Would you like to dance, Olivia?'

'Dance?' she echoed blankly, almost as if she had never heard the word before.

Matthew lifted a brow quizzically. 'The lights are low,

there's soft music and even at this late hour there are still couples dancing. Shall we join them?'

Olivia swallowed and raised her eyes to his, giving a be-mused nod to assent, then allowed him to lead her to the other end of the room, frantically regretting that last drink. He held out his hand and she hesitated fractionally before giving him her own, then she was in his arms and somehow her head was on his shoulder.

'Olivia,' murmured a voice after a moment, 'stop trembling and relax—I won't eat you.'

She lifted her head, but in the half-light could not read his expression.

'You won't?'

'No. Why should I eat one of the prettiest girls in the room and deprive myself of the pleasure of looking at her?'

Oh, Julian! Julian! she thought hysterically to herself—you were right! I do want to believe it when Matthew says it. She closed her eyes for a second and concentrated on being sensible, then taking a deep breath, said:

'I'm sorry, Matthew, but I'm afraid I can't accept this sudden change of attitude. It's too late in the day for me to relax in your company, and I feel it's also rather suspect when you ask me to do so the evening before I'm due to leave your house.'

'Mm ... you couldn't call a truce, for my father's sake? He's sitting over there with a benevolent look on his face.'

Olivia followed his gaze and Charles smiled and lifted his hand in an almost 'bless you, my children' gesture. She sighed.

'Very well, for your father's sake, a truce,' she agreed primly, and almost kidded herself that that was the real reason. She relaxed and gave herself up to the mood and the music and hoped that Matthew couldn't feel how hard her heart was thumping. It was a few moments before she realised that the music had stopped and the other couples were dispersing, and she took a hasty step away from Matthew. He had a faint smile on his face as he regarded her thoughtfully.

'I rather think it's time you went home, Olivia. It's late and the party is beginning to break up now anyway.' He led her firmly to the door. 'Get your things and I'll meet you at the stage door.'

Olivia found herself nodding, obediently fetching her cape.

Standing before the long mirror in the cloakroom, she studied herself seriously and shook her head at the starry-eyed girl facing her.

'Olivia Darcy, you are a fool.'

The girl in the mirror did not seem to mind the insult and with a curve of red lips and a swirl of cape she was out of the door, running down the corridor and out of the stage door before sense could prevail. Matthew appeared out of the shadows. Olivia breathed the night air deeply.

'What a pity it's too far to walk home.'

Matthew, amusement in his voice, answered dryly: 'You wouldn't get far in those shoes, my dear. I think you'll find the Lotus a more comfortable means of transport—but we'll walk if you wish.'

'How valiant of you, Matthew, but you're right. The Lotus it is.'

The car was in its usual spot. In silence Matthew unlocked it and helped Olivia into the passenger seat and when he climbed into his own, she said apologetically:

'I'm afraid this dress has a mind of its own—there's so much of it . . .'

Matthew leánt across and released the fabric from the door, so close that his warm breath touched her cheek and his arm leant heavily for a moment on her body as he pulled the door to and checked the lock. Nervously she fumbled for the seat belt and when it was taken from her, sat quietly, suddenly calm.

Nothing hurried, everything assured, Matthew kissed her.

'I've been wanting to do that all evening,' he stated, and kissed her again.

'You . . . have?' asked Olivia, when she could control her breathing.

'I have.' Matthew slipped the key into the ignition. 'You note that I made sure you were helpless first, before I did so,' and the amused note was back in his voice. He reversed the Lotus with practised ease and slowly accelerated towards the entrance of the car park.

For Olivia the world had turned crazily upside down. Feeling ridiculously weak and helpless, she lay back in the seat and turned her head to look at him. By the light of the solitary lamp fixed high on the corner of the building she saw he was

112

leaning forward slightly, peering through the windscreen, whistling softly under his breath. This broke off short when a couple rounded the corner and Matthew braked sharply, slowing to a standstill, allowing the couple to pass in single file through the narrow gap between the Lotus and the railings. As they neared, Matthew wound down his window.

'Goodnight, Elizabeth, Adam.'

The couple paused and a feminine voice exclaimed: 'Adam! Here's Matt ... Matt darling, we've been looking all over to say goodnight. Thank you for a lovely play and a lovely, lovely evening. Hasn't it been a lovely evening, Adam?'

Thus applied to, Adam grinned, white smile gleaming in the semi-darkness.

'Elizabeth should never touch wine,' he announced blandly, and received an indignant:

'And just what do you mean by that, Adam Carlyon?'

'I mean that we've seen a lovely play and had a lovely, lovely evening, and Matthew and Olivia are waiting to go home—and so am I.'

Matthew said indulgently: 'Elizabeth, I don't believe you've met Olivia.' He gestured to each in turn. 'Elizabeth Carlyon, Olivia Darcy. Olivia, this is Elizabeth, Adam's long-suffering wife.'

There was silence and then:

'Olivia Darcy!' Liz's face beamed through the open window.

'Liz Browning,' replied Olivia, forcing herself to speak, fatalistically calm. Matthew made a sudden half movement to speak and then sat still. Adam said quietly:

'You know each other?'

Liz laughed. 'I should think we do! We were at drama school together—oh, eons ago. Olivia, this is exciting. How on earth have we missed each other this evening?—except I've been sitting most of the time in a secluded spot owing to my rather obvious delicate condition. Oh, we must meet and exchange all our news.'

'Indeed you must,' agreed Adam as the silence inside the Lotus stretched longer than was acceptable, 'and we'll arrange something, but not now, Elizabeth. Now we must go. It's been a splendid evening, Matthew, artistically and socially, I congratulate you. Goodnight to you both.' Tucking his wife's

113

hand firmly beneath his arm, he drew her away from the window.

Liz managed: ' 'Night, Olivia, Matt,' before she was led away and continued: 'I just can't believe it, Adam. Why didn't you tell me her name was Olivia? Then I would have connected it with . . . at least . . .'

The roar of the engine drowned all further conversation and Matthew let out the clutch and the Lotus snarled forward. Street lights illuminated the interior and Olivia watched Matthew's face, now dark, now light, trying to read it, to gauge his feelings, but it was inscrutable, only a slight rigidity of the jawline proclaiming a degree of control.

The city centre was left rapidly behind and still no words had passed between them until Millbrook Road flashed by on their left and Olivia turned sharply to Matthew, demanding:

'Where are we going?'

'Somewhere we can talk.'

'I don't want to talk.'

'Well, it's certainly not what I had in mind earlier, I must admit.' His voice was wryly amused and Olivia felt her cheeks burn, remembering the long kiss they had exchanged only minutes earlier. Only minutes, but it could easily have been years—indeed, the whole of the evening had taken on a dreamlike quality. Dancing in Matthew's arms had been confusing enough, but the emotions that kiss aroused had been staggering, bewildering. Even now her whole being responded to the memory, a wild delight swept treacherously through her and she knew that had Liz not arrived on the scene, Olivia Darcy would have made a fool of herself. But not now . . . oh, no, not now. There was absolutely no fear of that happening. That dream sequence had been firmly squashed, trodden on . . . torn to shreds. A cold anger now consumed her, to replace the hot fire—a cold anger that she clung to for dear life, clung to as a dear friend, it being the inveterate and ingrained emotion that was part and parcel of her relationship with Matthew Raynor, and any deviation from that was to be rejected instantly.

Matthew swung the steering wheel over to the left and with a high-pitched squeal the tyres gripped the camber as they took the fork to the open country. The Lotus wound its way along twisting roads, climbing higher and higher until the headlights lighted up an open gateway, signposted 'Sentinel Hill'. Then they were bouncing over a stone track, sweeping to a halt, gravel splaying, a few yards from the edge of an escarpment.

Matthew leisurely switched off the ignition and the engine note died, leaving an oppressive silence. With a click the headlights were doused and before them, low down, was the dark expanse of Rotheringham, its scattered lights twinkling in the distance.

'So ... you don't want to talk.' Matthew reached out and turned her averted face, gazing at her steadily for a moment, grey eyes holding green. 'We need not talk, Olivia,' he continued softly. 'We could wipe out meeting the Carlyons and carry on where we left off.'

The words evoked the scattered, torn shreds of dream and they fluttered helplessly. Olivia jerked her face away, the imprint of his fingers on her cheek scalding her.

'You must be joking! No one can ever go back, even if they wanted to,' and her voice implied quite definitely what her feelings on the subject were.

His hand lifted in a curiously resigned gesture before resting on the steering wheel.

'So the truce is over?'

She gave a short laugh. 'It most certainly is.'

'Mm ... pity. As truces go, ours was beginning to be interesting.'

'From your point of view, no doubt. Open hostilities until the eve of my departure and then, when you're sure I'm leaving and have caused no trouble, you turn on the charm, condescend to give the poor girl a kiss or two, equal up the Raynor ratio and show her what she's missed.'

His voice was dangerously even. 'Yes, the truce is most definitely off—and with a vengeance, it seems.'

Olivia's head shot round, green eyes flashing.

'My God, Matthew Raynor, you're damned right it is! You decided how it was to be the first time we met, remember? So you shouldn't complain now.' She gazed challengingly at him and he returned her look with one of consideration, his thumb methodically tapping the wheel.

'You're angry. I expected some reaction, of course, but not

115

such all-consuming righteous fury. You're letting your emotions cloud your judgment, Olivia.'

Despite all her good intentions, Olivia's voice rose a fraction.

'Oh, I am, am I? And how else would you expect me to react, I'd like to know? Two minutes earlier and we would have missed Liz and I might never have known. How strange meeting her like that! On my last night too. Rather ironic, don't you think, Matthew? We could have met any time during the last three months and it has to be tonight. Quite spoiled your style.' She couldn't see his face clearly, but he was sitting unnaturally still and when he didn't speak she continued in a voice now so controlled that the words came out flat: 'You knew, didn't you? I was watching your face when Liz said we were at drama school together and there was no surprise there.' She expelled a sharp breath. 'All this time . . . and you knew!'

The accusation lay between them for a moment and then Matthew relaxed and leant back against the door, an arm across the back of his seat.

'Yes.' He was quite cool. 'I knew, Olivia, the first time I saw you. Surprising though it may seem, I was intending telling you this evening.' Olivia snorted derisively. He continued mildly, 'I still can't see why you should be so angry about it.'

'Well, isn't that just dandy?' retorted Olivia bitterly. 'You can't see why I should be so angry—who have been playing cat and mouse with me these past weeks?'

'Oh, come on, Olivia, be realistic, please.' Matthew's voice hardened. 'You can't have lived with us all this time without realising why I didn't trust you?' He waited, but she refused to answer. '*Knowing* you were connected with the theatre?'

Olivia struggled with her innate sense of fairness and gave an impatient shrug.

'I concede that it must have seemed suspicious—but you should have said something, not kept quiet and . . .' she floundered for a word, '. . . and persecuted me.'

'That's a little strong, surely?'

'Not from where I was standing, believe me.'

'You could have avoided all that by telling the truth at the beginning,' he pointed out with infuriating reasonableness.

Olivia pressed her hands to her cheeks. 'I did tell the truth. I was genuinely not working in the theatre and hadn't been for nine months. I didn't even know you were a director at the Royal or that the Raynor who was employing me was Charles Raynor. If I had I might ... oh, what does it matter now? It's all over and done with. I'm no longer in your employ, Matthew Raynor—go to hell!'

He gave a short laugh. 'I probably will.' He paused and then said abruptly: 'Tell me, why didn't you say afterwards, when you did know?'

Olivia felt suddenly stifled. The fact that Matthew was treating her reactions with a superior air, obviously considering them of little account, made her feel angrier than ever, but this had always been the case between them. She pulled open the door and scrambled out, taking a deep breath of fresh air. The wind, strong now that they were at a high altitude, tugged playfully at her cape, allowing the flame silk to escape and flutter delicately. She rescued the cape and hugged it to her, walking along the rough path with no regard to her evening shoes, the welcome breeze cooling her hot cheeks. The car door slammed and after a moment Matthew joined her, neither speaking. At the summit a tall stone monument stood in solitary splendour, and Olivia climbed the steps and leant against the cold marble, shielded momentarily from the wind. Matthew, hands in pockets, remained below, the wind ruffling his hair, the moon, suddenly free of scudding clouds, highlighting his watchful gaze.

'Why *did* you think I "persecuted" you, Olivia?'

'Why?' She frowned and said rather haughtily: 'How could I know why?'

'But you must, at some time, have given it thought,' Matthew persisted.

'Of course I did. Every time you were beastly to me.'

'And?'

She shrugged and half turned away. 'I supposed you'd taken an instant dislike to me,' she answered disdainfully.

'Isn't that rather unbelievable? That I should take one look at you and take such an aversion? I can't imagine that ever happening to you before.' He shook his head slowly, grey eyes hooded as he climbed the steps towards her. 'No, that is decidedly unbelievable.'

'How did I know whether it was unbelievable or not?' she

answered patiently, taking a step backwards. 'I didn't know you.'

'Exactly!' He caught her arm and pulled her round. 'You didn't know me.' He paused, emphasising his point and then continued ruthlessly: 'You didn't ask yourself *why* I held you in suspicion, perfect strangers as you thought we were? *Why* a normal man of fair intelligence should display such antagonism? That there was perhaps a more genuine reason than mere instant dislike—which, after all, is such an illogical emotion?'

'No, I didn't,' she flashed back indignantly. 'It's all very easy to give advice and profound theories from your lofty, secure position, Matthew. I needed that job. Have you ever needed a job so badly? When I found out you were a director at the Royal I was surprised and dismayed. I didn't tell you the truth then because I knew damned well you wouldn't believe that I was genuinely having a break away from the theatre, and I'd lose the job. So I said nothing and put up with you—and believe me, it took some doing . . .'

'You lapsed now and again.'

'. . . but because I loved every minute of working for your father I was prepared to do anything to remain.'

'I still say that your anger now is misplaced. You're judging the whole situation on the assumption of my ignorance. You must consider that I *knew* you were an actress. That you were posing as a typist . . .'

'I wasn't posing as . . .'

'. . . and because my father took an instant liking to you . . .' He broke off and gave a twisted smile. 'I wonder why it's perfectly in order to take an instant liking to someone and not the reverse? Could land you in just the same amount of trouble. Anyway, because I had a guilty conscience about the smash-up and the injuries he received, and I could see how well you would both get on together, I took a calculated risk and let you stay. But I kept my eyes open in case . . .'

'I conned him into marriage or into giving me the lead in his next play?' Olivia interrupted bitterly. 'You must have thought me . . .' She stopped short, an arrested expression on her face. 'Does . . . he . . . does your father know about me?'

'We've never spoken together on the subject, but you must be very naïve if you think a man of Charles Raynor's experience could be fooled by a girl as ingenuous as yourself.'

Olivia stood still, her face a blank. Charles had known all the time too, she thought bleakly. Had he been waiting on tenterhooks in case she broached the subject of a job? She swallowed hard.

'I was no threat to you, to any of you, but I don't expect you to believe me.'

'Even now I couldn't accept such a sweeping statement from you, Olivia, and certainly three months ago I wouldn't have. You've accused me in the past of being a cynic—well, if I am, my profession has made me one, but I must admit that almost against my will I began to suspect as the weeks went by that you were a rare species—an actress with integrity.' Startled, Olivia turned towards him, eyes wide and questioning. Matthew smiled thinly. 'It surprises you? That cold, hard-hearted, cynical Matthew can actually see beyond his pre-judiced nose? Well, my dear, I rather think I can see further—but we'll come to that later.'

'Yet you carried on, right up to the end, with your horrid watchfulness,' she interposed scornfully. 'I suppose that cynical streak wouldn't allow you to give up.'

'I'm rather wary of rare species. And if I still occasionally gave you a verbal dig, it was in the hope that you would tell me why you were no longer acting. But I doubt you could have told me anything I didn't know already.' Matthew lifted his face to the sky. 'We'd better make our way back to the car, there's rain in the wind.' Olivia shook off his hand on her arm and stalked a pace ahead, pulling the hood of the cape well over her head for more protection. 'Tell me, Olivia, if I were to offer you a job at the Royal, as one of the resident company, what would you do?'

It was a few paces before the meaning of the words pene-trated. Olivia stopped in her tracks and turned, staring speech-lessly. When she did, at last, find her voice it was only to stutter:

'Offer me ... what did you say?' as though it was incon-ceivable that she could have heard right. He repeated his words and her incredulous astonishment rapidly changed and in a shaking voice she burst out furiously:

'My God, Matthew, you've got a nerve! Still experiment-ing—still testing?'

119

'Maybe—but what would you do?'

'Hit you.'

He nodded. 'As I thought. There's no need to explain why you're typing instead of acting, Olivia.' His voice hardened. 'You haven't the fight, the tenacity, the ruthlessness or opportunism that propels actors to the top.'

Her hand flew out, almost of its own volition, and struck him hard across the face, and the fact that he didn't react in any way incensed her further.

'How dare you ... how dare you say that to me!' Her voice was low with suppressed rage. 'What do *you* know about it? About anything? What can a privileged Raynor know about what goes on in the lower strata? Nothing!' She gave a scornful laugh. 'What right have you to sit in judgment? Fight? I've fought all my life ... and just once I gave in, because I was so tired of fighting, and ...' She caught her breath painfully. 'Have *you* ever had to watch someone you love waste away before your eyes ... putting on a cheerful front, knowing he was doing the same, each protecting the other? When my father died I was left completely alone, and it's not easy to be strong when ...' Her voice broke and she rounded on him in contempt. 'How can you stand there and accuse me of not being an opportunist when I've had to put up with your damned cold grey eyes forever accusing, always suspicious ...' She flung herself from him and ran, stumbling along the path, tears streaming down her face.

Hateful, hateful man!

Olivia wrenched open the driver's door and thrust herself into the seat. She would show him ... she would teach him to stand there with a silly smile on his face. He'd soon laugh on the other side of his face when he found he'd had to walk five miles home! With a sigh of satisfaction the Lotus leapt to life and she peered frowningly at the gears, fumbled for reverse, eyes flicking up to the mirror to see if she was being followed, but Matthew seemed to be standing still where she had left him, just watching.

Headlights on, she let out the clutch, swept back in an arc and stopped, then driving forward erratically down the track, she shot through the gates and out on to the road. She forced herself to relax her grip on the steering wheel and peered anxiously through the windscreen, knowing she would have to

120

stop to find the wiper switch if the rain, suddenly covering the glass, got any worse. Five hundred yards further on she slowed to a halt.

Matthew was standing on the edge of the escarpment, his back to the monument, looking out over the city. The beam of the headlights caught him momentarily and then curved round. He waited while he heard Olivia get out and change places and when the passenger door banged shut, only then did he turn and walk casually over, to slip easily into the driving seat. By this time Olivia had gained some semblance of composure, outwardly at least.

'Why didn't you run after me?' she asked tautly, 'stop me taking it?'

He pursed his lips. 'I didn't want you to mistake first for reverse and kill yourself in your anxiety to escape.'

'That would be going rather too far in your persecution campaign!'

'You do have a delightfully dramatic turn of phrase, Olivia, it must get you into a vast amount of trouble. The real reason, of course, was that I considered my insurance company might have justifiable cause for complaint had I claimed for yet another write-off.' He engaged gear. 'It would have been a long, wet walk home—I'm glad you came back.'

'You've almost made me regret that I did,' she snapped, adding with a mutter, 'Anyway, you knew that I would,' and turning her shoulder she stared out of the side window, rejecting any further conversation. She felt completely drained and her head ached abominably. She couldn't seem to stop crying either, and didn't want to look for a handkerchief because she wouldn't give that hateful man the satisfaction of knowing she was upset. So the tears trickled slowly down her cheeks, to drip relentlessly on to the front of her cape. It was therefore galling to have a hand appear before her, holding a crisp white handkerchief, and a not unkind voice say:

'Mop them up before we both drown.'

Olivia almost snatched it from him and made rapid running repairs, but it didn't stop the flow. The dam had burst and there seemed nothing she could do about it, but at least, even if her turn of phrase was dramatic, her crying wasn't.

Although facing the window, Olivia was not conscious of direction or distance and it was with surprise and relief that

121

the Lotus swung into Millbrook Road. Matthew eased the car gently through the open gates, the throttle responding with a gentle purr as they moved slowly up the drive. They came to a standstill in front of the house, which was in complete darkness. Olivia reached for the door handle and Matthew's hand grasped her wrist.

'Aren't you interested in how I knew you were an actress, Olivia?'

She turned, not caring that he should see her ravaged face, and answered coldly:

'No—no, I'm not interested. Nothing you say or do interests me, or ever will. I shan't be sorry if I never see you again.' She looked down at his hand. 'Do I *have* to put up with you mauling me?' She was inordinately pleased to see a faint tinge of red creep into Matthew's cheeks and he relaxed his grip but did not release her. His voice was expressionless.

'But you'll be sorry not to see Toby, and the others ... and you may do so without the fear of seeing me. I shall be leaving here.'

'Oh, if you're not going to be around then I'll come back and see everyone—or will you be worried that I might ensnare your father or one of your brothers into marrying me?—for that's all I have left, isn't it, since you've decided acting is out.'

'You had already done that, Olivia, and as for the other—well, we all get what we deserve, sooner or later. When are you leaving tomorrow? I'll arrange for your trunk ...'

'There's no need for you to concern yourself. It's already packed and waiting in the hall.' She gave him a look of dislike. 'Now—will you kindly set me free?'

Matthew regarded her intently, taking in the tear-stained face, the pale cheeks, darkly smudged, cold green eyes.

'In this fight of yours—make sure you know what you're fighting about and with whom,' and on this cryptic note he got out and opened her door. 'Goodnight, Olivia.'

He was very close. Olivia had only to move a few inches and her head could rest on his shoulder.

'Goodbye, Matthew,' she answered firmly, and went into the house.

It was getting light rapidly when the taxi drew up at the gate.

Olivia asked if he would fetch her trunk and the driver gave her a sharp look as if he thought she was absconding with the family silver and would be needed to give her description later in the day. But he did as she requested and Olivia closed the front door quietly and walked quickly down the drive.

When the taxi drew away she looked bleakly out of the rear window, but the house had nothing to offer her, still wrapped in sleep.

CHAPTER SIX

'Direct thy feet where thou and I henceforth may never meet.'

'OLIVIA! Olivia Darcy!'

A hand grasped Olivia's arm and stopped her in her tracks. Her look of surprise changed to one of pleased recognition.

'Why, hello, Mr Carlyon.'

Adam Carlyon regarded her quizzically. 'I very nearly passed you by ... you've had your hair cut.'

Olivia's hand went self-consciously to her head and ruffled the short, smooth crop of hair.

'It takes some getting used to, but I didn't want to go to the expense of having another set of photographs taken—it seemed easier to revert back to the hairstyle of the ones I've already got.' She considered him gravely. 'I expect Liz told you that I'm an actress?' and when Carlyon nodded, she added wryly: 'I bet you knew anyway, I've been told I'm rather naïve. How is Liz?'

'Very well, but I hope you'll be able to judge for yourself in the near future,' answered Adam Carlyon, and glancing round at the busy High Street, he added briskly, 'Look, I want to talk to you and it's hopeless here. Have you time for a coffee?' He took her arm and began to draw her across the road to where his car was parked, dodging the traffic as they went. 'In any case, I can give you a lift to wherever it is you're going—that basket looks heavy.' He opened the passenger door invitingly while Olivia watched in amused helplessness as he took the basket from her and placed it on the back seat.

'I don't seem to have much choice, do I?'

He smiled disarmingly. 'Elizabeth always says that directors come out of the same mould, considering it their right to have their own way—and steamroller everyone into getting it.' He slid behind the steering wheel. 'All a pack of lies, of course.'

'Of course,' agreed Olivia, responding to the twinkle in his dark eyes. 'But, Mr Carlyon ...'

'Oh, Adam, please! I've been hearing so much from

Elizabeth about your drama school days that I feel I know you rather well. Now, I must remove ourselves from this yellow line before a warden comes along—is it coffee, or a lift home?'

Olivia looked at him uncertainly. 'I have the time for coffee, I'm not working at the moment, but ...'

'Good, coffee it is.' Carlyon waited for a gap in the traffic and drew out. It was soon apparent from the direction he was taking that their destination was the Theatre Royal. Concentrating on the road ahead, he said conversationally: 'The photographs you mentioned just now. I presume they're the ones you take round to the theatrical agencies?'

'Yes, although I haven't done so yet.' Olivia saw his questioning look and said ruefully: 'I know it's over a month since I left ... the Raynors, but I ... it hasn't been convenient to tout them around so far.'

'Why not?' asked Carlyon with inexorable persistence.

Olivia pulled a face. 'I've had the measles.'

'Ah! Which you caught, no doubt, from young Toby Raynor.'

'I suppose so.'

'Does Charles know?'

She shook her head. 'I didn't come out in spots until about two weeks after I'd left, although I was under the weather before that, but I put it down to being upset at ...' she broke off abruptly and bit her lip.

'Upset at ...?' prompted Carlyon relentlessly, swinging the car into the theatre car park.

Olivia said with some hesitation: 'I had a row with ... someone, and I hate rows, I always have, they stay with me for days ... stupid really, as the other person probably forgets about it five minutes later. It wasn't Charles, of course,' she added quickly, 'and as for telling him—why, I'm not Charles's responsibility any more.'

'Since you caught the disease from his grandson in the first place, I doubt Charles would agree with you. You know the way, don't you?' He held the stage door open and Olivia slowly entered the theatre once more and preceded him down the corridor. 'Here we are—go in and sit down, I'll organise some coffee.'

The room into which he showed her was a comfortably

125

furnished office and Olivia had hardly settled herself when Carlyon reappeared carrying two cups.

'Elizabeth was most disappointed to find you had disappeared so effectively, Olivia. I hope, now I've found you again, that you'll visit her. She doesn't get out quite so much now that she's near her time. Sugar?'

'No, thank you.' Olivia took the proffered cup and flushed slightly beneath his penetrating gaze. 'I did intend getting in touch with Liz, but becoming ill took me by surprise and I've not long been out of the infectious stage.' She sipped her coffee and said with just the right amount of interest: 'I saw your name on the door ... does that mean Matthew has left?'

'No. He wanted a couple of months or so off, and I was on the look-out for something to do—the mutual arrangement suited us both.' He paused and lifted a brow. 'You haven't seen him?'

'No,' said Olivia, slightly startled.

'You're not on your own. His family have no idea where he is or what he's doing, but I don't think they're unduly worried.'

'How ... are they all, do you know?'

Carlyon smiled. 'Very well, I believe. I see Julian and Charles, of course, and that brings me to the reason why I was so pleased to bump into you today. What is your American accent like?' and seeing her look of surprise he said crisply: 'I need an actress. In two weeks' time I start rehearsals on Mark Donaldson's play *Two for Joy*. Do you know it? Good. I would like you to take the part of Cassie.'

Olivia swallowed and gave an experimental clearing of the throat just to make sure she still had a voice.

'I don't quite understand ...'

'You're an actress—I need an actress. You're about to look for a job, I'm offering you one.'

'Aren't you taking rather a gamble, Adam? I mean, I could be awful.'

He smiled and said gently: 'Why don't you let me worry about that, Olivia? Do *you* think you're good?' The dark eyes were unwavering.

'Yes,' answered Olivia, almost defiantly. 'I know my limitations, but I also know that I've never really been stretched enough.'

'We'll have to see what we can give you to alter that, won't we? I met Frank Devine the other day. I understand he produced you at Cheltenham in *Innocents*, remember?'

'Of course I do. Frank was a grand man to work for,' Olivia said with enthusiasm.

'He gave me a very good report about you, and don't forget, I overheard you on the stage here, the first time we met.'

Olivia covered her face with a hand. 'Oh, my goodness! I wondered if you'd heard it all.' She considered him, tip of finger on lip. 'And yet you didn't tell Matthew?'

'Why should I have done that? If you wanted to be a secretary that was your affair.' Carlyon leant back in his chair impassively. Olivia pleated her gloves nervously as she explained her absence from the theatre. More than anything she wanted this man's respect and friendship and desperately wanted to work with him—but everything, this time, had got to be above board. He heard her explanation in silence and she added finally:

'I gave myself a year to decide, and the year's nearly up. I suppose I was in a state of dithering about, and someone ... something, made me decide to have another go.'

'We can go through sticky patches, all of us, and not just professionally. It adds to our experience, which in turn is never wasted.' Carlyon looked behind him and reached for a script from the shelf. 'Here, take this and digest. It's mostly duologues and the pace is quick, so you'll realise how exacting this play will be. Julian's the husband, Peter, by the way.'

'When do I start?' asked Olivia, trying for composure.

He studied a large desk diary, lips pursed. 'Come in on the twenty-first—all right?'

Olivia nodded, clutching the script tightly to her, and rose to her feet. Carlyon lifted a dark brow.

'Before you go write down your address and here's our telephone number. I'll tell Elizabeth to expect a call from you arranging a meeting. Don't forget!'

'I won't, I promise.'

He walked with her to the door. 'Go and sit in the car, I'll be with you in a minute.' Olivia was in the corridor before she realised what he had said.

'Oh, but there's no need——' she began, and stopped as she came face to face with Julian.

127

'Olivia, my favourite girl!'

Olivia was surprised to find how pleased she was to see him and suffered a bear-hug with laughing protest. Julian turned to Carlyon.

'Adam, you meanie, were you going to let her go without saying a word?'

'You'll be seeing plenty of her soon enough, Julian. Olivia is taking Pat's place.'

'Is she now?' Julian raised a brow. 'Well, well, that is a pleasant surprise. If you're leaving now, can I give you a lift, Olivia? I'm just off myself.'

'I'm trying to persuade Adam that there's no need for him to take me home,' explained Olivia, anxious not to be a nuisance.

'Of course you don't want a lift with an old fuddy-duddy like Adam,' agreed Julian, sneaking Carlyon a wicked glance. 'Time was, Olivia, when Adam ran a snazzy Morgan V8, but marriage soon takes its toll,' and he grinned at the 'fuddy-duddy', who shrugged philosophically.

'That's the way it goes, Julian, as you'll no doubt find out for yourself.' Carlyon looked at his watch. 'It would be a great help if you could take Olivia for me.'

'There's really no need for either of you to . . .'

'No sooner said than done. You may leave the dear girl in my capable hands, Adam,' assured Julian airily.

'I'm sure I can,' agreed Carlyon dryly. 'Goodbye, Olivia. I'm glad we met today, it saved me the trouble of searching you out. Don't forget to telephone Liz.'

Olivia took his hand. 'No, I won't forget. Goodbye, Adam, and . . . thank you.'

Julian sat for a few moments before driving off, eyeing her intently.

'Mm . . . yes, I like the hair. It suits you, gives your face a pixie look.'

'I'm glad I've passed the test.'

'Now, now, Olivia, sarcasm will get you nowhere.' He started the TR and drove out of the car park. 'Which way, madam?'

'I have a room on Poplar Road, which is a misnomer as there's not a tree in sight! Turn left into King Street and I'll give you more directions then.' She smiled demurely. 'I'm

128

glad you think I look nice. Fancy being married to me, Julian?'

He flicked her a wary glance and she laughed, 'Don't panic,' and waving the script, added gleefully: 'Adam wants me for Cassie!'

'Clever Adam . . . yes, Olivia my love, I fancy being married to you. I knew Adam was trying to contact a replacement, but never guessed it could be you. Mm, this is going to push a certain young lady's nose out of joint.'

'Oh?' said Olivia uncertainly. 'Who?'

'Our beautiful Philippa, that's who, and I for one am mighty pleased. I quite thought I'd be landed with her. She's all wrong for the part and too old as well.'

'Oh, Julian, she's not that much older than I am, surely?'

'She's the wrong side of thirty, darling, but would never admit it,' drawled Julian. 'Anyway, whatever her real age she wouldn't look young enough for Cassie. You will.'

'Did Philippa think she would be offered the part?'

'I believe so.'

'What will she do instead?'

'Be in the play that will run concurrently with ours in the Studio Theatre, I expect.' Julian pulled up at a set of traffic lights and gave her a benign look. 'So you're back to acting. My illustrious parent will be pleased to have you under his wing again.'

'You knew too, didn't you?' asked Olivia, voice all resignation.

'Had an inkling, love.'

'Did . . . did Matthew say anything to you?'

Julian raised his brows and shot her a penetrating glance. 'No. Should he have?'

'No, oh no,' replied Olivia quickly, thankful that Matthew had kept quiet about their fight. 'I didn't take the job with your father knowing he was an actor, Julian. It was purely coincidental.'

'I didn't suppose it to be anything else,' answered Julian, accelerating as the lights changed. 'Now then, you'd better give me some more instructions of where to go or else we'll be finding ourselves on the motorway bound for London!'

'At last! I began to think we would never manage a meeting,' exclaimed Liz as she opened the door to a smiling Olivia, and she gave her an enthusiastic hug. 'Oh, it is good to see you, Olivia. Come on in. I'm sitting in the garden sunning myself. You do look attractive in that halter neckline, so lovely and cool.'

'May I return the compliment?' answered Olivia, looking affectionately at her friend, who wore a gaily coloured sundress and positively glowed with her prospective motherhood.

'You may,' returned Liz complacently, easing herself carefully on to a sun lounger. 'I think my figure is rather super, but I don't expect others to agree. What would you like to drink?'

'The grapefruit looks most inviting, thanks.' Olivia stretched out happily and lifted her face to the sun. 'Oh, this is definitely the life.'

'Here's your drink, Olivia. Cheers,' and the two girls raised their glasses and then drank deeply. There was silence for a moment and then Liz said hesitantly: 'I rather think I put my foot in it when I saw you and Matt after the opening night of *Pilgrimage*. I hope I didn't cause any trouble between you?'

'Good lord, no,' said Olivia emphatically. 'You told Matthew nothing he didn't know already.'

'Oh, good,' and Liz gave a relieved laugh. 'I wouldn't like to have been instrumental in breaking things up.'

At the implication of that remark Olivia sat up quickly.

'What exactly do you mean by that, Liz?'

'Well, aren't you and Matthew ...' Liz opened her eyes wide, '... you know ...'

'I know—and no, we're not. Honestly, Liz, you haven't changed one bit!'

Liz pulled a disappointed face. 'Oh dear, what a pity. I like Matt immensely. He reminds me in lots of ways of Adam when I first met him. He would do beautifully for you, Olivia.'

'You wouldn't think so if you knew how we manage to rub each other up the wrong way,' returned Olivia dryly, 'so forget it.'

'Oh, all right, but I can't think how I got hold of the idea. I was so certain ...' She took one look at Olivia's face and laughed. 'Okay, I believe you. Now then, tell all. I know Adam's offered you a job, but he doesn't gossip and can be annoyingly close sometimes. Julian is my mine of information, but I haven't seen him for a few days.'

130

Olivia clasped her hands round her knees and hugged herself contentedly.

'Liz, this job is the most fantastic bit of luck for me. I'm absolutely thrilled and can't wait to get started. To play a lead with my very first show too! I mustn't let Adam down.'

'Stop deprecating yourself,' ordered Liz. 'You're not a beginner, Olivia. So you've been away from the theatre for a year?—one week of rehearsals will soon get you back in the swing. Pour me out another drink, there's a pal; once I'm down in this position it's a great effort to move!'

As Olivia poured out two more drinks Liz contemplated her erstwhile friend. She had always liked Olivia, although they had veered professionally in different directions, Liz to backstage work and Olivia to acting. Twice, when they were together at drama school, Liz had taken her home, but further invitations had been refused, mainly Liz was sure, because Olivia could not return the hospitality. She also knew how close Olivia had been to her father and listened now with sympathy as Olivia gave a brief and unemotional account of the intervening years.

'I've become a very proficient typist, but it's no good doing that when what you really want to do is act,' Olivia concluded with a wry smile.

'It's the devil when you can't get work, especially when you see females up there on stage who are no Sarah Bernhardts. Anyway, that's changed now. You've got a foot back in the door and you'll soon show 'em.'

'I certainly shall.' Olivia smiled grimly. 'Nothing's going to stop me this time.' Not even Matthew Raynor, she thought with satisfaction.

'Enough about me, Liz, tell me about yourself. I knew the name of Carlyon meant something to me, but I just couldn't fathom out what. I was sorry I couldn't get to your wedding. How long ago is it?'

'Three years. We went to Australia, paid a flying visit to America and have wandered round ever since.' Liz waved a hand at the house and garden. 'This is the first permanent home we've had, and we're only renting this at the moment with a view to buying later if we decide Rotheringham is a good base. It's only twenty miles from Queensbridge where Helen lives—you remember my sister?—and the parents are five miles on from there, so it's very convenient really. I'm enjoying being so near to my family after three years away.'

'It's a lovely old house and so private, with these trees making a screen all round the garden.'

'It's too big for us now, of course, but,' Liz patted herself approvingly, 'we'll soon be filling another room.'

Olivia laughed with her and said reflectively: 'I'm on the look-out for another place to live. The room I have now is rather grim, I only took it as a stop-gap, but decent places with reasonable rent are few and far between.'

Liz sat up. 'You can have ours.' She grinned at Olivia's bewildered face. 'We've a perfectly good furnished flat at the top of the house, empty; just waiting for the right person. In fact, we weren't going to let it at all unless it was to someone we knew. Didn't fancy a stranger on the premises, but Olivia, if you took it, even on a temporary basis, it would be perfect. We could come to some arrangement over the cost—say you will.'

'Wait, wait!' Olivia clasped her hands to her forehead. 'You mean to say that you have a flat ...'

'... on the top floor,' continued Liz impatiently, swinging her legs off the lounger and heaving herself upright. 'Come along, we'll go and see it. The flat's not large, small kitchen, small bedroom, and a sitting room. You share our second bathroom one floor down.'

Olivia followed, hardly daring to believe her ears. Liz took her all over the house, starting at the bottom and working up until they finally arrived at the flat. Liz leant against the wall and gasped for breath.

'It's times like this that I realise I'm not so agile as I was.' She flung open the door and exclaimed: 'Well, here it is, small but compact, lady, and note the white walls, cleverly painted to give an illusion of space.' She waited expectantly, a smile on her face, as Olivia walked slowly round, tentatively opening cupboard doors, testing the bed, turning the taps. 'Well—what do you think?'

'What do I think, you idiot?' echoed Olivia, peering out of the small gable window and visualising herself playing house among these lovely surroundings. 'I think it's wonderful, but before we go any further just consider ...'

'Not another word.'

132

'But you must discuss it with Adam, Liz. You can't go blithely ahead like this,' protested Olivia.

'The furniture's not new, but it's good solid stuff and ...'

'Liz! Did you hear what I said?'

Liz grinned and sat down heavily on the divan. 'Yes, Olivia, I did, and I promise I'll talk it over with Adam, but I know he'll agree.'

Hoping desperately that he would, Olivia pointed out that Adam might not think it policy to have one of his company as a tenant, adding: 'Discuss it with him when I've gone and if he says no—and I'm quite prepared that he may—then that's that.'

'Leave it to me,' said Liz regally. 'Now I'm going to bore you to death by showing you all the things I've bought so far for the new infant. This way ... I shall expect you to make the required appropriate noises and then we'll have lunch and continue catching up on our missing years.'

The first day of rehearsals arrived at last and Olivia viewed it with mixed feelings. Any first day with a new company was bound to bring on an attack of nerves, but a year away from the theatre to contend with as well added to the tension. But for all that, she was doing what she wanted to do, and suddenly having a horrified thought that she had left the script behind, she hurriedly searched her shoulder bag and heaved a sigh of relief. The script was there, slightly thumbed and not so virginal, together with two sharpened pencils for writing in the stage directions. She had been studying the play ever since Adam had given it to her, identifying herself with the newlywed Cassie, acquainting herself thoroughly with the plot and learning the first act dialogue, for they had only three weeks to rehearse and the quicker she knew her lines the better.

Olivia waited for the bus to stop and jumped off, walking briskly down the High Street, pausing to study some curtain material draped in a window display. For that was another wonderful thing that had happened. She was now installed in the Carlyons' flat and loving every minute of it, and the curtain material was just what she was looking for to renew the sitting-room ones, perhaps even take them right down to the floor. As Olivia continued on her way she thought over the past week, how careful she had been to keep herself to herself and not to take advantage of the Carlyons' friendship. She knew the arrangements were going to work beautifully regarding Liz and herself, but as for Adam, Olivia was going to be very careful at the theatre to give him no cause for uneasiness. She would not have presumed on her friendship with Liz in his direction in any case, but she didn't intend him having regrets for saying yes to her having the flat.

Olivia rounded the corner just as a shaft of sunlight struck the stone sculptures of the three Muses, Comedy, Dance and Tragedy, situated high up over the entrance. It was probably very fanciful of her, but they seemed to have a benevolent expression on their faces. She paused at the glass-fronted billboard on the pillar between the two sets of double doors. This told the public that the theatre was closed for its three weeks' summer break, but that on Monday, September 13th, Rotheringham Theatre Royal had pleasure in presenting that delightful comedy by Mark Donaldson—*Two for Joy*. Surrounding this notice were the photographs of the performers. Anthea Beresford, looking poised and beautiful, Charles, smiling his famous smile, matching Anthea for instant visual appeal. Julian, with laughing eyes, was the epitome of young, masculine vitality, guaranteed to flutter the heart of many a young girl. Olivia's smile faded as she came to the last photograph. Behind the glass it seemed to take on a different dimension, almost as if it were someone else. Surely her eyes were not as large as that? It must be the camera angle, she decided, and Julian was right, her face did look pixieish . . . and why on earth hadn't she smiled? She looked all eyes and mouth! Philosophically reflecting that she must have been going through her tragedienne period and that whatever photograph of herself that was put on display she would probably hate, she hurried to the stage door.

As it banged behind her, shutting out the brilliance of the sunshine, she saw the corridor stretched before her, cool and dark, and her footsteps echoed as she walked along the stone floor, up the steps, through the swing doors stopping in front of the rehearsal room door.

Olivia stood for a moment, took a deep breath and opened the door.

'Olivia, my dear!' Charles crossed the room and greeted her

with outstretched hands, holding her by the shoulders and standing back to study her face. His gaze was intent, his blue eyes kindly and showing concern. 'I did not intend for you to disappear out of our lives so completely, with no one knowing where you were or what you were doing.' His voice was mildly reproachful.

'I didn't mean to disappear, truly, Charles, and I left you a letter explaining ... why I felt I had to go, to make a clean break ... I was going to get in touch, honestly, only things seemed to happen to prevent me.'

'Mm ... becoming ill being one of them. What a lot we Raynors have to answer for!'

'Oh, no,' protested Olivia. 'It was just my misfortune that I hadn't had measles as a child.'

'You've made light of it, but it must have been a distressing time, my dear. Toby had you and Harry to look after him, but we were not allowed to look after you. Harriet was horrified when she was told. You're still looking rather peaky, but I'm glad you're settled in at the Carlyons',' he went on. 'I've heard all about your room with the funny-shaped ceiling and windows from Toby. I gather he spent a splendid day with you—he didn't stop chattering for at least an hour after his return.'

Olivia smiled. 'I loved having him, and he was most impressed at being my first guest.' She hesitated. 'It made up, in a small way, for when I left so quickly.'

Charles asked gently: 'Why did you run away, Olivia?'

'I ... hate goodbyes.'

'But it wasn't going to be goodbye—was it?' he persisted.

'Charles, you'd all been so kind, I didn't want to embarrass you. I had no idea you knew I was an actress until Matthew ...' she stopped short and Charles raised his brows.

'Ah ... Matthew. I wondered when we would get around to him. Are you sure that it wasn't Matthew who made you run away?'

Cheeks rosy, Olivia shook her head, brushing her short fringe through her fingers. 'Why ever should you say that?'

'My dear, I left you with him that night in seemingly perfect harmony and the next morning you'd both flown.' Charles smiled wryly. 'I must admit for one wild moment I thought you might have flown together, but I was a popular person that day—I had received letters from you both which soon dispelled that idea.'

'Oh?' breathed Olivia weakly.

'Matthew can be very high-handed at times. If I thought that he had been responsible for ...'

'He wasn't, Charles; it was because I felt so awful about deceiving you ...'

'Foolish girl! You didn't deceive me for one moment, and had I realised you felt so deeply about it I would have told you. Selfishly I thought I'd keep you with me until we had finished our work together and then afterwards help you if I could. But even in that I was thwarted—you do a quick getaway and leave no trace. I'm afraid we plagued the life out of the employment agency for news of you, but they were as ignorant as we were.'

Olivia lifted distressed eyes and stammered: 'I never dreamed you would go to all that trouble,' adding helplessly: 'I can't think why you did.'

Charles smiled. 'And there lies your answer. Never mind, all that's in the past. Adam has achieved what I hoped to achieve, and I couldn't wish for anything different if it means that you've joined us.' His blue eyes twinkled. 'Perhaps I'm only sulking because I wanted to be the one to restore you to the footlights. In any case, I think you prefer things to have happened as they have, and although I consider your reasons are taking altruism too far, nevertheless, I respect them. Be wary of pride, Olivia. It's a good thing to have, but only in small doses—it can sometimes confuse one's judgment.' He smiled. 'End of lecture. Be sure that now we've found you again we won't be so careless in the future.'

Olivia felt the warmth of his regard spreading through her and said shyly: 'I won't run away again, truly. How ... how is everyone?'

'Harry and Paul were most surprised when I told them you were working here—surprised but very pleased.'

'And Matthew?' Her voice was light and casual.

'I don't suppose Matthew knows. He disappeared as completely as yourself and has only been heard of in a roundabout way, and we understand he's somewhere in the north.' Charles lifted a brow. 'He didn't tell you where he was going or what he was doing?'

Olivia shook her head quickly. 'No. Did he tell you in his letter that I ... that we ...' she floundered to a stop.

'He didn't refer to you at all, Olivia.'

'Oh,' said Olivia, feeling foolish, and added feebly: 'I just wondered.' Would she, in fact, ever understand Matthew Raynor?

'You must come and meet the others,' Charles declared, taking her arm. He led her over to the far end of the room where he introduced her to a group of men and women who smiled at her in a friendly manner. This was, Olivia knew, tinged with curiosity, for their long conversation had not gone unnoticed. It was obvious from the way Charles was behaving that he wanted everyone to know that she was a protégée of his, and this news would be round the theatre before the day was out. And what do I care of that? thought Olivia, smiling in return and shaking hands all round the group. I'll soon show them I can act, and lifting her chin and mentally giving her armour a polish, she reiterated to herself the fact that from now on this was a new and tougher Olivia Darcy and to hell with whoever got in her way!

They were chatting generally together when Adam came in, followed by Anthea and Julian. He walked over briskly, greeting everyone, finishing with Olivia.

'Charles has introduced you, Olivia? Good.' He turned to his companions. 'Julian, of course, you know, but have you and Anthea ... ?'

'Yes, we have. Hello, Olivia. I think we're going to have fun with this play, don't you?' and turning to their director, Anthea smiled: 'I do thank you, Adam, for choosing such a lovely daughter for me.'

Anthea Beresford was dressed in a cream silk blouse and coffee-coloured pleated skirt. She looked as cool and as fresh as a fashion model. Olivia considered that her well-washed jeans and cotton shirt were a far cry from that deceptively simple outfit, but as the stage directions gave Cassie quite an amount of jumping on and over furniture, not to mention sitting and even lying on the floor, she had felt, when choosing what to wear that morning, that it should be something tough and durable. Had Olivia realised that her own outfit suited her to perfection she would have felt less conscious of Miss Beresford's cool sophistication. But for all her outward appearance it soon became apparent that the famous actress was as charming and delightful as she had been on their first meeting.

Adam looked round his company of actors and backstage crew.

'We know the state of most theatres at present, all struggling to keep their heads above water: mostly subsidised and having, to a great extent, to pander to box office. *Two for Joy* probably comes in this category, for we have to look to our patrons and count the pennies as much as everyone else. Nevertheless it's always been the Royal's policy to open the new season with a comedy, and this one had a long and successful run in London, so it's on the cards that we'll do good box office. As Anthea has said, we'll have fun, but it's going to be damned hard work. Ted's got an exciting set for us and Mary and Jeanette will dress the cast and the stage respectively, and anyone interested can see the designs afterwards. Shall we all sit down and have a read-through, just to get some idea of the continuity of the play?' He stood at the head of the table and they all gathered a chair and settled round. 'Ted, will you give it a rough time-out?'

Olivia was nervous at first, but gradually she forgot her surroundings and was transported to a basement flat in the heart of Manhattan. A good cast stimulates good performances and at the finish of the reading she was relatively satisfied, although eager to begin working with a director of Adam Carlyon's calibre.

They broke for lunch and Olivia was undecided what to do. Adam, Charles and Anthea walked out together and she didn't want to be dependent on Julian, she had to stand on her own two feet. The girl who was doing props was studying a list and at her approach looked up cheerfully.

'That went off rather well, didn't it? I reckon Adam's right and we're on to a winner.' She closed her folder. 'I think I've taken down all the obvious props, but no doubt as we progress Adam will add to them. Where are you going for lunch?'

'I was going to ask you if there was somewhere near that was cheap.'

The girl grinned. 'You may be sure that if there is we impecunious lot would find it! I'm Jeanette, by the way. Come on, follow me. The George and Dragon awaits.'

The pub was just around the corner and very full. They

managed to find a couple of spare seats and while Olivia stayed to save them, Jeanette went to fetch their lunch. Olivia looked around and recognised one or two faces from the Royal and wasn't surprised to see Philippa Markham in one of the groups. While waiting for Jeanette, Olivia opened her script and began to study it, looking up with a start when someone slid into the empty chair at her side.

'I'm sorry, but that seat is . . . oh.'

'Hello!' Philippa sat beautifully poised and sleek, not a hair out of place on her chestnut head and a smile on her face that Olivia did not trust.

'Why, hello, Philippa, how are you?'

'I'm fine, just fine.' Her eyes narrowed. 'And so, it seems, are you. At long last you've made it from typewriter to the stage—I only hope you'll think it worth it.'

'What do you mean, Philippa?' asked Olivia evenly.

'Oh, come on, sweetie, I don't have to spell it out to you, surely?'

'I think you do.'

'You know, that air of innocence and sweetness does you credit; it certainly worked with Charles Raynor, didn't it? But not, I can assure you, with Matthew. The things he used to tell me . . . oh, hello, Jeanette, have I taken your seat?' Philippa rose with a smile. 'Good luck with the part, Olivia, we'll all be waiting agog to see what you make of it. 'Bye, both.'

Jeanette passed over the plates of salad and sat down, giving Olivia a curious look.

'You know Philippa, then?'

'Not very well,' answered Olivia, thinking grimly—but well enough.

'I think you ought to know that she thinks she knows you well enough to . . .' Jeanette paused and gave a shrug, 'gossip about. And what she says isn't particularly complimentary.'

'I can guess,' said Olivia, hearing a burst of laughter from the group Philippa had just rejoined and knowing that she must not underestimate the redhead.

'Just thought you ought to know,' repeated Jeanette, tucking into the salad with relish.

'Thank you. Perhaps if I told you that I went to drama school with Adam Carlyon's wife and it was Adam who offered me a job here, then if you hear anything to the contrary you'll be able to put it right.'

'Sure ... glad to. Oh, good, here are the others—move up on the bench, Olivia, to make room.'

'Was that Coppernob I saw deigning to talk to you just now?' asked Julian, sitting next to Olivia.

'Now Julian,' admonished Olivia calmly, 'even Philippa's worst enemy would have to admit that her hair is her crowning glory.'

Julian grinned. 'Well?'

'She came to wish her luck with the part,' announced Jeanette blandly. She was rewarded by Julian throwing back his head with laughter.

'Damn it, Olivia, that's rich! She'd trip you at the top of the stairs if she could.'

'Stop exaggerating,' retorted Olivia, making a mental note to be wary of flights of stairs in the future.

They had now been joined by Ted, the stage director, who was a tall lanky man with an engaging lopsided grin; his young assistant Mick and Mary, the rather plump wardrobe mistress, and talk became general.

Afterwards, walking back to the theatre, Olivia murmured to Julian:

'I don't want you to think you've got to look after me, you know. I don't expect special ...'

'Lord, Olivia, what a worrit you are!' He ruffled her hair. 'Surely you know by now that we Raynors are selfish creatures and always do just what we want to do?' His arm round her shoulder tightened. 'Now here's someone you should be wary of,' he told her loudly.

'That's a mean trick, Julian old man,' complained the actor who had just joined them. 'Don't you believe a word he says.'

Julian gave a flourish of arm. 'This is Laurence Mayer, Olivia—come hotfoot to be introduced.'

'Welcome to our band of players, Olivia, and take no notice of this one's remarks, he's only jealous.'

Julian snorted derisively and then asked:

'Any idea what comes next on the programme, Laurence?'

'I would have thought you the first to know, dear boy.'

Julian's eyes narrowed, but his voice remained even. 'I'm a mere hireling like yourself, Laurence.'

'Well, I did hear some talk of a Tennessee Williams or a Shakespeare, but they were only rumours,' answered Laurence carelessly.

'Mm ... rumours seem to be given too much breathing space here at the moment,' said Julian rather pointedly to Laurence, and Olivia remembered seeing him sitting next to Philippa and wasn't surprised when he wouldn't meet her eyes.

'What's this Carlyon like to work for?' Laurence pushed open the stage door.

'Early days yet, but looks good. Matt has a high opinion of him,' and Julian's voice indicated that his brother's confidence was premise enough.

'Ah, well, Matthew would know,' Laurence acknowledged rather acidly. 'We part company here. Glad to have met you, Olivia. Perhaps we can have a long chat some time—when we're not quite so crowded?'

'Perhaps,' answered Olivia, and when Laurence was out of earshot she continued: 'Did I imagine it, or was there some veiled undercurrent in the reference to your brother in that last remark?'

'You didn't imagine it. Matt hasn't much time for Laurence. He's a good enough actor but a bit of a troublemaker.' Julian paused at the rehearsal room door. 'Remind me to ask Adam what's next on the agenda ... after you, Macduff.'

They both forgot, and it was a week later when they remembered.

'*Twelfth Night*,' Adam announced. 'Shouldn't be difficult for either of you as you've both played your parts before.'

'I'm to be Viola?' asked Olivia quickly, pleasure lighting up her face.

'Yes, and Julian is Sebastian. Philippa will take Olivia and Laurence the Duke Orsino.' Adam looked at his watch. 'There's time to do that scene again, and this time, Olivia, try and suggest that the words you say are the exact opposite to what you mean. Julian ... Peter is rather a conventional chap, but he did marry Cassie, so he must have a daft streak in him somewhere, and I think here is a good time for it to begin to show. Right—off we go, bottom of page thirty-nine.'

Olivia felt rather guilty about Rosemary. She had written her a short letter explaining about the measles but had not contacted her since. Therefore, on her first free afternoon, she hastened to her friend's house, ready to do penance. Walking along the avenue she could see Rosemary's figure in the distance, busily painting the front door a bright daffodil yellow. Olivia leant over the gate and groaned.

'I might have known that when I finally managed a visit it wouldn't be convenient!'

Rosemary looked over her shoulder and eyed her friend in surprised delight.

'Olivia, you wretch! Where've you been all this time? No address at the top of your letter. Fancy leaving me with "have got tons to tell, but it will have to wait until I see you", and then not to see you!' Rosemary's voice showed her disgust.

'I know, love, forgive me. Er—you're dropping paint off the end of the brush. Don't stop for me, Rosie.'

'I'll have to finish now I've started. Jamie's having a nap, so I thought I'd take advantage of the fact. Tell me what's been happening while I just do this bottom bit,' and Olivia complied, sitting on the step.

'Your luck's turned,' Rosemary stated emphatically, placing the brush in a jar of turps. 'I can't wait to tell Tom your news, he'll be as thrilled for you as I am. I very nearly rang the Raynors, you know, but Tom said no, wait. I was quite convinced that Matthew had done away with you. There, that's it. All I want is for it to dry before His Nibs gets his grubby paws on it. I'll go up and change and then we'll have coffee.'

Olivia made her way thoughtfully into the back garden and sat on the garden seat. She hadn't, in fact, told Rosemary 'all'. She had left out the meeting with Liz and the subsequent drive to Sentinel Hill. She had felt a reluctance to speak of Matthew and had concentrated on the new flat and rehearsals. She wondered why. After all, she couldn't ignore the fact that Matthew Raynor existed and in all probability would turn up out of the blue.

'You look ridiculously young with that haircut,' asserted Rosemary, carrying a tray from the house and placing it on the garden table. She passed a plate of sandwiches to Olivia and began to pour out the coffee. 'From what you say this Philippa person is a bit of a snake in the grass, but you always get one of that type wherever you work. She obviously sees you as a threat.'

Olivia wrinkled her nose. 'A threat to what? Not her career ... she must realise she couldn't have taken Cassie and she's just landed a lovely part, the Countess Olivia, in the next production. Which,' Olivia added reflectively, 'she will play beautifully.'

'Her man, then,' suggested Rosemary.

Olivia pulled a face. 'From all accounts that's Matthew—which makes your idea rather ludicrous. Anyway, I'm coping with her and everyone is very friendly. Once they saw that I didn't make a big thing of knowing both the Raynors and the Carlyons they accepted that I was a struggling actor like themselves.'

'When do you open?'

'Next Monday, and the thought of it makes me nervous!'

'I must organise a baby-sitter and book seats.' A yell was heard from an upstairs window. 'Oh, lord, your dearly be-loved godson is awake. So much for our peace and quiet—and as for your nerves, well, they're only to be expected, but from what you tell me about the play, you'll not have the time to be nervous for long, you'll be too busy.'

Olivia found a good friend in Jeanette. Anthea was of a different generation and however friendly and charming the elder actress might be, Olivia was restrained by this difference and also by a slight degree of awe. While Jeanette, who was working closely with the small cast, associated more and more with Olivia and their friendship blossomed rapidly. She was a good props girl, methodical and efficient, and if these attributes tended to colour her off-stage personality as well, she was goodnatured with it.

'I reckon Laurence Mayer's got a thing about you,' she remarked to Olivia as she checked her props table for the second act during the final dress rehearsal. Olivia, who was making sure her quick costume changes were all there, laughingly protested.

'Jeanette, really! I've hardly spoken to the man more than a dozen words since I came.'

'Nevertheless, he has interest in you, my girl. Why else has he sat in on these final rehearsals so often?'

'Perhaps he likes the play?'

Jeanette grinned. 'Come off it! This is a rattling good light comedy, but hardly the sort of thing you'd want to see over and over again—unless there's a dishy girl in it who floats around in a very alluring shortie nightie!'

Olivia returned her grin. 'It is rather provocative, isn't it, but they are, after all, on their honeymoon.' She peered out between the gap of the curtains into the semi-darkness of the auditorium, her gaze taking in the one or two dark shapes sitting scattered out front, and Adam, talking to . . .

'What's the matter? You look as though you've seen a ghost.' Jeanette came over to her. 'Olivia, are you all right?'

Olivia nodded and gave a laugh. 'I . . . felt a bit giddy, but it's passed now. Jeanette, who is Adam talking to out there? Do you know?'

Jeanette took a peep. 'Oh, that's the *Gazette*'s photographer. Quite a dish, isn't he?'

'Yes,' said Olivia vaguely. 'He reminded me of someone.'

Olivia was standing at the bus stop when Adam's Scimitar drove past and pulled up, reversing back. Adam thrust open the passenger door and Olivia climbed in.

'You really are an independent madam. Julian was looking for you, Laurence was looking for you and I'd sent word I'd give you a lift, but you'd already left.' Adam negotiated a crossroads and then said: 'Why don't you ask if I'm going straight home? I can always say no.'

'Giving lifts to people can become a drag.' She yawned. 'Golly, I'm tired!'

'All the more reason to make sure you travel in comfort. You've an exacting role to play and because you especially want to succeed in your first production you have all the usual traumas, plus a few.' He pulled up at traffic lights and turned to look at her. 'You've heard there's to be a gathering at the Raynors' afterwards?' Olivia nodded. 'You're going?'

'Yes, yes, I suppose so.' She hesitated. 'Will Matthew be there, do you know?' The lights changed and the Scimitar moved smoothly forward.

'Matt? I should think it highly unlikely. Why, would that make a difference to whether you go or not?'

'Heavens, no!' exclaimed Olivia, and looked sideways at him under her lashes. Adam was staring straight ahead, his

144

face immobile. You and Matthew Raynor make a good pair, she decided crossly, as inscrutable as each other. 'Have you known Matthew long, Adam?'

He pursed his lips. 'It must be over ten years.' He swung the car into the drive and on into the already open garage. 'What are you doing tomorrow, Olivia?'

'Being very lazy.'

'Good. Do I espy a copy of *Twelfth Night* in your pocket?'

'Oh, lord ... yes, you do, but I'm not learning it, Adam, honestly. Just browsing through.'

'Mm, you're a glutton for punishment, aren't you? In you go, and if you see Elizabeth on your way up, say I'll be with her in a minute, there's something I want to check on the car.'

'Yes, all right. Er ... Adam?' He turned and lifted an inquiring brow. 'I just want to thank you for giving me this chance. I ... I can't tell you what it means to me ... how grateful I am.'

He hesitated for a moment, a frown on his brow, and then he gave a quick smile and helped her out of the car, saying quietly:

'It wasn't a one-sided transaction, Olivia. I gained a good actress out of the deal. Goodnight, my dear. Sleep well.'

'Goodnight, Adam.'

Olivia lay in bed, tired but eyes wide open, knowing she wouldn't be able to sleep until she had sorted a few things out in her mind, the most important being Matthew Raynor. How had she mistaken the photographer for him? The only similarity had been the height and colouring. Had she wanted it to be Matthew? Did she, deep down, dread their first meeting so much that she wanted to get it over and done with as soon as possible? No one seemed to know where he was or what he was doing, but she felt in her bones that she hadn't seen the last of him. And if she were honest with herself, she was glad, for she wanted him to know that she was at the Royal; wanted him to see her act. She knew she was good as Cassie, exulted in the knowledge, and wanted to say to Matthew Raynor—here I am, back in the theatre through no help of the Raynors and an asset to the company! Yes, she wanted to crow.

Olivia pulled a face in the darkness. How contrary can you be, Olivia Darcy? One minute you say you never want to see

145

the man again and two months later you're wishing he was here. But then circumstances had greatly changed. The Olivia Darcy of Sentinel Hill and the Olivia Darcy, actress, The Theatre Royal Company, Rotheringham, were two very different people. She turned over and thumped her pillow. Perhaps he'll arrive unexpectedly for the first night—and surprisingly the thought didn't make her feel more nervous, rather the opposite, but then she'd always liked playing to an individual she knew than to an unknown mass. So—she would anticipate Matthew Raynor being there tomorrow night and afterwards—well, afterwards had better take care of itself.

First, she would concentrate on giving the performance of her life ... to Mr Matthew Know-it-all Raynor!

CHAPTER SEVEN

'My father had a daughter lov'd a man.'

CRESSIDA HOUSE seemed filled to capacity, everyone wearing that triumphant air of success that follows a good opening night, conveniently forgetting the tension and last-minute upsets of barely three hours ago. Olivia squeezed through the crush, the talk and laughter passing over her head. She was now convinced that Matthew was not here, and the disappointment this brought with it was ridiculous ... and positively childish. She made her way into the kitchen, which was blissfully quiet.

'Anything I can do, Harry?'

'I should think not, indeed. Famous guests do not help with the sandwiches!' Harriet laid down the knife with which she had been slicing tomatoes and shook her head wonderingly. 'I felt so proud of you tonight, Olivia. I can't get it out of my head ... how you kept quiet all those weeks, and you such a good actress. It was grand to see you up there on that stage with Charles and Julian with you. What a pity Matt hadn't directed it, then we would have had it all in the family—not that Mr Carlyon didn't do very well, of course.'

'Matthew isn't here, then?' Olivia asked casually, nibbling a slice of cucumber as she helped to arrange the rolls on the plate.

'Oh, that Matthew! I'll give him a piece of my mind when I see him,' declared Harriet passionately. 'He's never been this long without coming home, even if it were only for a few hours. Just a couple of postcards, the wish-you-were-here type, from somewhere remote in Scotland, is all we've had.' She wiped her hands on her apron. 'There, that will have to do. It's always the same, Charles invariably brings back more than I've catered for. You'll get indigestion if you eat all that cucumber. Take the plate through for me, there's a love.'

Olivia grinned and gave her a quick hug. 'You love every minute of it, so don't bother to deny it,' and holding the large plate filled with an assortment of delicious sandwiches and rolls, she left her and braved the crowded lounge once more. Soon after, Paul bent his head to her ear and asked:

'Do you feel like joining me in a walk? Caliban, poor fellow, hates large gatherings and he's missing Matthew into the bargain.'

Olivia nodded and they emerged triumphant in the hall. Olivia took a deep breath.

'Whew, that's better! Fresh air is just what I need.'

'Good, come along, then.'

'I think Caliban remembers me,' she said a few moments later as they walked along the bridle path.

'I'm sure he does. Remember your first meeting with him?'

'Oh, Paul! Shall I ever forget it? What a first day that was!'

'Can you see? There's a good moon, but perhaps you'd better take my arm, the going is rather rough.' They continued in silence for a while and then Paul said musingly: 'What a difficult position you must have found yourself in here.'

Olivia turned a surprised face to him. 'How strange—you're the only person to see it my way. Everyone else seems to think I should have said I was an actress, but how could I? It would have created a most awkward atmosphere.'

'Father was amazed when you left and none of us knew where you were.' He gave a short rueful laugh. 'He said the Lord had blessed him with three lily-livered sons and what were we thinking of, letting such a gorgeous girl slip through our fingers! Of course, he could only direct his sarcasm on two of us—Matt had flown too.' She sensed that Paul shook his head, puzzled. 'Father seemed as annoyed with that as much as anything else, although why I don't know. He ought to be used to Matt by now and it's not the first time he's disappeared without a trace. I think we'd better turn back,' and whistling to Caliban who had melted into the darkness, Paul transferred his other arm protectively round Olivia's shoulder and they retraced their steps. 'I enjoyed tonight,' he said rather abruptly, 'you were good. Wasted as a typist.' He gave her a gentle squeeze. 'You could go far—if you want to.'

Olivia was touched and answered quietly: 'It's sweet of you to say so, Paul, but you know how risky the theatre business is.'

'Nevertheless, now that you're back in, you must make sure that you stay in—that is, if it's important to you.' It was a half question and one that needed to be answered.

'It is, Paul.' A companionable silence stayed with them until they neared the house. Paul squinted at his watch.

'It's time I ran Laura home.' He smiled his slow smile. 'You've always liked her, haven't you, Olivia?' She nodded and he added: 'Toby does too.' He kissed her gently and calling to the Alsatian, tucked her arm through his and together they re-entered the house.

Later, being driven home half asleep on the back seat of the Carlyons' car, Olivia allowed their soft murmuring conversation to bypass her until a chance word made her ask sleepily:

'Hey, you two, is there a rota for my bathroom tomorrow? I don't mind, of course, but I intend to have a long soak.'

Liz turned in the front seat. 'What do you mean, Olivia?'

'Leaving for the theatre tonight I got as far as the gate when I found I'd left my purse, so . . .'

'. . . you went back for it.'

'Yes, and you were in the bathroom. Has something gone wrong with the plumbing in the master bathroom?'

'It had, but it's been sorted out. I didn't hear you come back.'

'No,' and Olivia yawned. 'I didn't shout, I was in too much of a rush. That's okay, then. No need to panic over bath times.'

'No, no need to panic,' agreed Liz, tucking a hand under Adam's arm and leaning her head on his shoulder.

Rehearsals for *Twelfth Night* began. Olivia found that being in the same play as Philippa was easier than she thought it would be, for the cast was so large that, without being too obvious, Olivia could steer clear of her when they were not performing. Philippa still managed a few sly digs at Olivia when they were alone, but refrained from doing so when anyone else was about as Olivia was a popular girl among the company and had been accepted. Laurence Mayer also was proving rather tiresome, and Olivia now regretted having gone out with him for a meal the previous night after the evening performance of *Two for Joy*.

'Honestly, Jeanette, he's got a one-track mind. I seemed to be fighting him off all night, verbally and physically,' declared Olivia indignantly.

'Well, duckie, there are those among us who would be grateful for the chance,' replied Jeanette, giving a thoughtful eye to Mary, 'but I must admit I'm not one of them.'

'The sooner he realises I'm not one either, the better,' grumbled Olivia. 'You don't think that because I'm supposed to be in love with him in the play he's begun to believe it in real life?'

Jeanette grinned. 'He's bigheaded enough to. You'll have to smile with your mouth and look daggers with your eyes.' She turned over the pages of the script. 'Doesn't old Shakespeare love a complicated plot? Identical twins, each believing the other dead, shipwrecked on to the same shore! Everyone in love with the wrong person—I mean, where else would you find a duke in love with a countess, who in turn is in love with the duke's page, who's in love with the duke because she's a woman disguised as a boy?' She giggled. 'Think what it must have been like in Shakespeare's day when they didn't have women on stage!' She frowned in concentration. 'That meant that a man took the part of a woman and then disguised himself back again into a man—golly, the mind boggles!'

'Do you think Julian and I will look like twins?' asked Olivia.

'Yes, I do, especially if you wear a fair wig. I say, Olivia, is that Adam's wife over there? She doesn't look very well.'

Olivia turned. 'Yes, it is ... quickly, Jeanette, go and find Adam!'

The two girls hurriedly parted and Olivia reached her friend's side to see Liz suddenly grimace.

'Liz, have you started with the pains? Come and sit down.'

'No, I'd rather stand, Olivia, thanks. Not to panic. I've had so many false alarms this week ... it could easily be the rhubarb pie I ate yesterday!' Liz managed a grin which changed into a look of concentration. 'All I know is,' she said at last, 'I want Adam.'

'Put your arm through mine and we'll walk up and down the corridor,' suggested Olivia. 'Adam won't be long, Jeanette's gone for him.' Hardly had she spoken when he came round the corner. He looked calm, the only sign of tension being a slight whitening round the lips.

'Elizabeth?' He took her hands, searching her face. 'Is this it, my love?'

'I think so,' responded Liz, smiling tremulously, tightening her grasp of Adam's hand. 'Yes, I definitely think so.'

Adam turned to Olivia. 'Find Ted. Tell him to take over, then ring the hospital and say we're on our way. Check in the office, I think I've an appointment later on—get them to cancel it for me.'

Olivia nodded and watched them go. As she made her way to the office she wondered if anyone would ever look at her the way Adam had looked at Liz. A rush of feeling for them both swept over her.

Julian, who gave Olivia a lift home after the evening performance, came up to the flat for coffee. Seeing him off later, Olivia listened to his suggestion that he stayed the night with interest; Julian was, if nothing else, a persuasive advocate.

'After all, Olivia,' he concluded, 'it's a large house, Adam's at the hospital with Liz, you'll be on your own.'

'It's very thoughtful of you to suggest staying, Julian, but I think I'll be perfectly safe.' She kept her face as straight as his own and added gravely: 'Probably more so.'

'Pity.' He grinned, took her in his arms and kissed her soundly. He sighed heavily. 'Yes, a great pity. Goodnight, love. See you tomorrow.'

'Goodnight, Julian. Thanks for the lift.' She stayed while he drove the TR out on to the road and waved before going back in, a smile on her face.

Some time later Olivia sat up and switched on the bedlight. Puzzled, she saw that the clock showed she had barely been asleep a quarter of an hour and she wondered what had woken her. Julian's words came back to niggle, giving her a sense of unease. What nonsense, she told herself crossly, getting out of bed. It's Adam back from the hospital with news of Liz. Running quickly down the top flight of stairs and along the landing, she hoped that he would be able to tell her that the baby had come and everything was well. Descending the main staircase by the light from the landing window, she felt a cool draught coming from the hall below. As her bare foot contacted the stone hall floor she collided with a figure coming the other way.

'What the ...?'

'Adam!' she yelped, and would have fallen had his arms not enfolded her in his own. 'Adam?' she said again, this time uncertainly, and even as her hand tentatively reached out and contacted a beard, her mouth opened to scream and she was thinking—how amazing! and it's no use screaming, no one will hear you—and indeed, she didn't get any further than a strangled noise in her throat, for the intruder came to life and with a muttered oath clapped a hand over her mouth.

'Quiet,' he ordered in a harsh whisper, 'you'll wake the whole house,' and almost lifting her bodily, forced her away from the stairs and dragged her, struggling and protesting, to beneath the hall window, where there was light enough to see.

As Olivia became accustomed to the half-light, her captor seemed all black—thick black sweater, black hair, black moustache and beard. He was tall and slim, but his physique was deceptive, for he dealt with her violent efforts quite easily. As she continued to fight he turned his face into the shaft of light. He might have seemed all black, but the eyes were grey. Her body went limp as she stared, wide-eyed. When he seemed satisfied that he had been recognised, he removed his hand from her face but still held her close in his arms.

'Hello, Olivia,' he said quietly.

Olivia fought for breath. She could feel his heart thumping beneath the rough wool of the sweater and knew her own to be racing just as furiously. She gave a shudder and when speech came she gasped:

'Matthew Raynor! How *dare* you frighten the life out of me like that!' Her hand fluttered helplessly against his chest. 'And what the hell are you doing here? Creeping in ...'

'Keep your voice down, for heaven's sake, woman ...'

'I will not keep my voice down!' yelled Olivia. 'You break in, scare me half to death ... to say nothing of bruising every bone in my body—and if I want to shout I shall damn well shout!'

There was silence for a moment and then Matthew said calmly:

'Very well, my dear. Shout as much as you want to.'

152

Olivia, to her utmost mortification, burst into tears and turned her face into his shoulder. After a second of immobility she felt Matthew heave a sigh and felt herself swung up into his arms, where she was carried into one of the downstairs rooms and deposited on to the studio couch already made up into a temporary bed. He drew one of the blankets round her shoulders and left the room. By the time he returned, a glass in each hand, Olivia's shudderings had stopped, although she couldn't stop trembling. Matthew handed her one of the drinks and sat down in the armchair opposite, thoughtfully contemplating her. She took a tentative sip, choking as the fiery liquid scorched her throat and the warmth spread through her body.

'Heavens,' she gasped, 'this is strong!'

Matthew smiled, his teeth shining white against the darkness of his beard. 'I thought you needed it.'

Olivia curled her feet under her. The light from a small table lamp cast a warm glow over the room. Matthew seemed in no hurry to speak. He lay back in his chair just outside the circle of light, and sipping her drink, Olivia studied him surreptitiously, wishing she could see his expression. He couldn't have dressed more aptly for the part if he had been a real burglar, she thought, although he looked too much of the aesthete to be really convincing.

'It's no wonder I didn't recognise you at first,' and putting her head on one side consideringly, she asked: 'Why did you grow it, Matthew?'

· Matthew lifted a hand and rubbed his chin. 'Pure laziness. And you, Olivia? Why are you so shorn?'

'Oh . . . I felt like a change.'

'I thought I had Peter Pan in my arms.'

His words were evocative, reviving memories that had been allowed to recede, and Olivia's head shot up.

'That reminds me—perhaps you will now tell me what you're doing here?'

'I will, of course, but I'm wondering, in the light of all your hollering, why Liz and Adam haven't joined us.'

'Perhaps because they don't happen to be here,' offered Olivia with spirit, satisfaction spreading through her as Matthew sat up in consternation. 'Liz is in hospital and Adam's still with her. That's why I came dashing down—I thought it was Adam with news. I don't,' she added dryly, 'usually greet my landlord so enthusiastically in the middle of the night.'

Matthew fingered his beard thoughtfully. 'No, I'm sure you don't.' He frowned and asked abruptly: 'Weren't you bothered about staying here on your own?'

'I wasn't until you grabbed me—and I had the offer of company, which I declined.'

'You should have accepted it. What would have happened if I'd been a real intruder?'

'You *are* a real intruder—and the offer was from Julian,' replied Olivia with acidity.

'I see.'

Olivia compressed her lips. You can see what you damn well like, Matthew Raynor, she thought, noting the decided coolness of voice. She frowned.

'How did you get in here? I mean, have you a key or did you ...' She stopped short, an arrested expression on her face, her gaze taking in the studio couch and blankets. Comprehension began to dawn and she said slowly: 'You've stayed here before, haven't you? When I came back for my purse ... I thought it strange ... Why didn't Liz say you were in the house?'

Matthew shrugged slightly. 'Because I asked her not to.'

'But why didn't you go to Cressida House?'

'You must forgive me, Olivia, if I show a certain amount of wry amusement over the almost reverential tone your voice takes on whenever my family touches the conversation. To one in your position it is, no doubt, something to be envied; to me, at times, it can be constricting. As my visits have been of such short term, I suggested to my good host and hostess that no one need know of them. There was another reason. I thought a certain Miss Olivia Darcy might have been persuaded to stay on.' He smiled thinly. 'Rather ironic, don't you think, Olivia, that instead of putting as much distance between us as possible I find that the Carlyons' new tenant is yourself? What were the words?' he taunted. ' "I shan't be sorry if I never see you again." I believe that is a faithful recap.' He downed the last of his drink. 'I'm sorry I wasn't able to oblige.'

Olivia turned the stem of her glass between her fingers, eyes downcast.

'You made me angry.'

'Yes, I did, didn't I?' Matthew smiled grimly. 'The feeling was reciprocated. But you learn fast, I'll say that for you.' He looked at his watch and stood up, walking over and taking her empty glass and placing it with his own on the table. 'It's late. I'll be off.'

'You ... you're going?' Olivia might have had enough pride to resist asking him if he had seen *Two for Joy* but not enough to feel dismay at his last words.

Matthew turned, brows raised. 'I can hardly stay here.'

'I don't see why not——' began Olivia, stopping when she saw his face.

'There is a difference, then, between Julian and myself?' he asked derisively.

'Well, Julian didn't really mean ... well, yes, he did, but ...'

'To spare your maidenly blushes I'll say I understand Julian's motives perfectly. I'm just a little unsure of your own.'

'As you are well aware of my feelings towards you, Matthew Raynor,' retorted Olivia icily, 'and having already informed me once before that you don't go in for caveman tactics, I don't think I need fear for my virtue—or start comparing you to Julian ... who knows exactly my feelings where he's concerned.' She jutted her chin, eyes sparkling with anger. 'Quite frankly, the idea of sleeping in the house alone has suddenly lost its appeal. So much so that I'll even put up with your presence just to know someone else is here.'

A pulse was jumping in Matthew's cheek and he said curtly:

'Very well. I'll be leaving early. If Adam's not back before I go I'll call in at the hospital. You'd better keep the blanket for the climb upstairs—I won't need it, there's plenty here.' He reached and pulled her to her feet and when Olivia jerked her hand away his face tightened. 'I'm sorry, I forgot you don't like me to maul you. It won't happen again.' The sarcasm was unmistakable.

'Could I have that in writing, do you think?' asked Olivia as she swept across the room. 'For your information, I've a whacking great bruise where you "mauled" me earlier, and that's why I pulled my hand away. But my feelings on the subject haven't altered any.'

The stared at each other across the room. Matthew had his

155

back to the light and in Olivia's overwrought state he seemed the stranger again, all black, even his eyes were dark now; and very tall, body dangerously still.

'Go to bed, Olivia,' he said harshly.

The faintest prickle of fear crept through her. She was, after all, completely alone in the house and in a very vulnerable position. Perhaps Matthew saw the flicker of apprehension in the wide green eyes or noticed the slight tremble of lip, for he turned away abruptly and said rather wearily:

'Go to bed, there's a good girl,' and Olivia quietly left the room, taking with her the view that Matthew Raynor was the most arrogant, self-opinionated ... aggravating man she had ever had the misfortune to meet.

Liz Carlyon gave birth to a son the following day, and it was a thankful but tired Adam who gave out the news that they were both doing well and that the baby was to be called Michael. He took Olivia to one side before leaving the theatre.

'I understand you had a visitor last night?'

'It's all very well for you to laugh, Adam, but he frightened the life out of me, and with the beard I didn't recognise him at once.'

'It was unfortunate happening that way. I gather that should you ever come to grips with a real burglar you'd put up a good fight. Matt said the thwack you gave him on the shins has lamed him for good.'

'He was exaggerating, of course. I was barefooted, and he's very strong.'

'Yes, Matthew's deceptive—in more ways than one,' Adam said mildly. 'By the way, Elizabeth thanks you for the flowers and hopes you'll visit her when you can.' He yawned. 'And now I'm going home to catch up on some sleep.' He turned, took two paces down the corridor and then swung back. 'Matt thought the fact that he stayed the night should be kept quiet, for propriety's sake. How do you feel about staying in the house alone with me while Elizabeth's in hospital?'

'I feel fine, Adam,' replied Olivia firmly. 'Just fine—and I'll leave all intruders specially for you.'

A radiant Liz came home clasping Michael triumphantly in her arms.

'I think he's beautiful, of course, but I don't expect you to agree with me. The nurses couldn't get over how good and contented he is, here's hoping he'll stay that way.' She looked round and smiled happily. 'Oh, it is good to be home! I didn't realise how fond I'd got of the place. Makes me hope more than ever that Adam decides to use Rotheringham as his base when he leaves the Royal.'

Startled, Olivia said: 'Oh! I didn't expect ... has Adam said when that will be?'

'My dear, I shall be the last person to know. It all depends on Matthew. If you like working for Adam you'll get on all right with Matt, they're very much alike in the way they go about things.' Liz lifted Michael on to her shoulder and patted his back. He obediently gave a small burp and Liz grinned complacently. 'How's *Twelfth Night* coming on?'

'All right, I think, but Adam's the one you should ask. May I hold Michael, Liz?'

'You may. Now's the best time, when he's full of lovely grub.'

The ensuing days passed quickly. Almost before Olivia realised it the last performance of *Two for Joy* was upon them and it was with a small lump in her throat that Olivia stood with Julian on one side and Charles and Anthea on the other, taking her bow before a capacity audience.

'Sad?' asked Anthea as they entered the dressing room and prepared to take off their make-up.

Olivia nodded. 'It's been so marvellous.'

'That is as it should be, Olivia. I hope you manage to feel that way about everything you do. Ah, here's Charles.'

'Well, my dears, another play over and done with.' He placed a kindly hand on Olivia's shoulder as he passed and stood before Anthea, bending to kiss her cheek. 'We shall miss you, Anthea. Don't forget us.'

Anthea smiled, taking his hand. 'I'm sorry it's all over.' She turned to Olivia. 'I do hope we have the chance to play together again, Olivia.'

'That's very kind of you, Anthea,' said Olivia shyly. 'You've been a tremendous help, I've learnt an awful lot from you.'

'It's sweet of you to say so, my dear, but quite untrue.'

'Nonsense, Anthea, of course it's true. We can still teach the youngsters a thing or two.' Charles beamed at each in turn. 'And now I'm going to take my two favourite actresses out to dinner. I suppose we'll have to take Julian along.'

'Try and keep me away!' protested a voice from the door.

'Exactly,' sighed Julian's father.

'Everyone back on stage for notes, please.' Ted's voice came over the tannoy and the cast reassembled on stage, still in costume.

'That was better the second time, wasn't it?' Adam glanced down at his notes. 'There's not much to give you, it's mostly technical queries. Is Mary here? No? Laurence, have you your cloak with you? Mm ... no, I'm not happy with it. Find Mary and say I want to see the black one again, come back with it on. Philippa, keep that pause before "Love sought is good, but given unsought is better." Charles, do you think that Malvolio would perhaps ... What the devil's that? Ted, go and see what's happened.'

Shouts could be heard off stage and someone wailing. Olivia pulled a face at Julian standing by her side and everyone remained grouped on stage, puzzled faces turned to the wings. Ted finally appeared and Adam asked abruptly:

'Well?'

'Not well, I'm afraid, Adam. Laurence has fallen down the stairs, tripped over the cloak, we think, and it seems very possible that his leg is broken. Says he heard it crack.'

'What's that racket going on?' demanded Charles.

'Mary having hysterics.'

'Go and shut her up, someone. Ted, ring for an ambulance. Everyone else leave a contact number with Mick and don't go out of earshot of the phone tomorrow morning. Right, Charles, have you any bright ideas?' Adam walked purposefully off stage with Charles, leaving a dumbstruck cast and stage crew.

'What'll happen if it is broken?' asked Jeanette.

'They'll get a replacement Orsino.' Julian ran his hand worriedly through his hair. 'That means extra rehearsals tomorrow, the principals at least.'

'What a thing to happen on the eve of opening!' groaned Olivia. 'Poor Adam!'

'If he can't find someone, he'll have to do it himself,' proclaimed Philippa, 'but standing around here won't help matters. Goodnight,' and with murmurs of agreement the stage gradually emptied.

Liz told Olivia the next day that Adam wanted her in at the theatre by ten, to be prepared for a long session. When she arrived the theatre seemed deserted, even the car park only sported Adam's Scimitar. Pushing open the stage door, she walked along the cool echoing corridor and made her way backstage, searching for a sign of life. There was a solitary spotlight left on and wandering over to the edge of the stage she sat down, dangling her legs. A door banged in the distance. Soon she could hear footsteps and Olivia turned, a welcoming smile on her face.

'Hello, Adam.' She swung her legs up and rose to her feet, dusting her trousers with her hands. 'Oh dear, you do look tired.'

'Hello, Olivia.' He looked at his watch. 'I don't feel too bad. I hope you had a good night's sleep—we have work to do.'

'Does that mean you've been forced to do the part yourself?' she asked sympathetically.

'Thank the lord, no, but it was touch and go. I rang round a hell of a number of agencies with no luck and then I had an inspiration ... and if I'm not mistaken, that sounds like my Orsino now.' Adam walked back through the wings and out of sight and Olivia returned to the edge of the stage to retrieve her script. She heard voices and Adam saying:

'Here's my inspiration, Olivia. He needs no introduction, does he?' and Olivia turned, moving slowly towards them, saying quietly:

'No, indeed. Hello, Matthew.'

Matthew returned a lazy, slightly mocking, 'Hello, Olivia,' and stood looking at her, waiting her reactions. In her first look, Olivia saw that the beard and moustache had gone, but he was wearing the same black cable rib, the texture of which she knew intimately. He looked tanned and well ... the eyes below a lank of untidy black hair were as cool and as keen as ever.

'If you thought I looked weary, consider Matt,' said Adam, searching through his briefcase with growing exasperation. 'He's been driving all night and has only snatched a couple of hours' rest. Allowing for the fact that he's recently had ...' He stopped short, deep in thought, then lifted his head and glanced quizzically at Matthew. 'Where was I?'

'Allowing for the fact that I've recently had ...'

'... two weeks idling through France it's no wonder you're looking remarkably fit, which, my dear fellow, is a good job, because quite frankly, Duke Orsino comes first on my list of priorities. Damn it, where is that script? I must have left it in the office.'

'I'll fetch it,' offered Olivia eagerly, glad of the chance to escape and collect her scattered wits. The fact that Matthew was to take over the part of Orsino was disturbing to say the least, and he knew it too—every time she glanced his way those damned grey eyes were gleaming with amusement.

Adam turned to her. 'Thanks, but I've a phone call to make and I can pick up the script at the same time. I won't be long.' He clapped a hand on Matthew's shoulder as he walked by and some form of unspoken communication passed between them. Olivia watched him go with dismay, but realising that an effort had to be made she asked brightly:

'Did you have a good holiday, Matthew?'

'Yes.'

'It's bad luck, isn't it, about Laurence.'

'Yes.'

'But I'm not a believer in bad luck, are you? I mean, some of the company are being prophets of doom and saying there'll be a jinx on the show.' She paused. 'Do you think there will be?'

Matthew pursed his lips and offered a long-drawn-out, 'No.'

Olivia swung round, her cheeks red. 'Oh, come on, Matthew. It's going to be hopeless if all you can say to me is yes and no.' She ran a hand through her hair. 'The situation is one we can neither of us enjoy, but we shall have to make the best of it. Besides, Adam's bound to notice and it's not fair on him. He has enough to worry about without wondering whether two of his cast are at daggers drawn all the time.' She took a deep breath and resumed on a quieter level. 'Can't we forget all that's happened between us and start again?' and thrusting her hands into the pockets of her jeans she flicked him a quick glance from under her lashes before contemplating the tip of her right toe. The glance, though fleeting, was enough to show Matthew at his most uncompromising. Leaning against the proscenium arch, arms folded, he considered her request for a moment and then leisurely straightened and walked across the stage until she was forced to take a step back.

'No, Olivia,' he drawled at last, 'I don't think it possible to forget all that's happened between us, and only someone as soft as you would suggest it.' He took her chin between thumb and finger and forced her to look at him. 'There's a simplicity about you that never fails to astound me—but for the sake of your green eyes I'll give it a go, if you will.' Olivia jerked her face away and half turned. 'And I can tell you now,' the cool voice ventured, 'that Adam Carlyon, being a highly astute and perceptive man, already suspects that our relationship is not one hundred per cent congenial, and if you want to set his mind at rest, now is the time.'

'Oh.' Olivia chewed her bottom lip, dropping her gaze.

'Oh,' mocked Matthew.

'All the more reason,' flared Olivia, 'for you to say something other than just yes and no!'

'All the more reason for you to stop being as nervy as a kitten in my company and learn to look at me for more than two seconds without feeling compelled to look elsewhere.' He smiled grimly. 'I quite realise that this particular Raynor face isn't your favourite, but it's the one you're stuck with at the moment.' Narrowing his eyes, he added: 'Do you think you're actress enough to hide your true feelings? You're supposed to be in love with me, so much so that you're willing to die for that love ... will you manage to gaze at me lovingly, Olivia?' he taunted.

'It will be a mammoth task and take all my reserves of ability to achieve,' she retorted, goaded into being as sarcastic as he, 'but I'm confident I can do it.'

Matthew smiled and warning bells rang for Olivia. That smile was definitely not to be trusted.

'Mm ... it's reassuring to find you so confident, because there's one other phobia regarding myself that we should tackle and which you will do well to overcome.' He voice was smooth and Olivia looked at him suspiciously, giving a nervous jump as he reached out and touched her cheek caressingly with his hand. 'Even Elizabethans, although not so permissive as these days, touched each other, and if you're going to flinch every time we come into contact you'll be making me as nervous as yourself.' He paused and surveyed her averted face. Olivia was straining to hear Adam's footsteps and then Matthew was saying: 'The best thing with a phobia is to face up to it squarely

161

and admit first of all that the thing exists, then find the reason behind it and finally make some attempt to overcome it. I can't help you with the first two,' he added dryly, 'but the last comes into my milieu.'

'How magnanimous of you,' scoffed Olivia.

Matthew continued in a practical voice as if she had not spoken.

'The first thing one is taught at drama school regarding physical human contact—as I'm sure you know, Miss Darcy —is to put the smallest amount of distance between the two persons involved. Nothing worries an audience more than a supposedly passionate embrace with the lovers standing a yard apart! Therefore ...' he pulled her forward, holding her close. 'What a good little actress you are, Olivia. Full marks for knowing that the eyes must be closed.'

'That way I don't have to see you,' she ground out.

'Doesn't matter about the reason, it's the look of the thing that counts—on stage, that is. Off stage is a different matter entirely—then the feel of the thing is more important, but we'll deal with that at a later date.' He sighed with exaggerated heaviness. 'You're forgetting, Olivia, that you are a woman, and society demands that the female of the species is soft and gentle, not stiff and straight as a ramrod.' His hands began to massage the tense spot between her shoulder blades, moving gently and very professionally to the nape of her neck. 'And I heartily concur with society. I believe, given more time, we could become quite proficient, but,' he lifted his head, listening intently, and her eyes flew open to meet his. 'I rather think this is Adam returning.' His hands moved down and locked in the hollow of her back. 'We'll try and kill two birds with one stone, shall we? Satisfy Adam that we're ... not enemies, and take a stab at your phobia.' His mouth twisted. 'Don't spoil it all by slapping my face, will you?'

'Matthew ...' and then his head came down and blotted out the light.

'Break it up you two, time for work.' Adam strode on stage, his face bland.

'We are working,' replied Matthew easily, unhurriedly turning but retaining an arm around Olivia's shoulder.

Adam was amused. 'I hate to have to tell you, Matt, but we haven't updated the play, so if that was intended as a rehearsal of the final scene you'll have to make do with kissing her hand.'

'What a spoilsport you are,' complained Matthew. 'Never mind, Olivia, we'll make our hand-kissing just as effective.'

'Good, for that's all you'll be allowed. Here's your script. Laurence's handwriting leaves much to be desired, but the moves are just discernible. It remains to be seen how much of Orsino you'll remember, but if my memory serves me correct, yours is pretty good, isn't it?'

'We ... ell, used to be.' Matthew frowned. 'It must be two years since I produced *Twelfth Night* and at least six since I played Orsino.'

'Ah, well, we'll soon see. I'm going to break it down into sections, starting with the Orsino/Viola partnership, and I'll read in the other parts as necessary. The full cast will be here at two and we'll have a run through, without costumes, and with any luck finish in time for you to have a couple of hours' rest.'

Matthew nodded and removing his hand from Olivia's shoulder opened the script and scanned the pages. Olivia made her way to the wings in readiness for her first entrance. Once safely behind the curtain she lifted hands to warm cheeks and concentrated on regaining some degree of composure.

The nerve of that man! she thought bitterly, watching Matthew work out the first set of moves with Adam. And why, when she started off being determined to remain cool and calm, did he always manage to rile her?

Adam crossed the forestage and joined her. 'You're looking very pensive, Olivia. No need to be unduly worried, you know. I have every faith in both of you to rise to the occasion. Now don't forget, the audience must be made aware of your feelings for Orsino, and Matt, you know as I do what a tricky part Orsino is. Here's a man, supposedly desperately in love with the Countess, and declaring it openly, yet finding himself growing more and more attached, despite himself, to his new page. I'll leave it to you to put all the subtleties into this relationship, but I want to see him pulled both ways.'

Afterwards, Olivia tried to remember the next three hours, but they were a blank, only certain things standing out. The discovery that Matthew had inherited his father's love and skill of Shakespeare, the two not necessarily going together, and the thrill this discovery gave her, all her professional feelings delighting in playing opposite him and responding. The knowledge that Matthew, relieved of his burden of discipline and command as a director, could enjoy a bantering, teasing relationship with Jeanette who brought in coffee for them, very reminiscent of Julian, and the unreasonable feeling of disappointment that she was not included. The obvious rapport between Adam and Matthew. As Olivia had a high opinion of Adam as a man and a director, and considered he had a sound judge of character, she wondered with a sinking of heart whether she had allowed her emotions to blur her vision, as Matthew himself had accused her. One other moment stood out. Only the once did she forget she was Viola, and it was Matthew's fault that she did, for he stepped out of character, his eyes mocking as she came to the lines: ' "My father had a daughter lov'd a man, as it might be perhaps, were I a woman, I should your lordship." ' Ironically her reaction pleased Adam and he afterwards told her to keep in the movement away and falter of voice, as he liked it. Her eyes had swung round to Matthew and he had smiled derisively.

'What a slavedriver you are, Adam,' Matthew said, when Adam made them go over a scene again.

'Just giving you a taste of your own medicine, Matt. You can do all the relaxing you like tonight, at about ten-thirty, with my blessing.'

Matthew lifted a brow at Olivia. 'Care to make that a date?'

'Don't you think we ought to wait and see how the show goes? After all, we might make a bosh of it and have to go into hiding,' replied Olivia, playing the game.

'I've always found relaxing in hiding the best way to do it,' was the swift reply, and before she could think of a reply Adam called:

'Finished coffee? Right then, let's go from Matt's speech —"If ever thou shalt love, in the sweet pangs of it, remember me," and take heart, children, it's coming on beautifully.'

It was with a certain amount of relief that Olivia welcomed the arrival of the rest of the cast and crew. Philippa made a beeline for Matthew and linked an arm possessively through his.

'Matt darling, how about making history tonight? Shall I confuse everyone by accepting your offer of marriage instead

164

of spurning it? It would be rather fun, wouldn't it?'

Matthew smiled, responding with easy familiarity. 'I need more warning of that idea, Phil. It's taken me all morning to learn the correct lines, I don't want poor Mick on prompt to have any more problems than he already has.'

'Besides,' broke in Julian, 'if you did that, my dear Philippa, we'd have no play.'

'Very well,' she sighed graciously, 'I'll stick to the script.'

'Make sure you do,' ordered Adam as he passed by. 'Ted, everything set? Clear the stage and we'll begin.' He looked round the assembled cast. 'Don't forget we go up in,' he looked at his watch, 'five and a half hours, so make it good.' A huge groan went up as he made his way to the back of the auditorium.

'You did some hard work this morning, you two,' remarked Adam later, walking to the car park with Matthew and Olivia.

'Poor Olivia has the worst burden, I'm afraid,' commented Matthew, placing a cool hand on the nape of her neck. 'She copes marvellously well with me and I'm very grateful for her support.'

Olivia coloured slightly, 'You're easy to work with,' she murmured, and the hand ruffled her hair and was removed.

'Thank the lord Orsino's not a mammoth part,' continued Matthew easily. 'Imagine if you'd been doing *Hamlet* or *Othello*!'

'Mammoth or not, there are words to be spoken, and you appear to have mastered them,' replied Adam with satisfaction. 'Did Mary find you another costume?'

'Yes, an all black with gold trim . . . rather splendid.'

'Good.' Adam pushed open the stage door. 'Good lord! Sunshine! Back in there it's possible to forget there's a real world going on outside. Are you staying with us, Matt? Liz specially asked me to say you're welcome.'

'Thank her kindly, Adam, but I'll go to Cressida.' He stopped and smiled, giving Adam a wicked glance. 'Actually, I daren't. Liz so extols the virtues of married life and fatherhood that if I stayed with you for any length of time she might convert me. You're a lucky man, Adam.'

'Yes, I think I am,' responded Adam complacently, adding reflectively, 'I might not have been, if I'd allowed my pride to stand in the way.' He searched for his keys. 'Such a stupid emotion, pride. In you get, Olivia. See you later, Matt.'

Adam hummed contentedly under his breath as he drove home and Olivia was pleased to stay silent. As he pulled the Scimitar to a standstill in the drive he paused before getting out.

'Nervous?'

Olivia smiled. 'A little,' she admitted, 'although I find I'm more worried for Matthew than myself.'

'You have no need to worry on either count. Matthew has a great deal of experience which will hold him in good stead and a well-rehearsed company to back him up. As for you, I always knew you would finally achieve exactly what I wanted, but I thought I'd have to wait for tonight. Funnily enough, it came in rehearsal today. You've always been excellent in your dealings with the Countess, bringing out the humour of the situation of one woman falling in love with another. You look the part beautifully, I've never seen such an attractive long-legged boy, and with your fair wig you and Julian make a remarkable set of twins. It was in your association with Orsino that I felt you could give me a little more ... with any other actress I'd have been satisfied, for what you were giving me was a good and competent performance, but today you've shown me that I was justified in my expectations. For all we were without costumes and effects, it came suddenly to life. I knew my instinct was right about you and as Matt had it too, chances were that we couldn't be wrong.'

Olivia's head swept round. 'Sorry ... what ... did you say about Matthew?'

Adam looked at her consideringly, lips pursed. 'Have you ever wondered how Matt knew you were an actress?' he asked abruptly.

Olivia shook her head and looked away. 'He was going to tell me once ... but I cut him off. Since then the subject has never arisen.'

Adam thoughtfully tapped his fingers on the steering-wheel.

'It may help you,' he said at last. 'You were in a play once, at Cheltenham. I mentioned it to you before when I spoke of Frank Devine who produced it. *Innocents*, it was called, and I believe you took the part of a girl who became blind.'

Olivia smiled at the recollection. 'Yes, it was a good play and Isobel a lovely part to do.'

'Matthew was in the audience,' Adam said evenly.

Olivia stared wide-eyed for a moment and then covered her face with a hand, sitting very still.

'Exactly. It's a small world, isn't it?' Adam gave her a quick look and then transferred his gaze out of the window. 'For a particular reason which I won't go into now, Matthew wrote to me about this play, I was in Australia at the time, Elizabeth and I were not long married. He was enthusiastic about an actress in it, who he felt had outstanding ability—a touch of the star quality were his words, if I remember rightly. She made quite an impression on him.' Adam turned to her, a rueful smile on his face. 'You can imagine his feelings, therefore, when he found this same actress applying for the job of a typist.'

'Yes,' said Olivia, 'I can imagine his feelings.' She collected her things together and opened the car door. 'Thank you for telling me, Adam. It's explained a lot,' and deep in thought she went slowly up to the flat.

CHAPTER EIGHT

'Then come kiss me, sweet and twenty.'

THE noise had reached an incredible level in the crowded
theatre bar. Liz fought her way through the mass of people
and hugged Olivia enthusiastically.

'Olivia, you were super ... and you looked so lovely, no
wonder Matthew fell for you!' She looked round, her bubbling congratulations enveloping all of them. 'It was terrific,
and you were all marvellous.' She slipped an arm companionably through Matthew's. 'No one, my dear Matt, would ever
have suspected that you'd had only a few hours' rehearsal, it
was a trojan performance. I started off on the edge of my seat
but soon realised I didn't have to worry for you and just sat
back and let it all happen.'

'Why, thank you, Elizabeth,' said Matthew, amused. 'Had I
known that I would have felt much better myself.'

Liz wrinkled her nose at him and turned to Charles. 'And
my darling Charles, you actually made me feel sorry for
Malvolio!' She beamed at everyone and added: 'It was all
fantastic.'

'We gather, Elizabeth, from your abundant use of adjec-
tives, that you enjoyed it,' remarked her husband dryly, coming up quietly from behind.

'Oh, poof,' scoffed Liz. 'If I like a thing then I say so.'

Julian laughed. 'Yes, but it must be rather apparent when
you don't.'

Liz put out the tip of her tongue and Adam said:

'There's no guarantee for silence when that happens.'

'We've heard Liz's reactions, what about our director's?'
asked Charles quizzically.

'I shall allow myself a glow of satisfaction and say I'm very
pleased with the way it went. Laurence is here, by the way,
encased in plaster. He'll be a write-off for a few weeks, I'm
afraid.' Adam turned to Matthew. 'Care to take his place indefinitely until his return, Matt?'

168

'Oh, no! I'll see *Twelfth Night* out for you, but you'll have to replace me for the next. I've other plans in the offing,' declared Matthew in mock horror.

'May we ask what those plans are, Mr Raynor, sir?' asked Philippa, smiling coaxingly.

'You'll know them soon enough,' returned Matthew easily.

Philippa pouted prettily but didn't seem put out, placing a sleek, well-manicured hand on his arm and whispering something confidentially to him, her red curls very close.

'The bar's about to close,' said Julian suddenly. 'We can't just wander home, we must celebrate in some way. Any ideas?'

'Why don't you come back to our place?' suggested Liz. 'We can collect a Chinese take-away on the way home.'

'That is an inspired scheme,' approved Julian. 'May we have a sanction from the head of the house?'

'It wouldn't hurt to unwind,' agreed Adam, adding with a smile, 'and Elizabeth knows my weakness for Chinese food.'

It was pleasant to sit talking quietly. Not everyone came back, but those that did found chairs, and where there were none available, sat on the floor, tucking into the delicious food with relish, most agreeing that food had been something not to be thought of before the performance.

Olivia found a place on the floor beside the armchair in which Charles was sitting. He turned to her in the course of the evening, saying with a warm smile:

'Do you remember the first day we met and I quoted *Twelfth Night*?'

'Yes, of course I do,' responded Olivia eagerly. 'And I said how much Viola appealed to me, and here I am, playing her! It's ... unbelievable.'

'I couldn't have planned things better if I'd personally broken Mayer's leg,' announced Charles, the gravity of voice belied by the twinkle in his eyes. 'I shall have to make the most of having Julian and Matthew with me in the same play —it probably won't ever happen again. It's a pity that Matt prefers to direct, he's a good actor, has a way with Shakespeare.'

They both turned their gaze across the room to where Matthew lay sprawled on the floor, talking to Philippa. He was dressed casually and his hair fell across his forehead, making him seem younger than usual, and when he suddenly laughed, Olivia was reminded of the day when she had taken the toss from the horse and he had laughed with such abandon in the bracken.

'You know it's on the cards that I may be having a new daughter-in-law in the very near future?' Charles murmured in her ear, still looking at Matthew and Philippa as they left the room.

'Oh! Yes ... yes, I'd guessed.' So ... Matthew and Philippa.

'Not before time.' Charles glanced sideways at her. 'You don't feel like making it a double?' His blue eyes were very blue and direct.

'It's not leap year, Charles,' managed Olivia with a laugh, cheeks rosy. 'A girl has to wait to be asked, you know,' adding mischievously: 'And when it is, you just watch out!'

'If I were twenty years younger, my dear, you wouldn't have to wait for leap year!'

'What is my illustrious parent whispering in your ear, Olivia?' demanded Julian. 'Do not trust him, gentle maiden! You've had a monopoly of her long enough, Father. They've put the record player on in the other room, twin—care for a smooch?'

'Yes, of course she does,' said Charles briskly, adding with a pained expression on his face, 'although your terminology leaves much to be desired.'

Laughing, Olivia permitted herself to be hauled to her feet and led into the adjoining room, which because of its size, proved that smooch was indeed the correct word. The only other couple in there were Philippa and Matthew, who were dancing gently to the slow, dreamy music, heads close. Julian drew her to him and Olivia closed her thoughts on the last time she had danced in such a way and allowed Julian's arms to protect and wipe out any silly memories that had the tenacity to linger where they were not wanted.

'Just listen to this!' exclaimed Liz the next day, eyes bright with excitement, waving the paper at Olivia. She began to read out aloud. ' "The Theatre Royal, Rotheringham, has for some time now been giving work worthy of more universal notice. Adam Carlyon's direction of *Twelfth Night* is no exception. A lively and invigorating production; he gives us

170

Shakespeare at his best, allowing the text to be meaningful without destroying the beauty of the words. This should be no surprise to us, however, for Mr Carlyon has long been one of our more distinguished men in this field." Whoopee!' Liz lifted her head. 'How I do love thee, C. W. Longford, you are my favourite critic! To continue—"He is richly served by his strong cast. Philippa Markham, a beautiful Olivia, is regally scornful, transformed from icy coldness to awakening passion with clever bewilderment but throughout never losing her dignity." Huh!' snorted Liz impatiently, 'she's always on her dignity, it comes naturally to her. If she finally hooks Matt I shall have to put up with her, but I'll rue the day she does.

'Where was I? Oh, yes ... "Matthew Raynor's brooding, melancholic Orsino is strongly portrayed and his performance is delicately drawn. Orsino usually annoys me, but Mr Raynor has at last made him believable. Olivia Darcy, a newcomer to the Royal, is a modest, unassuming Viola, giving us a glimpse of reserved passion. She steals into our hearts and that of the Duke's with masterly playing and her sense of comedy is a delight to see—an actress to be watched." Olivia! How marvellous! "Julian Raynor, the youngest member of the talented Raynor family, gives to Sebastian a fresh and roguish charm, making the usually insipid role one of note. As if two Raynors in the programme were not bonus enough, Charles Raynor is a mesmerising Malvolio, building up dislike and contempt for this bumbledom, this social climber, only to leave us at the end feeling almost sorry for him, a victim of blundering ambition." There's more about the rest of the cast and quite a bit about set and costumes. Oh, how pleased I am for you all. Isn't it a super crit?'

Olivia, as thrilled over the review as Liz, nodded and said with a grin: 'I wonder why when a crit's good it's the truth, and when it's bad then it's only one man's opinion?' she asked teasingly.

'For that you can come and help me wash up all the coffee cups from last night,' demanded Liz, marching into the kitchen.

'Have you decided whether you're buying the house yet?' Olivia asked, following her and donning an apron.

'No. Adam's being very cagey, as usual. He has something up his sleeve, but until it's definite he's keeping mum.' Liz looked sideways at Olivia and asked casually: 'Are you renewing your contract?'

Olivia shrugged. 'I ... I haven't made up my mind yet. I've loved working for Adam, but ... I don't know whether I could work as well for Matthew.' Liz showed surprise and Olivia added defensively: 'Just because you get on well with him ...'

'But I thought you liked him, Olivia.'

'I don't think he'd be happy to have me in his company.'

'Rubbish! Adam doesn't often indulge me with theatre business, but what he's told me makes nonsense of what you say. Why on earth should Matt not want to renew your contract when it was he who wanted you at the Royal in the first place?'

Olivia gripped the edge of the sink. 'Wh ... what did you say?'

'I couldn't understand why it had to be so hush-hush, and it's obvious you ought to know. Adam thought you'd leave a forwarding address and when you didn't he began contacting the agencies and then luckily he bumped into you, but I know for certain that Matt gave Adam explicit instructions before he went in for observation that he was to contact you and offer you a job.'

While Olivia digested this amazing piece of news, Liz sat still, a hand to her mouth, a horrified look on her face. Olivia, following through Liz's comments, suddenly lifted her head, frowning.

'What do you mean—"go in for observation"?'

Liz covered her face and sighed. 'Oh, lord, I'll get shot! I knew I'd open my big mouth sooner or later. Can't you forget I said it?'

'No, I can't. Observation for what?'

Liz thought hard for a moment, chewing her lip, then: 'Promise you'll keep it to yourself, unless Matt says otherwise?' Olivia nodded. Liz continued quietly: 'Ever since that wretched car crash Matthew has been having spasmodic but blinding headaches and occasional blurred vision. He saw a specialist who advised a series of tests. Matthew contacted Adam, who he knew to be free, and Adam agreed to come and take over at the Royal.'

'Wh ... what was the matter with Matthew?'

'Apart from superficial cuts he was concussed after the accident, but he didn't realise that the bump he'd had was serious and he seemed to recover and everyone concentrated on Charles, who had the more obvious injuries. No one knows about Matt's operation, by the way, not even his family. That's why he stayed with us that couple of times.'

'Operation?' echoed Olivia faintly, busying herself at the sink. 'Er ... he went into hospital ... and had an operation?'

'Yes.' Liz looked at her friend closely, a puzzled frown on her brow. 'Are you feeling all right, Olivia?'

Olivia managed a creditable laugh and turned on the taps. 'Yes, of course I am.' She swallowed hard. 'So all the time I was working for Charles, and Matthew showed such concern for his father's welfare and recovery, he suffered his own ill-health in silence.'

'Mm ... well, he's like this, is our Matthew—and it wasn't all the time.'

Olivia said thoughtfully: 'There were, now I think back, obvious moments when he was not well. If only he'd said something then ...'

'... then they'd all have been fussing around. Matt would have hated it.' Liz smiled grimly. 'Especially as he didn't know whether everything would turn out well. What was the point, he said, of worrying them unnecessarily?'

'What exactly was the matter? What did they find?'

'Heavens, it's all rather technical, but I gather that if you have a bump on the head this sort of trouble can manifest itself later; weeks, months or even years later. Something to do with pressure inside the head. Evidently, once the trouble has been diagnosed, the chances of success are high, but for all that, it's still a delicate operation and anything can go wrong.'

'Where ... did he have it done?'

'Derby,' said Liz briefly, and peered anxiously into the sink. 'Er ... don't you think you've squeezed enough washing-up liquid in there, Olivia?' she asked gently, eyeing the mountain of suds creeping up the side of the bowl.

'Oh!' Olivia gave a laugh which didn't quite make it. 'I ... I wasn't concentrating, sorry.' She turned her face away from her friend and began to wash the cups vigorously. 'What drama going on beneath our noses and we knowing nothing about it! Matthew is perfectly all right now?' she added in a voice which did not seem to belong to her.

'Perfectly all right,' repeated Liz firmly. 'The surgeon is very pleased with him.'

Olivia expelled a deep breath and said lightly: 'That's good. Is that Michael crying?'

'Yes, he's having his morning exercise. If you'll be an angel and carry on here, I'll go and feed him.'

Liz went thoughtfully up the stairs to Michael, whose face was bright red with frustration. He immediately stopped crying when she lifted him, although his mouth worked hungrily.

'You've an appetite like your mother,' Liz reproved fondly as she carried him over to the chair, collecting a clean nappy and the baby basket on her way. In a few moments she was sitting listening to the contented sounds coming from her son. 'I ought to have guessed, Michael,' she told him confidentially. 'Poor Olivia!' And then she smiled at the determination on his face and held him close.

By Friday evening of the final week of the run, Olivia had decided not to renew her contract. She had been engaged for three plays and she would see the third through, but after that she would move on. She found herself drawn compulsively to the side of the stage, standing quietly in the darkness of the wings, her eyes never leaving the tall, dark figure in black and gold. Watching him, her throat aching with ... well, with what? she asked herself dryly ... hardly memories! Two kisses did not constitute memories—the only memories she had a right to were ones of anger and mistrust. Regret, then? A negative emotion maybe, but she could daydream a whole new set of circumstances where she could meet Matthew on equal terms, have a normal beginning, one that could flower and grow. Watching him, indulging in this daydream ... and her resolve wavered. How could she leave, never to see him again?

And then Philippa came on stage, regal in black, her beautiful auburn hair piled high on the top of her head, a black veil thrown aside to reveal her face, subtly pale—and Olivia knew she would have to go, that there was no future in living in a 'what might have been' world, in being tortured daily seeing them together. Matthew as director could be endured, Mat-

174

thew married to Philippa would be unbearable—and so she would go.

A shadow appeared by her side and an arm placed round her shoulders. She smiled at Julian and his arm tightened and together they followed the action of the play. Dear Julian, she thought gratefully, what a friend he had turned out to be, looking after her and making her laugh, almost as if he knew she was unhappy. Only two more performances, she thought with a pang of dismay. Like Charles she had made the most of the past three weeks, but now that the end was near it made everything so much more bitter-sweet.

Olivia disengaged herself from Julian and moved two paces nearer her entrance. Nearing her cue line, she took a deep breath and strode on stage, a slim, boyish figure, dressed in browns, and allowed her love to shine from Viola's eyes. She had very little recollection of how she arrived back in the dressing room afterwards. Only could she remember Matthew, grey eyes intent as he kissed her hand before they began the final Elizabethan dance, steps measured and poised, hands touching briefly, then away, and Feste the clown singing his song.

Olivia went through the methodical motions of hanging up her clothes, listening half-heartedly to the chatter of the other girls, purposely taking her time removing the stage make-up. One by one the dressing-room emptied until Philippa, the only other person left, stopped by Olivia's chair on her way out, a slightly triumphant air about her, although her words were all concern.

'Are you well, Olivia? I was saying to Matthew how tired you were looking these days.'

Olivia eyed her through the mirror. Dressed for a party, Philippa looked absolutely radiant and bursting with health and vitality, and beside her, Olivia felt washed out and insipid, but she wasn't going to admit it.

'I'm fine, thanks,' she answered, and continued greasing her face, waiting, for there was obviously more to come.

'I'm looking forward to next week, aren't you? I'm ready for something different.' Philippa pulled one of her curls into place.

Olivia nodded. They were doing *Oh, What a Lovely War*,

a satire with a musical score which expounded the stupidity of war.

'And then *Blithe Spirit*—I adore Coward.' Philippa paused. 'I shall just love playing Elvira.' She smiled sweetly. 'Well, I'm off for a gay evening, which will only just make the thoughts of a matinee bearable. 'Bye!' she trilled, and swept out, leaving a waft of heady perfume behind her.

Olivia gave a bitter smile. She was no threat to Philippa and she gave her joy of Elvira. By that time the Theatre Royal, Rotheringham would be well and truly behind her and no doubt its associations would fade with time. Olivia sighed, pressing fingers to her throbbing temples. She now had the mother of all headaches and was not surprised at the fact. Since her talk with Liz her head had been buzzing round, going over and over what she had learned, reliving moments in the past. So much now made sense.

'I love Matthew.' There! The words, thought often during waking hours, were now said. And what did they alter? Nothing! Matthew wasn't going to rush in and declare passionate love to her accompanied by a heavenly choir! She grimaced derisively to herself and moving languidly over to the wash-hand basin, wetted the corner of a towel and placed it across her forehead. It helped, but not much.

This was how Matthew found her; a slim figure in a silk slip, leaning against the wall, every line of her body depicting weariness, eyes closed in a too pale face.

'Olivia,' he said sharply, 'are you ill?'

Her eyes flew open and she stared, startled, her heart thumping rapidly.

'I knocked, but you didn't hear.' Matthew came close, a frown on his face, and he repeated his question, giving her a searching look.

'I ... I'm just cooling down, it's so hot, isn't it?' Olivia flung away the towel and crossed back to her chair, picking up her dress.

'Do you want to go straight back to the flat, or would you like a drink first?' Matthew asked, adding quickly: 'Hold on, stop struggling, a button has caught in your hair.' He released it and Olivia emerged, fiery-faced, and allowed him to button her up, moving abruptly away when he had done so, the skin on her back scorching where his fingers had touched. Matthew

176

repeated his question verbatim and Olivia said awkwardly:

'Julian did say . . .'

'That he would give you a lift home—I know. He's sent me with his apologies, but a party's cropped up at the last minute.' Something in his voice made her look up. His face was inscrutable, but she had a sudden vision of Philippa proclaiming that she was off to a party and floating out of the room, a vision of smoke blue chiffon. No wonder Matthew was sounding so bleak. Whatever was Julian playing at? she wondered.

'Oh . . .' she began uncertainly.

'If you don't much care for a lift with me, say so and I'll get you a taxi,' he said curtly.

'Of course I . . . it's just that I didn't want to take you out of your way,' she floundered. Matthew rose to his feet, lifting the chair on which he had been sitting and forcing it beneath the dressing table with a clatter.

'In case you've forgotten, I live in the same house as Julian. What's out of my way is out of his too—but then we've agreed that we'll not compare me to Julian, haven't we?'

'Why do you always twist everything I say?' Olivia thrust her feet into her sandals.

'I don't believe I do.' There was silence and then: 'Adam tells me that you haven't renewed your contract.'

She stood upright and turned to face him. 'No . . . no, I haven't.'

'May I ask why not?'

'I haven't made up my mind what to do.'

'Aren't you happy here?' he demanded shortly.

'Yes, but . . .' Olivia hesitated, unable to cope with Matthew in this mood and her thumping head at the same time.

'You want to go on to greater things.'

Goaded by his tone, she swung away and began to clear her table top. 'Well, honestly, Matthew, I can't make you out. One minute I haven't the guts to fight and get on and the next you're bawling me out for doing so.' She brushed a hand across her eyes. 'I can't argue with you . . .'

'I'm not arguing, just asking. If you're thinking of moving on, I have a contact in Edinburgh who would be interested, if you care to take it up.'

Olivia stood still, conscious of despair sweeping over her.

How easily did he contemplate her going. She said in a low voice:

'I understand from Adam that you were responsible for my job here.'

There was silence. Matthew picked up a pot of cream, tossed it in his hand a few times and eventually said brusquely:

'Adam isn't usually so talkative—and in any case, I merely suggested your name as a possibility when the vacancy came up.'

Olivia swallowed hard. 'And now you're offering to help me again.'

'That's how things work in the theatre business. I help Jim Stone in Edinburgh this week, he may be able to help me the next.'

She nodded, daunted by the practical tone.

The Lotus was parked in its usual spot—Olivia wondered if Matthew remembered the last time he had given her a lift. She half expected to see Liz and Adam walk down beneath the solitary lamp, ghosts of their former selves. If it were possible to turn back the clock, how differently would that evening have turned out, if she had reacted more rationally? she wondered. But no phantoms appeared and she laid her head on the back of the seat, thankful that Matthew seemed indisposed to talk also. Her feelings were shortlived. When Matthew brought the Lotus to a stop at the kerb he switched off the engine and turned to her.

'I shouldn't worry about Julian,' he said evenly.

Olivia threw him an uncertain glance and then comprehension darted through her. He thought she was brooding about Philippa and Julian!

'No?' she managed, and added more firmly: 'I'm not worried about Julian.'

'Good.'

Olivia was glad to be out of the Lotus, it was too intimate, and the night air was cooling and fresh. Matthew held her arm as he led her up the dark drive. At the porch he paused.

'Only two more performances to go.'

'Yes,' Olivia agreed bleakly.

'Standing in for Laurence has been most enjoyable. It seems that's my fate at the moment. While standing in for

Julian,' he pulled her to him, slowly but firmly, 'has attractive perquisites.'

Three kisses to be stored away in the memory chest.

'You won't change your mind, even at the last minute?' Adam swivelled his chair round, eyes intent.

Olivia shook her head. 'I'll never forget my time here, Adam.'

He rose to his feet. 'I should hope not. Send us your address when you have one. When does the bus leave?'

She looked at her watch.

'In half an hour. My case is at the bus station and I've said my goodbyes ... at least ... when you see Matthew, you'll pass on my regards?'

'I will.'

'You haven't heard from him since he left?'

Adam shrugged. 'You know Matt for going into retreat.'

'He's not ill again?' Olivia asked quickly, anxiously.

'Good lord, no.' Adam lifted a brow. 'How did you know about that?'

'Liz let it out quite recently, but she made me promise not to say anything to anyone, and I haven't, truly.'

Adam shook his head, smiling ruefully. 'I don't expect it matters now.' He stood up and held out an envelope. 'My secretary asked me to give you these, they're tax papers—I'd better check that ... yes, B. Olivia Darcy, all correct.'

'Goodbye, Adam.' She impulsively reached and kissed his cheek. 'Thank you for everything. I promise I'll keep in touch.'

'Goodbye, Olivia my dear. I ...' the telephone rang and with an apologetic smile he lifted the receiver. 'Carlyon here. Oh ... yes. Very nearly. Hold on a minute.' Adam put the receiver down on to his desk and walked with her to the door. 'I hope you'll be very happy, Olivia. Don't forget us.'

His words echoed as she walked purposefully towards the bus station. No, she wouldn't forget them. The bus was a luxury, streamlined tourer in kingfisher blue and shining chrome. The day was hot and part of the roof was pulled back for coolness and Olivia sank thankfully on to the comfortable seat, pleased to find she was near the window, and closed her eyes to discourage the portly gentleman by her side should he have any inclination for conversation. A door slammed and they were off. Leaving had not been without its difficulties. Liz surprisingly had not opposed it. Charles had remained silent for a few moments and then offered to get in touch with a colleague, saying with a smile that then he would know where she was, but he had been short-tempered for the rest of that day. Julian had looked thoughtfully at her and shaken his head.

'I was wrong about you, Olivia my love. You do need to be protected.' He had kissed her gently and patted her back in a fatherly gesture. 'Harry always knows where I am should you ever need me.'

Rosemary and Tom took the news as a normal progression. They were sorry to see her leave Rotheringham but pleased she was, at last, doing what she wanted to. The irony of it! That was the last thing she was doing, but the time for confidences was long past.

The miles slipped away comfortably and Olivia dozed. She was first made aware that something odd was happening by the increased volume of conversation within the bus. The driver was saying cheerfully:

'I don't know. He's been following us for the last hour. In a car like that we oughtn't to see him for dust, yet every so often he overtakes us and then pulls off the road and tags behind again.' He lifted his voice above the babble of his passengers. 'Anyone know a gold Lotus registration KNR847R?'

Olivia froze in her seat, aware of the growing speculation surrounding her, and of heads craning to see out of the windows. She had no need to do so, knowing in intimate detail the gold Lotus, registration KNR847R! Shrinking into her seat, her brain working furiously, she rejected one idea after the other, each seeming more ludicrous than the last.

'There he goes again,' the driver announced. 'Might as well see what the bloke wants. It's obvious he wants something and although he's been driving with the utmost courtesy I don't fancy having him tag along indefinitely,' and putting his foot firmly on the brake and sounding his horn in a series of blasts, he began to slow the bus to a halt.

'What happens if he's a hijacker?' someone called from the back.

'You've been watching too much telly, mate, but I tell you what . . . I'll go and have a word with him and if I come back on my own, you'll know everything's okay, but if he comes back with me, one of you gents take over and belt off. How's that?' With much good humour the driver climbed out of the bus and strolled towards the Lotus which had pulled up a few yards ahead.

Olivia stared down at her lap, but a running commentary was being given by a woman on the front seat, who suddenly realised that she had achieved fame at last.

'Our driver has reached the car now and leaning to speak to the driver through the window. He's talking—now he's listening and nodding his head.' She gave a strangled yelp. 'The driver of the car is getting out! Oh no, our driver's coming back alone, thank goodness.' The passengers responded diversely, some with annoyance for the delay but mostly with interest and curiosity. The bus driver climbed the steps, mopping his balding head with a handkerchief. He stood on the platform surveying his passengers, holding up his hand for quiet.

'Well now, it seems we're going to have the opportunity of playing fairy godmother. The gent out there fully intends travelling all the way unless a certain young lady gives him the pleasure of her company. Now that car might be a strange one for most of you, but not to her, so while she's deciding what to do I'll just say that he was most civil but sounded very determined.'

'Lovers' tiff, eh?' offered the man from the back, who was enjoying himself.

'Something of the sort,' admitted the driver, looking at his watch. 'I can't allow any more time, it's see him now or later, lady, but don't forget we stop for lunch in half an hour anyway.'

'Go on, love, make it up,' called a voice, and there was an indignant giggle from a girl in front who said:

'Don't look at me like that—I'm not the one he wants, more's the pity! Shouldn't mind him or his car.'

Everyone's attention was directed once more out front and Olivia, fascinated, followed their gaze. Matthew was leaning indolently against the bonnet, map outspread.

The various explanations that had beset her had left such confusion that Olivia abandoned the lot. Taking a deep breath, she rose, excused herself past the portly gentleman and, scarlet-faced, walked steadily down the bus, which had become instantly silent.

'Wh ... what about my case?' she asked as calmly as she could.

'That's all right, miss. Your gent said to leave it off at the next stop to be collected.' He beamed at her. 'Never let the sun set on a quarrel, my old woman always says.'

'You go and make it up,' advised the lady commentator in a motherly voice. 'If he's willing to go to all this trouble then he's got it badly.'

Olivia, who had been thinking along these lines and rejecting them, felt a warm glow creep over her. She turned sparkling eyes to the woman and said wonderingly:

'I think you must be right.'

The driver assisted her down the steps.

'Good luck, miss.'

Cheeks still flaming, Olivia began to walk towards the Lotus, her heart thumping madly, telling herself that as soon as she could see him clearly then she would know. But she had reckoned without Matthew's enigmatic expression. He had straightened and was now standing, hands on hips, facing her. As she drew near her steps faltered.

'Running away again, Olivia? Dear, dear, this is becoming a habit,' he said evenly, 'but perhaps it's not such a bad thing, after all.' He paused. 'You see, I've decided to change my way of life and both of us being unpredictable would be too confusing. Before you, my dear Miss Darcy, stands a twentieth-century caveman.' He looked at her intently for one moment and said softly: 'Had I perhaps made this resolve a few weeks ago you wouldn't have been forced to run away from me for a second time. Would you, Olivia?'

The look in his eyes made Olivia catch her breath and she gave an imperceptible shake of the head.

'Now for revelation number two—the bended knee. I do happen to be wearing a remarkably expensive pair of trousers, and the terra firma appears rather gritty, but never daunted, I ...'

'Oh, Matthew! You are an idiot,' and she was in his arms just as a voice said:

'Get on with it, mate—I've a timetable to make up!' The bus had silently moved alongside and a sea of faces was waiting expectantly behind every window. Matthew grinned and kissed her. A rousing cheer issued from the kingfisher tourer and, hands waving, it sailed on, faces beaming.

'Do you always,' Olivia complained breathlessly, 'make love before an audience?'

'I did so, for a certain three weeks,' Matthew answered whimsically. He lifted a brow in the direction of the passing traffic. 'As you see, we're much too public here for what I want to do,' and taking her hand, he led her to the waiting Lotus.

It was not long before they caught the bus up, and flicking the indicator Matthew said with amusement:

'We're about to pass, so if you want to hide your maidenly blushes, use my shoulder,' and pipping cheerfully on the horn, he overtook and received a delighted volley in return.

'If you think I'm calmly going to collect my case at the other end you're mistaken, Matthew Raynor!' protested Olivia, thankful to see them leaving the bus behind at a rapid rate. 'I've already made a fool of myself in front of those passengers and I'm not ...'

'All the world loves a lover,' quipped Matthew, giving her a look that sent her pulse racing. 'Your suitcase will prove no problem. The driver was willing to drop it off at a pub I know in Banbury where we'll eat, it's right on the main road. That's where the bus is stopping,' and he nodded at a hotel on the right which had an enormous car park and a sign 'coaches welcome' hanging on the wall, 'that is if you can wait until Banbury before eating? We'll stop nearer if you're famished?'

Olivia shook her head. 'Matthew,' she asked softly, 'it is all happening, isn't it? I haven't fallen asleep on the bus and dreaming?' He took her hand and kissed the palm. 'It's real, very real.'

'I ... I still don't know what happened,' began Olivia, and seeing his sceptical glance, laughed in confusion. 'Oh, I know full well what's happened to me ... and almost incredibly, it seems to have happened to you too, but ...'

'But what, my dear?'

'Why didn't you say something before? Why wait until now?'

'Believe me, had I the slightest inkling that you had begun to see me in any way other than one of acute dislike I would have acted before, but after Sentinel Hill you made it quite plain that I was not your most favourite of men!' He gave a self-mocking smile. 'I kept in touch with Adam, of course, and heard how well you and Julian were hitting it off, and when I came back I could see for myself ...' He shrugged and was silent for a moment while he overtook a long vehicle. 'I wasn't going to contest my own kid brother, and in any case, our relationship, although improved, could hardly have been called encouraging.'

'I ... I thought you disliked me—I mean, I offered to start all over again when you took over Orsino, forget what had happened between us, and look how sarcastic you were about that!'

'You're damned right I was. I knew it would be impossible. In any case, the fact that every time I touched you you flinched didn't help.'

Olivia pulled a face. 'Because I was fighting a losing battle, trying to keep up my dislike of you and failing completely. The minute you touched me complications set in! Er ... am I allowed to ask where this kidnapping is ...'

'Kidnapping? The bus passengers are witnesses that you came of your own free will.'

Olivia snorted. 'Rubbish! I knew darned well whatever I decided you were going to get me off that bus somehow—I know you, Matthew Raynor, you're much too used to having your own way.'

A dark brow lifted. 'You came because you were afraid of me?'

'No,' answered Olivia softly, 'no, I came because I was in love with you.'

'That settles it!' Matthew swung the Lotus off the road on to the grass verge and pulled to a halt. He peered through the windscreen, eyes narrowed against the glare of the sun. 'I seem to have chosen a particularly pleasant spot. We'll take a walk down by the river, shall we?'

They left the car and made their way down the sloping meadow to the water's edge. The sun was hot on Olivia's bare arms and Matthew took off his jacket and held it over one shoulder.

Olivia suddenly was tongue-tied, ridiculously shy. She glanced beneath her lashes at the tall, dark figure by her side. This self-possessed, unapproachable man had dominated her life for three months as a threat and then gradually he had become important to her—the respect and admiration she had always hoped to find in a man growing slowly, firmly, hopelessly. She was compelled to see her prejudices for what they were—a fight for recognition, a reaction to the force of this attraction, sublimating love for dislike. And now the world had gone topsy-turvy. What had seemed hopelessly out of reach was within a hand's touch away, but she was powerless to make the first move, so used was she to suppressing her feelings that it was difficult to break the habit.

She stumbled over a clump of grass, turning her ankle, and fell against Matthew, who saved her from falling. Laughing at her clumsiness, she lay passive in his arms, the laughter dying in her throat as she looked up into his face, and then his head came down and their lips met.

After a long moment, when she had breath enough, Olivia murmured:

'We do seem to attract an audience, don't we? There's a fisherman sitting over there.'

'So there is.' Grey eyes smiled down at her. 'We mustn't disturb his concentration, must we?' He looked over her head. 'We'll leave him in peace and go this way. There's a shady tree further along and the ground is so dry we can sit and watch the swans go by.' He lifted a brow. 'How's the ankle? Shall I carry you?'

'Certainly not. It was only painful for the moment and after that I had other things on my mind,' and giving him a mischievous grin, she began to run along the river bank with Matthew at her heels, to finish up helpless with laughter on the grassy bank beneath the tree. Lying in his arms, she said contentedly: 'How nice this is. To think it was only this morning that I was feeling so miserable for having to leave, knowing I'd probably never see you again.'

'Foolish girl!'

'I used to stand in the wings every night during the play and secretly watch you.'

'Mm . . . I know you did,' Matthew admitted smugly.

She twisted round in surprise. 'Did you? How?'

He kissed the tip of her nose. 'Julian.'

'Oh . . . yes, well, I suppose it must have been rather obvious to him, although at the time I didn't think of it—and even if I had, I wouldn't have minded Julian knowing. When did he tell you?'

'Last night. I'd rung home and Julian answered. He told he he'd landed the Aldwych job and I duly congratulated him and steeled myself to ask if any other congratulations were in order. When he found out what I was talking about he said he'd met some prize idiots in his time and I was to come home.'

'But how did you know I'd be on that bus?' Olivia settled her head on his shoulder more comfortably. 'You seemed to have everything well planned.'

Matthew laughed ruefully. 'Not quite. I didn't plan the puncture I picked up on my way in which made me so late. I rang Adam and he gave me all the information needed to carry out my kidnapping.' He leant against the trunk of the tree, looking down at her through half closed lids. 'I admit I couldn't believe completely the encouraging noises from baby brother, but if he was out of the running, and I was sure I hadn't imagined the odd moments when electricity seemed to spark between us, then it did indeed seem time for me to return.'

Olivia traced his profile with a blade of grass. 'Where had you been staying?'

'In Suffolk. I have a cottage there that sadly needs a woman's touch.' He captured her hand and held it. 'See what I mean about electricity?' he drawled softly.

'I do indeed,' Olivia said weakly, as she was released from a nerve-shattering kiss. She pulled her scattered wits together. 'So it's Julian we have to thank.'

'Not completely. I arrived at your flat this morning, hat in hand, to find you'd already left. Liz berated me soundly and said what the hell was I doing, letting you go, when it was as plain as the nose on my face, etc ... I politely asked how she knew and she said if I hadn't been such a fool as to go away again I would have seen for myself how you'd been mooning around, following this up with a detailed account of your reactions when she told you about my op.'

Olivia turned her face into his shoulder. 'How awful for you, Matt. To think you might have died! And apart from Liz and Adam you'd not said a word—how I admired your strength for that, except I desperately wished I'd had the right

186

to be the one to worry over you and look after you. When Liz told me, it was the final revelation. I had to admit to myself that I didn't hate you—far from it, I loved you.' She pulled a face. 'I didn't realise that the fact I was upset was so obvious.'

'I'm glad it was, my dear. For one thing it was most satisfying for my ego, and for another, if you hadn't been, Liz would never have guessed how you felt. She, in turn, convinced me that no woman would act as you did unless her feelings were deeply involved.' He rested his lips against the top of her head, asking softly: 'Are they, Olivia?'

'You know they are.'

'And you're willing to become a member of the Raynor family?'

'Try and stop me!' she replied with a grin, adding dreamily: 'Mrs Raynor. Mrs Beatrice Olivia Raynor. Mm ... it sounds very impressive.' She was jolted into a sitting position by Matthew saying explosively:

'What did you say?'

Olivia stared and repeated in bewilderment: 'It ... it sounds very impressive.'

'No, not that, the other.'

'Er ... you mean the Mrs Beatrice Olivia ...' answered Olivia, confusion growing as Matthew interrupted her with a tremendous roar, rolling over to lie on his back, helpless with laughter. 'Matthew, what is it? What have I said? Matthew, you wretch, let me in on the joke!' she yelled, beating his chest with her hands until Matthew pulled her down, eyes wickedly amused.

'My dear, darling, beloved Olivia. You never told me your name was Beatrice.'

'You never asked,' protested Olivia indignantly, 'and I don't think it's very polite of you to laugh so. I know the name is rather uncommon these days, but it was my mother's and I'm very fond of it, although I never use it. So why you have to ...' She was stopped most efficiently by a long and satisfying kiss. 'Oh ...' She smiled demurely. 'Is that how you intend to govern the conversation?'

'If you don't behave,' Matthew said slyly, 'I have more drastic measures to hand.' Rosy-cheeked, Olivia asked quickly:

'Do explain, Matt. Beatrice isn't that funny, surely?'

'No, my darling, but the fact that I happen to be a Benedick is!'

'You? Your name is ...'

'Matthew Benedick Raynor. For our sins we are Paul Valentine, Matthew Benedick and Julian Sebastian.'

As the implications struck her Olivia's lips quivered and she began to giggle.

'Oh, Matthew! Your father!' Laughter broke from her and she managed to splutter: 'So keen on Sebastian and Olivia pairing off, and now ...'

Matthew grinned. 'I'm going to find the nearest post office and send him a telegram saying he'll have to include *Much Ado About Nothing* in next season's repertoire or else you'll not marry me.'

'Beatrice and Benedick—how appropriate! They fought continually, didn't they, just like us.' She thought deeply for a moment and then said slowly: 'Your father, Matt, what will he say?'

'Charles? My dear, he'll be delighted. You know he's very fond of you and nothing will please him more. He's a wily bird. On thinking about it, we might have fooled each other, but I fancy we didn't fool him.'

'I think we did. I think he expects you to marry Philippa.'

'Philippa?' Matthew's voice was sceptical and Olivia nodded. 'Nonsense, there was never any chance ... why ever do you say that?'

'It was something Charles said at Liz's after *Twelfth Night* implying that he was about to have a new daughter-in-law, and he was looking straight at you and Philippa.'

'He may well have been, but he was talking about Paul and Laura, you ridiculous girl,' adding in disgust, 'Philippa!'

'Oh.' Olivia smiled widely. 'Oh, Matt, I'm so pleased for them both.'

Matthew tightened his hold. 'And you believed that Philippa and I ...'

Olivia pulled a face. 'Well, she seemed so possessive, and she's very beautiful,' this last was said a trifle wistfully.

'My dear, the Philippas of this world know where they're going and she hoped I'd help her to get there. And as for beauty—I have a preference for green eyes, ridiculously short brown hair, freckles and a very kissable, smiling mouth.' He looked at her gravely. 'I know that Adam has told you how I knew you were an actress. I very nearly missed seeing you altogether as the plane I was in was delayed and we arrived in England two hours late. I dashed over to Cheltenham and saw threequarters of *Innocents* and then had to dash away again to catch a train, or else we might well have been introduced there and then—I know Frank Devine quite well. When you came to Cressida I could hardly believe my eyes. I was a man torn both ways—you had impressed me at Cheltenham and I wanted to believe in you, but I knew too much. You gave me a hard time, love.'

'I gave you ...! Why, Matthew Raynor, you were horrid to me!'

'Yes, I know, but I promise to make it up to you.'

She smiled. 'I'll hold you to that. Don't think me unduly inquisitive, Matthew, but what happens now?'

Matthew looked at his watch. 'Something to eat first. Then back to Rotheringham where I'll ring Len Ward and tell him he'll have to find another actress because this one is getting married as quickly as the law allows and her husband intends taking her to Italy for her honeymoon.'

'I see,' said Olivia sedately, her heart thumping rather rapidly. 'Just like that.'

'Just like that.' He levelled her a long look. 'Do you mind getting married without paraphernalia and time?'

Olivia shook her head. 'I ... I still can't believe it, Matthew.'

'You will.' He rose and pulled her to her feet.

'Will you be going back to the Royal?' Olivia asked as they made their way across the meadow.

'No. I've sounded Adam out and he's willing to carry on indefinitely.' Matthew ran a hand through his hair. He stopped and faced her. 'I have a confession to make, Olivia. Would you mind if we based our home in Suffolk for a start?'

'No, of course not. I'm not bothered where we live, so long as we'll be together.' She looked inquiringly and gave a teasing smile. 'Well?'

'The fact is, the cottage is my bolt-hole when I have a spell of writing. There's another play buzzing around in my head and the sooner I can get it down on paper the better. I've already made a start since doing Orsino.'

Olivia shook her head wonderingly. 'What a strange man

you are, Matthew. I didn't know you'd written a play. Would I know it?'

He smiled wryly. 'Intimately. I have it on the best authority that you loved it and that Isobel was the best part you'd ever played.' His dark brows lifted quizzically.

'*Innocents*!' breathed Olivia, delightedly, and then frowned. 'I thought the name of the playwright was a man called Ben Holland—we never met him because he was in America, but Frank knew him and ...' Seeing him smile she stopped short, an arrested expression on her face. 'Ben Holland! Ben for Benedick and Holland was your mother's maiden name! Oh, Matthew, how exciting—I think I love you even more knowing this. What a secretive man you are!' She hugged him enthusiastically and arms around each other they continued walking towards the road. 'How many more secrets have you up your sleeve? I now find I'm in love with two men—Matthew Raynor, actor and director, and Ben Holland, writer!'

'No more secrets,' promised Matthew, helping her to climb the gate. He left her sitting there while he went to unlock the Lotus.

Olivia swung her legs contentedly. Soon she would be able to take it all in, but it was very difficult to do so now. Mathew had often called her naïve, but she was not naïve enough to suppose that the future stretching out before them would be a bed of roses. What marriage ever was? It was a partnership which had to be worked at, but they had love and laughter, companionship and respect on their side and if any sticky patches came along she was sure they would be strong enough to sort them out. Anyway, she was darned well going to have a try. An exclamation from Matthew brought her thoughts winging back to the present. He was standing in the road gazing down at the Lotus. Olivia went to his side and followed the direction of his gaze.

'You'll be able to change it, won't you?' she asked, slightly bewildered by his expression of disgust.

'Your belief in my powers, though flattering, is misplaced, my love. Not even I can have two punctures consecutively and come out on top.' He eyed her suspiciously. 'Don't you dare laugh!'

'N ... no, of course not. What shall you do?'

'Give you a good hiding if you don't behave,' he warned, eyes gleaming. 'Well, there's not much that we can do, except wait for something to come along and try and hitch a lift to the next garage.' He looked back down the road. 'It's always the same, too much traffic when you don't want it and when you do ...' He turned a rueful face to her. 'Darling, I'm so sorry ...'

'Don't be silly, it's not your fault.' Olivia lifted a hand to shield her eyes from the sun's glare. 'Matt, there's something coming now. Shall I thumb a lift for us?'

'Yes, do,' he said quickly, adding dryly: 'I'm sure you'll be more acceptable, especially if you smile nicely. I'll check the doors.'

'Here goes.' Olivia positioned herself in a good place and stuck out her hand, thumb uppermost. 'M ... Matth ... ew!' she wailed, and holding her other hand to her head hooted: 'Oh, Matt! I can't believe it!'

Following her gaze Matthew stared, impatient query rapidly changing to incredulous comprehension. He struggled to keep his composure, but his sense of the ridiculous coupled with the outrageous coincidence proved too much. He joined Olivia and putting an arm round her shoulder, thumbed vigorously, both of them laughing helplessly.

The large, sleek kingfisher blue bus swept by in a cloud of dust, gradually pulling to a stop seventy yards further on, its passengers waving like old friends, the horn tooting away like mad.

Matthew looked at Olivia and grinned.

'Madam, your chariot awaits you,' and taking her hand he ran her towards the waiting bus.

Send coupon today for
FREE
Harlequin Presents
Catalog

We'll send you by return mail a complete listing
of all the wonderful Harlequin Presents novels
still in stock.

Here's your chance to catch up on all the
delightful reading you may have missed
because the books are no longer available at
your favorite booksellers.

Fill in this handy order form and mail it today.